PRAISE FOR THE FRANK SWANN SERIES

'Hard-boiled and riveting writing... A notable addition to Australia's crime-writing canon.' *Crime Factory*

'Like Peter Temple, Whish-Wilson tells a cracker of a yarn while wielding language the way Sachin Tendulkar wielded a bat.' *The West Australian*

'Fast-paced, complex and with some excellent twists, this is quality crime.' *The Australian*

'Classic crime noir.' *The Australian Book Review*

'A hard-boiled, vivid examination of crime and corruption in 70s WA.' *The Guardian Australia*

'Combines the pace of a hard-boiled thriller with a lyricism that makes you pause and catch your breath, before plunging in for more.' *Angela Savage*

'*Zero at the Bone* is a gritty and utterly absorbing read.' *Good Reading Magazine*

'Frank Swann is an attractive lone wolf, and the period is perfectly drawn ... *Zero at the Bone* delivers on a whole series of levels.' *The Newtown Review of Books*

'Unexpected, intriguing and beautifully written, you won't want to put this one down until the very last page.' *The West Australian*

'First rate crime noir.' *Sun Herald*

'*Line of Sight* is beautifully crafted. The characterisation is flawless and economical, the plot has a creeping intensity that grows greater and greater as it progresses to the unexpected conclusion.' *The West Australian*

'Against an intimately realised Perth backdrop three stories intertwine ... gripping and well constructed ... there is a satisfying twist to the end of the tale ...' *The Advertiser*

'Well written and meticulously researched, it's a wonderful piece of hard-boiled writing and an incisive analysis of the changing nature of corruption in Western Australia.' *crimefictionlover.com*

'A tightly plotted, well-textured story of shady figures contesting a lease at the beginning of the mining boom ... fast-paced, complex and with some excellent twists ... *Zero at the Bone* is quality crime.' *The Weekend Australian*

'Like an expert surgeon, Whish-Wilson cuts away to reveal an anatomical dissection of corruption and street level history: Perth's geography, class relations, its tribes and sub-cultures, including the most ruthless tribe of all, the cabal of bent cops who act with impunity. Whish-Wilson's writing is terrific, taut and lyrical.' *Crime Factory*

David Whish-Wilson was born in Newcastle, NSW, but grew up in Singapore, Victoria and Western Australia. He left Australia at eighteen to live for a decade in Europe, Africa and Asia. He is the author of *The Summons*, *The Coves* and *The Sawdust House,* and four crime novels in the Frank Swann series: *Line of Sight, Zero at the Bone, Old Scores* and *Shore Leave. True West* (also featuring Lee Southern) was published in 2019 and shortlisted for a Ned Kelly Award for Best Crime. His non-fiction book, *Perth*, part of the NewSouth Books City series, was shortlisted for a WA Premier's Book Award, and in 2022 David was shortlisted for a Western Australian Writer's Fellowship. David lives in Fremantle and coordinates the creative writing program at Curtin University.

Old Scores

David Whish-Wilson

First published 2016 by
FREMANTLE PRESS

Fremantle Press Inc. trading as Fremantle Press
PO Box 158, North Fremantle, Western Australia, 6159
fremantlepress.com.au

Cover photograph by: Phil Melling; background image Shutterstock
Designed by: Nada Backovic, nadabackovic.com

 A catalogue record for this
book is available from the
National Library of Australia

ISBN 9781925164107 (paperback)
ISBN 9781925164138 (ebook)

Fremantle Press is supported by the Western Australian State Government
through the Department of Cultural Industries, Tourism and Sport.

Fremantle Press respectfully acknowledges the Whadjuk people of the
Noongar nation as the Traditional Owners and Custodians of the land
where we work in Walyalup.

For Luka Fergus

I.

Blake Tracker laced his Dunlop Volleys with the green ribbons he'd stolen from the sewing shop, tied the double knot his father taught him.

'Bout the only useful thing he *had* learnt from his pops, this knot – specially good for footy boots; never came undone.

He'd learnt how to fight from his mum. That and how to run.

His Longmore cellie, Peter Parkhill, was still awake. Skinny white arms catching the moonlight, pale face and nothing eyes. Was looking at the calendar blu-tacked to the wall, as he did every night. No titty shots were allowed in juvie, so the calendar picture was of the Perth beach: cobalt waters and white sands and brown bodies. November, 1983. Parkhill liked to cross the days as they passed – the last thing he did before going to sleep. November 23 waiting for the rip-slash of a Parkhill fingernail.

Parkhill was a skinhead and as soon as he turned eighteen was going to be deported to England. Seemed happy about it. Had taken a shotgun to a posh party in Claremont and blown the feet off a mod enemy.

In Longmore the Nyungar boys had done Parky over so many times they'd got bored of it. Skinhead style, the way ten of *them* would bash a black kid if they got you cornered on Hay Street, day or night.

But they hadn't broken him. Just one of his eyes drooped beneath the waxy scar that his father had caused, when Parkhill was a kid.

Not a bad cellie, for a Pommy bastard. Had even learnt a few words of Nyungar from the others, and Wongi from Blake. Reckoned that Nyungar sounded like Klingons speaking, but Wongi sounded like wog lingo.

Blake stood and swung his arms, jogged on the spot, tried to settle the nerves. He adjusted his balls, smoothed his green tee-shirt, pushed curls from his eyes.

Felt the bruises. Still had a broken nose and three bust ribs. Fingers on his left hand no use.

Soon as he decided, he'd stopped being afraid. It was all about *the thing* now, getting it done. Before and after, gone. Just the thing, what he had to do.

No ifs or buts. It was kill or be killed. Him or them.

He took his ID card and showed it to the light. Pressed it lengthwise in his fingers, felt the blade drop through the slit he'd worked in there. Drew the razor blade out with his teeth until it formed a nice long edge. Cut a man's throat, no problem – and it was men he'd soon be fighting.

Blake'd used the razor blade to make tattoos on the others, had driven the screws mad trying to find it. Every time he showed his ID to get through a door he'd wanted to laugh. 'Here you go, Boss.'

But they never found it. Had confiscated all the Bics instead.

Cigarette ash worked just as well.

Carve the design into the flesh, rub in the ink, or the ash. Let it heal.

Ten ciggies per tatt. Had 'em lining up. His own designs, mostly.

Parky had one on his left forearm. Spurs, whatever that meant.

It was nearly time. The hour after lockdown, time for the screws to watch a bit of TV, eat their dinner, share some jars. Make sure the Super wasn't working late.

Blake had taken the beatings every night for a week, but he wasn't going to take it any longer. He knelt and ducked and weaved, solid on his base, feet spread. Sparred with his moon shadow. Bust ribs slowing him down. Unable to close his left hand. Right hand OK.

He still had his blade. He had his legs. He had his teeth.

Whatever it took.

He looked down at Parky, and for the first time saw him afraid. Eyes bright. Parky sighed, started to get up.

Blake stood over him. 'You stay down. What your white mates say? You fightin' on a blackfella's side?'

The words had their effect. Parkhill turned to the wall.

The lock clicked in the door.

It was a screw, but alone. Irish Pete. Truncheon still belted down. Face red, ciggie burning at his side. 'They ain't messin', Blake. They're comin' shortly. No point bein' stubborn.' He looked warily over at Parkhill. 'You don't get to say no, not after tonight.'

8

Blake dropped his shoulder, took the stance. 'You a good bloke, Irish Pete. But I ain't sayin' yes. That last boy got caught, they added two years. I'm goin' to Freo in a week, black 'n' blue maybe, but I'm walkin' into my adult time, not lookin' back.'

Irish Pete shook his head, looked again at Parkhill, trying to work out if he was asleep. 'You don't understand, son. You don't *get* to say no. Not anymore. They're gonna make an example.'

The Irishman did an imitation of a noose around his neck, and tugged, bug-eyes and tongue lolling out.

Blake's body understood, before he did. Knees went wobbly. Guts coming up inside him. Power out in his arms.

Held the stance, breathing like he'd run a mile.

Nowhere to run. He shook his head, tried to clear his ears.

'I ain't sayin' yes.'

He didn't know where the words came from, but he meant them.

Irish Pete shook his head. Looked down the row of cells, to the staff-room. Looked at his watch. Spat on the floor.

'C'mon boy, get ...'

Blake didn't need to be told. He slid past the Irishman and skidded down the hall. Past the dark cells of his mates. Past the roster board where the bastards had crossed out the 'e' from his name. 'Blak Tracker.' Discovered the door to the yards ajar. Bloody Irish Pete. The moon on his swollen face now, arms pumping, feet slapping the packed earth as metre by metre he built his run-up to the wall, taking off and flying, flying ...

2.

Frank Swann parted the bedroom curtains. It was a spring day and the pigface was flowering in orange dabs across the garden. The sky was a cool blue and stitched with threads of white cloud, the southerly tousling the heads of the street trees. He checked his watch and went to the telephone in the front room. Just on seven it rang, as he knew it would. Dennis Gould was as punctual as he was reliable. Swann answered and flicked the switch to initiate the recording. Gould was Swann's best researcher, you could even call him a partner, but now he was on the run. Trevor Dragic's thugs had seen to that.

'Dennis.'

'Swann.'

Their code for everything's well. Swann heard a road train rattle past, the wind in the mouthpiece. Imagined the dust and heat of the Nullarbor – red dirt and hot wind and crows moaning on the wires, Gould limping to the public phone at whatever roadhouse.

'I'm staying at a surf break called Cactus just the other side of the border – there's a campground there. Got a caravan with a view of the Bight.'

'Right for money?'

'Right enough. Any sign of Dragic?'

Swann grunted. 'Presumed overseas. Think we should give it a week.'

'Alright. It's not too bad here. Been getting a bit of fishing done. Salmon are on. Bloke next to me's got a jerry-rigged smoker, a converted fridge.'

'How far to the roadhouse?'

''Bout fifty k, round trip. I'll check in every two days, same time.'

'Make it earlier. The new job – I've got to be on deck at seven, in town.'

Swann hung up, checked his watch again. Three days ago Gould had been snatched from the street by four bikies, taken to the hills and made to dig his own grave. Forced to lie facedown and make his peace with the dirt. Had genuinely thought it the end. No mercy in the voice of the man with a shotgun. Gould still had no idea why they hadn't finished him off; instead asked him how much money he had – a few grand in cash at home. They gave him a ride back into town, blindfold on. Waited on the street while he packed a bag, then forked over his life savings. They followed his Triumph out onto Great Eastern Highway – the road to Adelaide.

Swann cinched his suit jacket around the top button, heard the sound of the V8 chugging down the street.

The delivery of his new staff vehicle was scheduled for seven am.

He gave himself a once-over. His old police boots had come up with polish and the blue woollen suit fitted him well. His hair was combed and his eyes were shielded by new sunglasses, chosen by his daughters.

Ray-Bans, cut in hard angles like he remembered from the fifties. Expensive, but then again, he had just been paid. Enough to gift each of his three daughters a grand and to bury the rest under the lemon tree out the back. Trevor Dragic had apparently fled the country, back to Macedonia, forfeiting his bank accounts and property to the company liquidator, who in turn had paid Swann in full.

For the first time in months, Swann was ahead of the game, and today was a fresh start.

*

The Holden Statesman reared into the driveway and settled like a giant cat, purring deep and regular.

A Stato would do him just fine. Bigger than his usual ride, the five-litre beast made affordable by the deal he'd signed – staff car and petrol costs in the contract.

He'd been sharing his wife's Datsun 120Y these past years through a long run of sixties Holdens – bought cheap and fixed on the weekends and given to his daughters as they came into their majority. A Kelly-green HK for Louise, a red-over-white EK for Sarah and, most recently, at her request, a Lincoln-green Brougham for Blonny, his youngest. It'd taken him three years to restore the salvaged car to its former glory, long enough to get used to the air-conditioning, the electric windows and leather seats.

Heenan, the premier's flunky, stepped out of the Holden onto the driveway, but the driver did not.

Swann raised his eyebrows at Heenan, who hoisted his trousers over his gut and cracked his ankles, rolled his neck. 'Nice suit,' he said, in that quiet voice of his. Quiet and wet like medicine in the ear. 'Your car's down the street, Frank. By the bakery. Here are the keys.'

Swann took the keys from Heenan's hot fingers and saw the Holden logo and nodded his thanks.

'You got the pager?' Heenan asked, and Swann showed it, although he didn't know how it worked. 'You'll get a number when it's time to meet. Call it and get directions. We could be anywhere this morning. Wait in your office. The phone there hasn't been security cleared. You might start on that.'

Heenan clambered behind the dark doors of the Statesman, which rolled into the street. Its tinted windows revealed nothing as it cruised up the hill.

Swann turned the keys and retrieved his tool bag off the front porch. The Gladstone bag was filled with electronic equipment related to his core trade these past years: surveillance devices, bugs and tools to detect bugs. His cameras and recorders.

Down the street was the corner bakery that wafted the smell of bread into his bedroom every night. Beside the bakery was the parked car.

Not what he expected. The peach-coloured VC Commodore was the 1981 model, and although only a couple of years old, it already looked tired.

Swann walked a lap of the Commodore, hoping it'd look better from a different angle. It was a fleet vehicle, sure enough, but the duco chips around the fenders meant it had driven the stone roads of the outback, and the egg-crate grillwork at the front was hatched and holed. The bonnet antenna was rusty and bent. The badging on the boot was missing. The petrol tank cover was scratched and prised away, where someone had forced it open. The tyres were nearly bald.

None of this would matter, except for the reputation of the 1.9 litre model as gutless – two cylinders sawn away from the regular six – the motoring equivalent of riding a heavily laden three-legged horse.

Swann opened the door and tossed in his tools, and sat behind the wheel. He adjusted the sun visor and turned the key, settled his shoulders into the nylon cream, waited for the engine to take. The radio was tuned to talkback, John K. Watts riffing on the need for a national footy competition, and a representative WA team. Swann had served with Watts back when he was a copper and footy player, before he reinvented himself as a comic.

Swann had gone the more traditional route – copper to security agent – or what most people knew as a private investigator.

Swann killed the radio so that he could listen to the engine, which was at least in tune. Except that the fuel gauge was ticking empty, and the battery light was flashing.

He turned the radio on and punched the board with a finger. A man was singing about a car. The tune was familiar from one of Blonny's tapes ...

Here in my car, I feel safest of all ...

Swann laughed. His last car, his beloved 1962 EK Holden, had been blown up by Gus Riley's bikies, back in '79, not twenty metres from where he sat.

Swann tilted the rear-vision mirror and made sure the street was clear behind him.

*

The freeway into the city droned in the morning heat, the Swan River buffed to a glossy sheen. Pelicans sat on the pylons of the old Como jetty, and shags dozed on the bones of a limestone reef. Some of the cormorants looked like morose old men, others like skinny black angels.

Swann lit a cigarette, the Commodore struggling along in the lane closest to the foreshore. The polymer box in his pocket began to beep loudly. Then a phone began to ring. With his left hand, he lifted the lid off the centre console. Inside was a plastic phone, straight out of *Get Smart*. He hoisted the receiver.

'Swann? The pager working?'

Swann held up the black box and read the digital display – a seven-digit number.

'Yep.'

'Means you're in or near the city. Thing's got a five-kilometre wireless radius,' said Heenan. 'Bugger going to your office. We need you to clear the office and meeting rooms at Parliament House. A pass is waiting for you at the door. That all needs to be done before the morning presser ...'

'Presser?'

'Press conference.'

'At your service.'

The Commodore ground its way across the freeway lanes to the West Perth exit, the limestone face of Mt Eliza at his shoulder.

'This phone – I can call anywhere with it?'

'Anywhere metro. No STD.'

The self-importance in Heenan's voice – clearly enjoying being the premier's big man, as well as bag man. Swann cut him off. 'I'm hanging up ...'

'Oh really, why?'

'I'm there.'

3.

Des Foley leaned between the front seats and placed his hands on the shoulders of both men. Five hundred kilometres into his ride they were all great mates. The bush weed that Cameron, in the passenger seat, kept stuffing into a clay pipe and passing around, had rippled the bush with a golden light and deep watery texture, made the car feel like it was floating over the blacktop. But it was the sulphate in the bag on the driver's lap that really had Des flying. It was good stuff, and the bag seemed bottomless, despite Reggie's dipping his finger in every five minutes and rubbing it around his gums. Reggie had started taking the goey orally after his nose began to bleed. The two men had driven from Sydney without sleeping, and were nearly there. That was three nights and four days of smoking and snorting and foot-to-the-floor. The new model Mazda, which Cameron admitted they'd stolen in Dubbo, seemed up to it so far, but that burning plastic smell wasn't a good sign. Not that Cameron and Reggie noticed.

Reggie was AWOL from the army, having met Cameron in a bar in Wagga. Cameron was headed to Perth to see his three-year-old son, and the impromptu trip had seemed to Reggie like a good idea. They had picked up Des this side of Kalgoorlie, where he'd had his finger out for three hours, with no luck. They'd skidded down the hard shoulder and nearly off into the jam-tree scrub.

Des could see that they were tanked, but their being out-of-towners suited him. Des' face was well known around Perth, despite his beard and long hair.

And they were clearly in a hurry.

It was all fun and games for the first few hundred k's, until the wheat-belt receded around York and Cameron started to rant.

His three-year-old son, stolen by his fucken ex. The stolen TV on the back seat was for him. Cameron was going to shower and shave and sleep it off, then visit him, take the little fella the TV, say sorry for scaring him that last time.

But the closer they got to Perth the more agitated Cameron became. There was no talk now of sleeping it off. *He was going straight over. If she didn't let him in, that TV was going through the fucken window, and he was goin' in after it. Where the fuck in Perth was Thornlie?*

Des kept his mouth shut.

That fucken bitch. That freckle-faced moll. If she says a fucken word. Thinks she's smarter than me. But I've tracked her down. Like every time.

Cameron began punching the dash. What he intended doing to her head. Fucken improve her looks. Little facial reconstruction. Reggie bellowing like a wounded bull, getting off on Cameron's wildness.

It was none of Des' business, he told himself, once. But not twice. He was through lying to himself.

Instead he looked down at his hands, which were clenched.

The car was swerving as Reggie laughed and battered the steering wheel. Cameron getting off on what he was gonna do to his ex, recited at the top of his lungs, so mad it had a rhythm now, a beat punctuated by his punching the dash.

This wasn't good.

Des was one of Australia's most wanted. The Good Morning Bandit. Named after his habit of entering banks through side walls and ceilings and waiting for the manager to arrive. 'Good morning' was the first thing they heard. He was out of there by the time any punters arrived. No-one ever got hurt.

The mutts in the front seats were too drug-fucked to recognise him, but any copper would ID him with a passing glance.

That wouldn't do.

He wasn't going back to jail. He was polite to civilians but would shoot any copper who looked twice. And he was *never* going back to jail.

His only mantra.

Wanted in four states, and they all had a prison cell waiting for him. He'd do time in one state then they'd send him along to the next. He'd never get out. And it wouldn't be easy time. It'd be super-max and solitary, after his last escape from Pentridge.

They were getting close now. Five kilometres ahead, Des saw the crest of the Darling Scarp over the grey ribbon of the Great Eastern Highway, the marri and jarrah forest on either side.

It wasn't unusual to have a copper stationed before the peak, to observe the behaviour of the long-haul truckies coming home. Hundreds of tons bustling along at a hundred k's headed for a sudden forty-five degree decline. The odd truckie asleep at the wheel, or with busted brakes. One or two going off the road and taking out a whole street of brick homes the other side.

'Pull over here, Reggie. I'm home.'

Surprisingly, Reggie heard him over the noise. Des had spoken quietly but firmly. Perhaps the AWOL corporal had sensed it, trained to be hyper-vigilant.

'Thought you lived near the coast?'

Cameron ceased his pounding of the dash.

'Aren't you gonna come over with us, see my son?'

Des didn't dignify it with an answer. 'I always walk the last part home. A thing I do. Let me out at the next turn right.'

Down a winding street into John Forrest National Park.

'Keep going. Here.'

Des got out and hoisted his duffel bag, leant it against the trunk of a giant marri, white flowers scattered in the dust at his feet.

He heard the driver and passenger doors open, as he knew they would. The view from the little carpark on the western edge of the scarp was always a treat; the city of Perth sprawled across the vast sandplain, the wide blue dome of the Indian Ocean curved across the horizon beyond, but the two travellers weren't getting out to appreciate the view.

Cameron and Reggie were a long way from home. Stealing the car and driving west was a spur-of-the-moment decision. They'd driven off from the last two servos without paying. They were living off the land.

Des closed his hand around the cool, cracked butt of the Browning pistol in his duffel bag and turned, kept it concealed. Like a game of statues the two men froze, tried to relax their hunter's posture into something more deceptive, rictus grins on their dials and hands on hips and arms folded.

Des took a deep breath and turned to look at the view. Wanted to know if he still had it – that radar he'd learnt in the borstals as a kid, and had honed in all of the prisons since.

He sensed Reggie come at him from behind and sidestepped and clocked him with the butt of the Browning and allowed the man's momentum to carry him over the edge of the granite cliff face, down into the nothing.

That felt good. Good enough to put a round in the breech of the pistol and, before Cameron had a chance to wipe that mincing look of shock, Des had crossed the distance between them and kicked out his legs. Des knelt on Cameron's back, so that he was facing the man's feet.

'You know, mate, you remind me of my father. My mother raised me up on *her* own, and my brothers too. She kept my father out of it, until we were old enough to keep him out of it. He was a nasty cunt, just like you ...'

Cameron was getting his breath back, starting to struggle.

'You won't be visiting your son, Cameron. And you won't be putting no TV through your ex's window. No more hidings for her.'

Des put the Browning against the back of the man's trouser leg, behind the kneecap, put in a bullet. The dirt absorbed most of the blunt force, the shattered bone and the brute sonic shock, and the forest drank up Cameron's scream. Des put a bullet through the other kneecap and stood. Took up the man's hands and ignoring his screams and eyes drunk with pain dragged him over to the cliff face and kicked him off the edge. Heard the branches in the taller marri crash and break as he fell towards the granite below.

'Give yer mate a kiss goodbye.'

It was a start. Think of it as training. He looked over the city, river curling like a lazy snake through his hometown. His mother was down there, getting ready to be put onto the street. That wasn't going to happen.

He'd burn the city to the ground.

4.

Swann passed the wand of the wireless signal meter along the skirts of the wall opposite the premier, who was reclined with his feet on the desk, taking calls. Swann paused at the end of the wall, and waited for some of the staffers to move. The premier appeared relaxed but his eyes were keen, and his reddish-brown hair was parted down the side. The characteristically longer hair had gone in the months leading up to the election, as had the sideburns and moustache. He looked like a young JFK without the roving eyes.

The last two premiers had resembled military men, or even detectives – square-jawed and thickset, both tall. Rob Farrell, however, was short and what Swann's daughters would call 'willowy'. His blue-green eyes said mischief and excitability, but his voice was deep and modulated. Unlike the previous two premiers, who'd spoken in the mock-Pommy cadences expected of their generation, Farrell spoke the working class vernacular he'd grown up with, and the voters loved it. 'Prime Minister, I appreciate you calling on your holiday ... thanks mate, yep, straight into it. You like the haircut? Heenan, my right-hand, forced it on me. It's the eighties, he reckons. New look for a new start. Short back and sides, little cowlick at the front ... yeah, Mary did it, I wouldn't trust anyone else. And how's Hazel, the kids?'

There were a dozen men and women in the premier's office, clustered in the shadows away from the lamplight. The room was all varnished sheoak panelling and heavy drawn curtains, but the premier sought out Swann with his eyes and winked.

It was an odd gesture, intimate and cheeky, although Swann was the only person in the room obviously watching the premier, and perhaps he'd sensed this. The others were all staffers, busy with paperwork and waiting to speak to him, but all of them had their eyes averted, pretending they weren't listening to his every word.

Even Heenan, standing at the premier's shoulder, glancing at his watch. The two of them reminded Swann of the book described to him by Louise, his eldest. *The Picture of Dorian Gray*. It looked like Heenan had taken on all of the premier's exhaustion and anxiety, while the premier had never looked younger.

It was Heenan who'd called Swann a month ago. Should the election go as expected, the premier intended taking a new broom to the office staff. He was also keen to create some new positions, and Heenan had Swann in mind for one. Heenan was the Leader of the Opposition's fixer, and he needed a fixer for himself.

Swann was in the middle of the court case on behalf of small investors trying to retrieve money from Dragic, an ex–smack dealer turned property developer who'd claimed bankruptcy and pocketed the coin. Swann's surveillance and trailing of the money through shell companies had demonstrated the theft. Swann had since been approached by dozens of other stockmarket and real-estate investors who'd been scammed – a whole new line of work in a city where hustlers in business suits had always thrived.

The problem was that Swann didn't like the people. Not the charming reptiles who stole the money or the victims who'd risked their life savings on something too good to be true. Both sides of the scam were greedy, but one side was cleverer than the other. He'd hated the desperate looks in the eyes of the ripped-off, and their nagging him day and night. He felt sorry for them, but he didn't respect them.

So when Heenan called a meeting in the front bar of the National Hotel in Fremantle with the prospect of a full-time, salaried position, working exclusively for Heenan in an as yet undisclosed role, Swann was curious. Over a few middies Heenan talked of utilising Swann's counterintelligence skills to keep the premier's offices 'clean', and of other roles security-vetting new employees and the like. All contingent on the election result and the state of the coffers. Was Swann interested?

Yes, he was. He'd been living hand-to-mouth these past eight years and he wasn't getting any younger. On the subject of *why him?* Heenan had been equally vague, except to say that he'd been monitoring the Dragic case and was an admirer. This last statement said with a tone that indicated its double meaning, made explicit in the searching look in Heenan's grey eyes – Dragic was a bad enemy to have.

Any port in a storm?

There in Heenan's eyes, behind the vague offer.

They shook on it and necked their beers.

*

'Let's walk and talk, Frank. Come and watch history being made.'

In the crush of the narrow corridor, Heenan and Swann fell behind, leaving the premier to stride ahead. Having spent the last half-hour receiving calls from wellwishers, the premier looked flushed and jumpy, kept running a hand over his hair and wiping his mouth, bouncing on the balls of his feet. Heenan huffed alongside Swann, looking protectively ahead, whispering to Swann as an aside, 'The ones who've been calling him, owe him; the ones he's got to call, he owes. At the moment there's more of the former. Let's hope it lasts ...'

'This the first time he's spoken since last night?'

'Yep. I was up all night writing it. It's about starting on the promises he made. The best way forward. Some of them will affect you. There are the security cameras he wants around the city. An Australian first. I want your oversight on that. There's the new police commissioner, a Victorian – I might want you to liaise. Then there are the big-ticket items – the big promises. Look, the place is packed ...'

In the atrium of Parliament House, the busts and portraits of premiers past lining the walls, cool Donnybrook stone underfoot; the gathered journos filled out the hall, waving their cameras and fluffy mikes.

Heenan stood beside Swann while the premier took the stage. The glare of the lights didn't seem to bother him. Swann loosed the top button of his jacket, straightened his cuffs. The faces in the crowd were eager. After decades of terse, wooden premiers the journalists had a new, younger and more flamboyant leader to work with.

The premier cleared his throat, drummed his fingers on the sides of the podium, shared a smile with a familiar face in the crowd. 'Ladies and gents, I'll be introducing my cabinet this afternoon. Tomorrow, I'm recalling parliament to get the death penalty abolished, as promised. And that's just the start of the legislation we'll be putting forward. With both houses in our control, there's no time to waste. But first, in line with my core election promise of looking after our workers and maintaining the entrepreneurial spirit of our big end of town, I want to talk to you about infrastructure. I've been scant about the details, and I apologise for that, but I have a vision for reshaping our beautiful city for the following generations that I think you'll be excited by – and I think our first premier, Big John Forrest over there, would be excited by, too, were he with us today ...'

The premier's smile was sincere but the wave of his hand towards the bronze bust of John Forrest was peremptory. The son of an indentured servant, Forrest had been an explorer and surveyor in the years before Australia was born as a Federation. With the wealth of the first gold boom he'd built most of the state's rail networks, the Fremantle port, the weirs and the pipeline out to the goldfields while his brother, also larger than life, ran for mayor and made his money dividing up Peppermint Grove into some of the country's most valuable real estate.

The premier's comment and gesture were casually made, but they sparked a new frenzy of camera whirring and snapping, painting him in hot flashes of light. Was he seriously intending to be as vigorous in his nation-building as the first premier, who had transformed the city from a small colonial outpost to a booming young metropolis?

'I don't pretend to know what Big John would make of me personally, but he'd sure be an interesting bloke to have a beer with. What I aim to have in common with him, however, when my time is done – is for people to say that my government also capitalised on the current mining boom and built the city we need for our children, and our children's children. What I have is a new vision of the role of government. To lessen the burden on Western Australian taxpayers, this government is going into *business*. I don't mean nationalising industry or any such thing, but actively putting taxpayer money to work in the financial and industrial and mining sectors, reinvesting all profits into infrastructure and state services. Thinking of the government as a profit-making entity is revolutionary, folks, but is something that will characterise this government. As a first priority I aim to redevelop large parts of Burswood and East Perth into desirable residential and office zones, fix up the city's derelict buildings, including the Old Swan Brewery. As of an hour ago, the tenders have gone out to local construction businesses first, because I intend to see these plans fast-tracked. Life is short, people ...'

The premier stood aside to allow the cameras to fix him to the wall with little spears of light. 'In a conversation recently with a major figure of the Western Australian business community, I was paid what can only be described as the highest compliment – when the man in question described me as a businessman at heart. I embrace this compliment wholeheartedly ...'

Swann nudged Heenan with his elbow. 'That speech you spent all night writing. This it?'

The barest shake of his head. 'This is going to be hard to sell. Damascene conversions always are.'

An aide sidled up to the premier, whispered into his ear. The premier's face became grave, and he turned to the journos and spread his hands wide. 'That's all, folks. No questions I'm afraid. Something's come up. I'll be back here in a few hours with the new cabinet, when you can ask all the questions you like. There's tea and coffee set up in the room over there and, as always, the parliamentary bar is open. Thankyou.'

He turned his back to the audience and slipped off the stage, sauntered over and took one of Heenan's lapels, leaned into his ear. Heenan rolled his eyes, reached into his pocket and passed Swann a set of car keys. The keys to the Statesman. 'You can't use the Commodore for this. Take these. We've got a small problem that requires the utmost discretion ...' Remembering that some of the journalists were still milling around, hoping to catch the premier's eye, Heenan backed into the corner. 'It's the premier's father. You need to stop him. I'll call you on the car phone while you're headed over. Quick, this is urgent ...'

The premier watched them, his hands thrust into his trouser pockets.

*

Swann was on the freeway, as directed, when the car phone began to trill in the centre console between the deep leather seats of the Statesman de Ville. He was enjoying the ride so much he'd forgotten why he was headed to Salter Point. The arctic-white Statesman surged towards the horizon like a great land yacht. There was the legroom, too, and the fact that Swann could ease back into the seat and spread his shoulders and enjoy the audio-extravagance of the Bose stereo system, tuned to a classical station that he'd never heard before, but the bass and the treble and the female soprano voice so clear that it felt like she was singing to him alone.

'Maria Callas,' said Heenan by way of hello. 'And very loud.'

Swann tweaked the dial and listened to the voice fade, drawn back into the speakers like a reluctant ghost.

'This is a sensitive matter,' Heenan said. 'It's Stormie Farrell, the premier's father. He's about to do something on the front lawn of his place. We pay the neighbours and the local Bentley coppers to tip us off, for this exact bloody reason ... She couldn't say what he was up to, except that he's naked and turfing things onto the front lawn.'

'I know Stormie, at least I've met him. My stepfather took me to hear him speak at a funeral, at the Freo cemetery ...'

'Yeah, he's a legend, as they say. But he's a sick man now, Frank. His liver's shot, his blood's poisoned and his head isn't right. He's becoming increasingly erratic, volatile even. Before the press get wind of it, I want you to have a word with him, talk him down from whatever trip he's on. I'd do it myself, but Stormie hates my guts. Reckons I shave my legs. Calls me the hairless catamite – in public. And that's when he's sober.'

Swann eased the Statesman off the freeway down the long concrete curve onto Manning Road. Glimpses of the Canning River between the playing fields of Aquinas College, some remnant banksia scrub and the old workers cottages dotted around patches of the pine plantation that had once stretched to Victoria Park.

He pulled into the street of weatherboard cottages built up from the riverbank, the tannic smell of tea-tree wetland soaking the still air.

Swann could see the address without having to check the letterboxes. A single-storey salmon brick cube with orange terracotta tiles, built into a slope of limestone rubble and casuarina needles. No front lawn, like the other neatly tended gardens around. And smoke, from a bonfire, the wrong colour – thick, black and turbid, pulsing into the midday sky. There were neighbours standing on the edges of their properties, not daring to go further, one or two of them shouting.

Swann glided the Statesman along the curb opposite the fire and caught the stink of burnt plastic and hot metal. He ignored the jeers directed at the old man standing near the fire under the shade of a casuarina, in his underpants, stroking a large white rabbit. Next to him, leaning on the trunk of the sheoak, was an ancient, single-barrelled shotgun.

The old man watched Swann with a squint as he walked up the drive.

'You mind?' Swann asked, indicating the garden hose coiled in a dried-out tangle of nasturtium. Without waiting for an answer he leaned over and hefted the hose and twisted the rusty tap on. Water trickled then grew in pressure as he approached the fire, uncoiling the hose as he went.

Televisions, four of them, laid at crazy angles on a jumble of car tyres, burning little jets of incandescent green and sparks of gold and red, sucked into the blackening sky by the roiling heat coming off the tyres. They looked like they might explode at any second. Swann could see his reflection in the screen of a big TV on casters that dated from the sixties, wood-veneer and steel dials, would have once been top of the range. Besides that, two small black cubes that motels favoured. On the apex of the burning tyres was a newer model, all chrome and sleek plastic with a built-in VCR, which looked new despite the melting base and blackening glass.

The fire didn't like the water that came out with a surprising pressure; it gave a startled and angry hiss. Swann had a sense of the shotgun behind his back, glanced to see the old man now perched up the driveway on the rear bench seat of a cherry-red Thunderbird convertible, the rabbit on his lap and now a rooster under one arm, swigging from a goon of wine. The T-Bird was garaged under a pergola roof. The shottie remained leant against the casuarina.

Not all the tyres had caught fire, and Swann angled the jet of water into the base of the flames, snuffing out the burning tyres one at a time. He circled round the fire and and watched the old man standing out of his seat on the massive boot, trying to encourage the rooster back into the car.

'Bloody vandal!' Stormie Farrell shook his fist and gave Swann the forked fingers. 'A man's allowed to light a fire!'

Swann lifted the jet of water for a moment and sprayed the old man, who dropped his goon and tipped back into the seats. The rabbit leapt out and followed the rooster inside the house. Stormie Farrell scampered after them.

There were cheers from across the street. 'First wash he's had in years!' shouted one of the neighbours, an outraged codger with dagwood wings of grey hair, dressed in footy shorts and thongs.

The fire guttered down to a few twists of smoke. Swann soaked the periphery of the scorched grass and laid the hose on an unlit tyre so it continued to gush into the cinders. He wiped his hands on the blanket of needles and cracked the shotgun to make sure it was unloaded, and wandered up the slope towards the T-Bird. From a distance, the late-fifties model looked in mint condition, but up close it was pitted with dents and dings and scrapes of different coloured paint. The roof was down and the interior was covered in fish'n'chip wrappings and empty goons.

They were all the same brand, which told Swann the old boy was a steady but serious drinker – liked to maintain the charge and not get buried under sleep, like most spirit alkies he knew.

The front door remained open, and Swann entered. All the rooms branching off the central corridor were dark but the kitchen at the back was noisy with the sound of a record scratching under a needle at high volume, static crackling and a background seashell hiss.

But the kitchen was empty, except for a square outline without dust on the formica table where Swann presumed the newest television must've rested.

He heard the engine of the T-Bird turning over but not sparking, and went back out the front. The old boy was behind the wheel now, dressed in a faded purple safari suit and Elvis shades, pumping the gas with a bare foot. He'd found the time to comb and oil his grey hair, which glistened in the sun.

Stormie Farrell gave up when he saw Swann, took his hand off the keys. His eyes sparkled. 'Frank Swann, home-delivered,' he said. 'What say we get down to Coco's for happy hour? My shout.'

The sickly aroma of cheap wine that settled around Stormie wasn't enticing, but Swann was curious. How had the old boy known Swann was coming over?

The engine kept ticking without sparking. Stormie Farrell cleared some space on the passenger seat with a sweep of his hand. Rabbit pellets in the floorpan. 'What are you doing, Frank?'

Swann circled the car and reached by Stormie's arm and took out the keys, popped the bonnet. Went out front and lifted the heavy steel lid and fastened it. Removed the distributor cap. Just as he suspected – someone had taken out the rotor button. He refitted the cap, dropped the hood. Went round and took a seat beside Stormie Farrell and passed over the keys. The sabotage was probably Heenan's, clipping the old boy's wings.

26

'Come on, Swann. Fix 'er up. You owe me, mate.'

Swann's eyebrows rose to say, 'How so?'

Stormie Farrell's face wrinkled like he was about to shout, but it was just him trying to think.

'How did you know I would come?'

Farrell threw back his head and laughed. Beyond him, across the other side of the street where the neighbours had gathered to snipe, the old man's laughter turned heads. Presumably, they had called the police, who'd been schooled, for favours accruing, to call Heenan. The recognition that Swann wasn't there to arrest the old man, or put him in a straitjacket, began to dawn. One young man in board shorts and singlet picked up a rock and approached the verge.

More nimbly than Swann might have expected, Stormie Farrell flipped his legs out of the T-Bird and scrambled over to the shotgun. Hefted and waved it around. The young man backed away, showing Farrell the rock.

The shottie wasn't loaded, but according to the law, going armed in public was still an imprisonable offence. Not that the Tactical Response Group ever made any arrests. In every case that Swann could remember, once the call went out the black-clad TRG simply turned up and shot dead the offender, before returning to their black van.

'Mr Farrell!'

At the sound of Swann's voice the fierce grin slipped away, revealed the face of a resentful schoolboy. Stormie even dropped his chin and rounded his shoulders. Without being asked, Farrell handed over the shottie, stock first, eyes down. But when he spoke, his voice was a rumble, and Swann remembered his stepfather Brian's words that Stormie Farrell was the best bloody orator he'd ever seen, could inspire a corpse to stand up and march, rally against the bosses.

Swann could see the premier in Farrell Snr's sharp blue eyes, the underbite in his jutting jaw when enraged on the podium; hear the boiling tar in his voice.

Whatever netherworld Stormie Farrell now inhabited dropped away, and his eyes were lucid, and angry. 'You owe me, Swann. Or have you got selective hearing too? Who do you think gotcha yer new job? My son? Surrounds himself with arse-clowns and thinks he's ready to swim with the sharks. Fucken idiot. He's traded on my name all the way. And that's all I got left. Look around ya. Had to burn all my tellies just to get his attention. Couldn't stand the sight of him grandstanding, on every fucken channel. Wants to be a businessman eh? Whaddya reckon about that?'

'Certainly nailed his colours to the mast, Stormie.'

'Yeah, the mast of a fucken pirate ship.'

Stormie Farrell ran the sole of his bare foot over a chunk of limestone. 'I'm not a well man, Frank. I should shut my mouth.'

With the anger gone out of him, Farrell Snr looked frail and thin and sickly, barefoot in a purple safari suit two sizes too small, picking up pebbles with his toes.

'When was the last time you spoke to your son?'

Farrell Snr shrugged. 'Months, years, dunno. He used to trot me out. Now he's ashamed of me, just like his mother was. She used to call me The Goat, in front of me own kids. He was her golden boy, doted on him, the little Prince, but I've always been tough on him ...'

'You want me to pass on a message?'

Stormie grunted, the words not easy. 'Yair. You can tell him that he's off his rocker. That you lie down with dogs, you get fleas. That he's betrayed the workers and the whole fucken movement. But that if he wants any advice, he knows where to find me.'

Swann cursed Heenan under his breath. Babysitting the premier's father, keeping him out of trouble, hiding from public view the premier's shame – he hadn't signed up for this. Swann glanced at the shotgun, thought about taking it with him.

'Don't worry, don't have any shells. I was in the second sixteenth. Since the desert, and then Kokoda, I can't sleep unless I've got my gun around. She goes everywhere with me.'

Swann heard something behind him and turned to see the rabbit, bigger than any he'd ever seen, staring at him with rheumy eyes. 'Barry goes everywhere with me too, don'tcha Barry?'

The rabbit hopped over to Stormie and sniffed at his feet. Swann took it as his cue. The sea breeze whispered through the casuarina, releasing the smell of tea-tree and pine sap and childhood memories; a note of nostalgia that took him by surprise. He felt a pang of sadness for Stormie Farrell, something he often felt around old men. Farrell Snr's race was run. His mind was going, and his body was failing, but to Swann he looked like a boy again, crouched over in badly fitting clothes, barefoot, rubbing the rabbit's soft coat.

5.

Des Foley was tired by the time he reached the tin wastelands of East Perth. He needed to sleep but continued to his mother's house. Once this caper blew up they'd have surveillance on her, night and day, and she'd be lost to him again.

The coppers didn't know he was coming, but he still needed to be careful. There was always a chance a neighbourhood-watch dobber or someone with an eye on the hundred-thousand bounty would put him in. He'd grown up on the street and many would recognise him, even if he looked the part of a wandering dero. Having parked the stolen Mazda on a backstreet in Maylands, he'd followed the river dressed in a stinking old bluey that'd belonged to one of the men – he'd already forgotten their names.

With his dirty sandshoes covered in red dust and blue overalls and dyed black hair under a truckie's cap, he looked like any number of the black, white and brindle vagrants who drank in Hyde Park.

Foley entered the street but had to stop, to check again. There was his mother's rental down the road, a two-storey Federation made of red brick with a sagging balcony and rusting lattice, the tin roof stained and buckled. But half of the other buildings on the street were gone. A few weatherboard shacks and bungalows remained, but were spaced with blocks of vacant grey sand, littered with plastic scrims and broken glass.

This had always been a busy road, part of the reason his mother established the shop there, having moved Des and his brothers out of the nearby housing estate, to try to get them square. It was a steep rent even then, and her clothing alteration business – a trade she'd learnt in Fremantle jail, working with an old Singer and a steam press – brought in just enough to cover the bills.

She worked long hours, his old mum. Made all their clothes too. The other kids at school soon learnt not to laugh at the Foley boys' custom slacks and denim shorts, the shirts of cast-off cotton.

One thing hadn't changed on the street: the grit underfoot and the black smears under the eaves of the remaining houses, a product of the recently decommissioned power station a block away. As a child growing up, the puddles nearby had all been heavy with grey sludge. He'd thought it beautiful after a rainstorm when the macadam of the road shone with a petrochemical rainbow.

Foley skipped over the low wire fence and went down the side gate of his mother's house. He could hear the whirring of her machine in the ground-floor shop, a new sound on an obviously new machine. He leaned against the back door to listen for voices. When he was sure that his mother was alone he took out the spare key from its hiding place behind a loose brick, turned the lock and slipped inside.

Quietly at first, but finding it hard to keep a straight face, Foley forced himself to sing loudly, and proudly, the *Catalpa* song. It was a code between them, the song of Fenian heroes rescuing Fenian convicts from Fremantle last century, a banned song during his mother's childhood. She had taught it to him and his brothers, and Foley had sung it at a school assembly in such a pure voice that the deputy principal, an Irishman who openly despised the Foley boys, had wiped tears from his eyes with a cotton hanky.

She didn't shout his name, or yelp for joy. Laurel was too smart for that. She merely pulled the sliding door and fell into his arms, a small lady and getting smaller with age. He buried his face into her long loose hair, felt her ribs tremble at his fingertips.

His poor ma. And he, the best of the sons, although equally lost to her. He wouldn't be at her bedside when she died, or at her funeral; he'd be on the run or locked up. Just turned thirty, he'd spent eleven years in jails and borstals, more years lost. Of his two brothers still alive, one was jailed in Victoria and the other was a career soldier, stationed in the Top End. He had two dead brothers: one from an overdose, another killed in a knife fight with American sailors.

She stood and petted him, pressed her hands over him, making him real. 'Yes, yes,' she whispered. 'You're looking after yourself. Good. Come through upstairs.'

He climbed the creaking staircase while she returned through the shop, pulled over the open sign, locked the door.

She made him tea and crumpets, and then pikelets with butter, and then two rounds of corned beef and mustard sandwiches, his favourite. He guzzled away a king brown while she made the rest of the loaf into sandwiches to take with him, the fact that he'd leave unspoken. Her eyes were sharp as ever. She still had the prison wariness, the reading of signs, after all these years.

'Who's the landlord?' he asked, getting down to business in case they were disturbed, or he had to leave suddenly.

She sniffed. 'You remember old Schloime Mostel, ran the drycleaners round there on Royal Street?'

'Old Slimey, yeah, I remember.'

'Don't. He was a good bloke. Sent plenty of business my way. If he noticed a loose hem or a worn collar...'

Foley shrugged. 'Ma.'

'His son. Goes by Sam. He bought this place about a year ago. Put the rent up right away, nearly doubled it. If it wasn't for your brother, and you...'

Foley waved his hand. 'And now?'

'He wants me out. Won't say why. But there's something in my contract with him, reckons I've got to make it good, fix the place up to its original condition...'

'This place was a *tip* when we moved in. Compared to how we found it, this is a fucken palace. Hang on. You mean original condition? Like when it was built? Brand new?'

'What he reckons. It's in my contract. Making good, he calls it. I admit I didn't read it too close.'

Foley laughed bitterly. 'Fucken hide on him. Shekel grubbing –'

'Remember how you was brought up, Desmond. It ain't him being a Jew, it's him being middle-class now. He's a big-wheel accountant.'

'Fucken slumlord, more like it. He's trying it on. Who's his flunky? Real estate agent?'

He hadn't needed to say it, but she could read it in his face. *This wasn't going to stand.* As always, when he or his brothers made fierce, his ma looked proud.

'Yair, there's an agent, the local fella. But Mr Mostel does most of it himself. Keeps coming around, reminding me I've got to make it good. Hassling me 'cos I haven't started.'

Foley put out his hand and took his mother's. It was dry and limp. 'Don't worry, Ma. I'm home now. I'll sort the bastard out. Promise.'

'You won't be able to stand over him, not even you. He's mean. Mean and short.'

'Like I say, Ma, it's my problem now. Does he know I'm your son?'

His mother nodded. 'You won't scare him. I can tell. He's like Keith.'

Foley's oldest brother, who took on five sailors with knives, and lost.

'You'll have to be smart. Threatenin' his wife, kids won't work.'

'I'll take your word for it. What's old Tom driving now?'

She gave him a sly look that folded into a smile. 'You wouldn't?!'

Old Tom, who lived in a bungalow across the road, and who'd cursed her sons as animals, who'd dobbed them in a dozen times. Last time Foley was in Perth he'd stolen Tom's Falcon, used it in five bank robberies before torching it in the wheatbelt.

'You forgiven him, have you?' Foley asked.

'That bastard? Never. He's driving a new Fairlane.'

'That'll work. Now, Ma. This is for you.'

Foley passed over a worn manila envelope, heavy. 'That's four thousand in small notes. Hide it in your usual places around the house. When they come, you can say you saved it up, in bits.'

But his mother wasn't listening, instead staring at the bedrooms off the side, empty now but for the dents and scrawls her boys had made, and the posters on the walls.

6.

The alarm clock trilled its way across Swann's bedside table and fell onto his head. It was old and heavy, large as a grapefruit, and its ticking during the night made him bury his head beneath his pillow. The clock rolled off the bed and onto the floorboards. He buried his head again.

'Come on, lazybones. Where's my cuppa?'

Swann groaned. 'Time is it?'

'How would I know? It's next to you.'

Swann opened his eyes and Marion's face was right there; her brown eyes flecked with gold, her buck teeth and tousled hair. He kissed her and tasted the mustiness of his own breath, rolled onto his back and hefted up the clock, the weight of a dinner plate.

Marion was the early riser. Swann preferred to sleep from midnight through to mid-morning, and over the previous years he'd been able to rise just as Marion was leaving for work.

But the premier wanted his offices debugged before the day's business started, and that meant Swann getting up at 5.30. Because of the ticking clock, and the amount of celebratory rum he'd drunk the night before, he'd got off to sleep sometime after three.

'Thing's stopped. Ok, I'll get going.'

Swann kissed Marion again and pulled the sheet over her warm shoulders, the sight of her pale outline another reason to stay in bed.

He pulled the curtains and made a face, the light fierce. Padded down the hall past the empty bedrooms where his daughters once slept. Blonny, their youngest, had moved out a fortnight ago to live with friends, and they were still getting used to it.

*

Swann's new office was in one of the beige blocks that had appeared across the city in the sixties. The style was brutalist, the fabrication materials on show. Pale cement and brown anodised glass, layer upon layer, resembling the carpark alongside it. The tenth floor was open-plan with a view over the Swan River and the Narrows Bridge. Out of the stainless steel Schindler's lift, Swann made his way though islands of boxes and files and men in overalls wheeling about filing cabinets. His cubicle had a view of more cubicles and a plain concrete wall. There was a clock above his desk, the size of a truck wheel, visible to everyone in the vast room. A red second hand the length of his arm crawled around its plain face. He prayed it didn't come with an alarm. To avoid looking at the clock, which wasn't easy, he eyed the nearby stairwell while the young, bright-eyed secretary in a pencil skirt pointed out his electric typewriter and described how to dial out on the phone, and relay messages, and press hold.

Swann didn't know how his position as Heenan's fixer related to the desk, but all of the people around him, mostly young and on the telephone, worked in what the secretary called Media & Comm. Some of them smoked and read the newspaper and others wore headphones plugged into transistor radios. They had the look of Louise's university friends: serious and smart and sleepyheaded at the same time. The young man in the nearest cubicle, wearing jeans and desert boots and a shirt and blue tie, his hair short on the back and sides but with a mop of curls on top, gave Swann the thumbs up, and then watched with curiosity as Swann laid down his Gladstone bag and tested his chair.

The cubicle, desk and chair were new, smelt of acetone, hot glue and plastic, but the set-up was comfortable. Swann took the Statesman keys from his pocket and slid them into his pencil drawer. Heenan hadn't asked for the keys back, and Swann hadn't offered. He'd swept the premier's offices at Parliament House for bugs and two of the adjacent meeting rooms, as instructed, his daily duty while Parliament was in session. Heenan suspected the Libs of planting bugs before their retreat to the other side of the building, but Swann hadn't found any. His duty for the rest of the day was to examine the building's internal telephone network, to check its overall security. But first he needed a coffee, and a cigarette.

He was just about to dig out his chipped enamel mug from the Gladstone bag when he felt someone behind him.

He turned, and there was Gregory Corvo, dressed in black, from his cowboy boots to his crocodile-skin belt to his black leather necklace and onyx pendant. Two gold earrings in each ear offset his slicked hair, the dark eyebrows and the five o'clock shadow over his pale jaw. His hands were held in an oddly gentle embrace, fingers interlocked, placed at his belly.

'Mr Swann. My apologies for not formally making a meeting time.'

Swann was so shocked at the plaintive note in Corvo's voice that he swivelled around in his chair, and gave young Gregory his full attention. Corvo took this as a sign that he might approach. He dragged across the nearest seat, and placed his hands on his knees, cocked his head, licked his lips. Blinked.

Gregory was a notorious thug, and the sight of him making a small target was so unusual Swann found it hard to keep a straight face. Swann had watched Corvo grow up in Northbridge, always around his father Tony's illegal gambling club, sometimes acting as cockie before graduating to running his own gang of teenage kids dealing pot and rebirthing stolen cars, standing over the smaller local businesses, trading on his father's name.

Swann wanted to ask Corvo how he'd found him, and why, but first there were the formalities. 'Congratulations on your wedding, Gregory. I saw the pictures in the paper – very tasteful.'

Corvo smiled, but immediately looked worried. 'My Sophia, she's pregnant. I'm happy. My mother and father are happy.'

Gregory had married into the Adamo clan – Sicilian into Calabrian. Swann had heard on the grapevine that Corvo's new venture, a club owned by himself and two of Tommaso Adamo's wilder sons, wasn't working out so well.

Swann could guess – the Adamo boys helping themselves to the till, drinking all the profits, harassing the dancers, bashing the punters.

'What can I help you with, Gregory? You seem nervous.'

The observation was a provocation, and it worked. A flash of pride in Corvo's eyes, and the setting of his shoulders. His hands stopped their false wringing.

'My father sent me. He's the nervous one. There's a rumour in all the clubs that the Burswood development, the one the premier announced yesterday, is for a casino. Not housing, like the premier says. Our interests ...'

Swann nodded, and Corvo didn't need to say more. The illegal Northbridge clubs had operated since the 1920s. The clubs were well run and attended, and their success made little kings out of the likes of the Adamo and Corvo men. But if a legitimate casino opened up, they'd be out of business, putting to waste the fortune they'd paid in bribes over the years.

Corvo was showing a deal of interest in his hands again, tamping down his natural pride, for the sake of his father's orders. Clearly it was his first time acting the diplomat.

'Spit it out, Gregory. No need to be coy. You're not a good enough actor.'

That got the reaction Swann hoped for. A renewed flush of anger in his eyes, and an immediate relaxing of his body, settling into its usual posture of menace. Swann could see the desire for violence in Corvo, but also the desire to please his father, the anger swallowed down, balanced out in a jittery calm.

'We want to know what's going on. And if there's going to be a casino, how we can get in on it. Any information you might have, it's valuable to us. Very valuable.'

'Is there something else?'

Now Corvo's true nature revealed itself in a malicious smile.

'There is. My father told me to ... convey this ... He said that there was no point offering you money, but that some information we have might be useful to you, and your response may be useful for us.'

Just as Swann suspected. 'Go on.'

'Trevor Dragic. I heard this from one of Adamo's sons, Sep. Trevor's trying to get someone to knock you.'

'What do you mean, trying? No takers?'

Corvo looked a little embarrassed, on Swann's behalf. 'You didn't leave him with much money. He's only offering two thousand. That's walking-around money for the Adamo boys.'

Swann rubbed his chin. 'Cheap prick. Two *thousand*. What'd Sep say?'

'Said he knew some smackhead cray fishermen who'd do it. But not until they've blown their money. The season's only just ended. He reckons it'll be weeks before the boys have put their wages up their arms.'

'Just thinking aloud, Gregory, and feel free to stop me anytime. Dragic wouldn't be that stupid, would he? Those cowboys of the ocean are wild, but they'll spill soon as they're arrested. Why wouldn't they?'

'You're right, Mr Swann. But I wouldn't underestimate Dragic. They say he's back in Macedonia, and that he's in with some Albanians. There's plenty owe him favours here too, and he's got the ear of the coppers from ...'

Corvo didn't need to say it. Dragic was one of a number of Perth businessmen who'd come up through the smack trade. He would have paid bent coppers like Benjamin Hogan over the years, and perhaps still contributed to the Christmas fund. But not even Hogan would knock Swann for a couple of thousand. He was now chief of the CIB, and had revenue streams coming out of the brothels, illegal casinos and dealers all over the city, without having to lift a finger. He'd tried to kill Swann once, but was making too much money to bother with an old vendetta.

'Thanks, Gregory, but I don't think Hogan would waste his time.'

'I hope you're right, Mr Swann. To the matter of Burswood, our business ...'

'Tell your father I haven't heard those rumours. But if I do, I'll be in touch. Between us, only.'

'Thankyou Mr Swann. And goodbye.'

'No need to thank me, yet.'

Swann turned his back on the departing Corvo, pulled open the Gladstone and fished out his enamel mug. He replaced the bag under his desk, where it couldn't be seen. The bag contained his tools, many of them expensive, some of them illegal.

He patted his shirt pocket and took out a cigarette. He dug into his trousers and found his zippo lighter.

He was just about to stand when the secretary who'd shown him to his desk arrived, glanced at the mug, the cigarette and the lighter in Swann's hands. 'Mr Swann, your next visitor is waiting. Shall I bring him over?'

Swann couldn't hide his surprise. 'Next? You mean there's more?'

She pursed her lips. 'Yes. They've been here all morning. They're waiting in the atrium. But we only have four seats there.'

'How many?'

'Last time I looked? Eight.'

Swann saw his next visitor coming, a rogue giant among the boxes and cubicles, shoulders hunched and fists clenched, followed by the stares and whispers of the young workers.

Gus Riley was dressed in his regular stained denim jeans and steel-capped boots, but was also wearing his sleeveless leather jacket bearing the club patch. His goatee beard was trimmed but his red hair was long and lank.

Riley was the new president of the Nongs, Perth's third largest bikie club, but its most notorious.

'Swann! You fucker!'

There was blood on the knuckles of Riley's left hand. Swann looked at the secretary, still frozen to the spot, and put two and two in the hat. There were people waiting in line to see Swann. One of them would be nursing a sore head. Riley wasn't the type to wait in lines.

Riley threw himself down into the seat and smiled. 'Last time I saw you, you was black and blue. Landed on your feet mate. Fucken foreman material ...'

'How did you find me, Gus? Not like I've been here long.'

'The fat bastard works for the premier. Heenan. Has a taste for some of our strippers. I went to him, and he said come to you. Said he can't be seen talking to me, but that you could pass on the message.'

The last time Swann had seen Gus Riley, Swann had needed a .38 revolver to negotiate his way out of the Nongs clubhouse. Riley and his mutts had taken on a contract to kill him, paid for by the current head of the CIB, Ben Hogan.

'You still owe me an EK Holden, Riley.'

Riley laughed. 'I know, I know. Good news is that train's about to arrive. But first I've got a little something to run by you.'

'I'm all ears.' Swann leaned back in his swivel chair, put his hands behind his head.

'Look at this.'

Riley leant forward and produced a crumpled brown paper bag that smelt like bad polony. He curled the edges of the bag until Swann could see the dried apricot-shaped meat at its bottom.

'An ear.'

Swann felt his stomach tumble. The ear didn't look good, and it didn't smell good, but he'd never let Riley see his discomfort.

'Yeah, Swanny. An ear. A human ear. Belonging to my mate Stiggs. Been missing since last week, when I sent him on a recon mission.'

'Do tell.'

'It's these Kiwi bastards. The Outlaw Mob. You heard they've been muscling in?'

Swann shook his head. He genuinely hadn't.

'Well, it's not like they've been advertising. No bikes yet, and no patches. But they've set up a tattoo parlour in Beckenham, and a bike shop next door. Kawa-fucking-sakis and other Jap crap. They've bought a big old factory on a block up the street. Started fencing the place off.'

'And you sent your mate Stiggs to have a stickybeak at the place. Stiggs isn't exactly suited to undercover work. He still have tatts on his face?'

'You can laugh, Swanny. Stiggs was one of my best mechanics. Best enforcers too.'

'Was? There a body to go with the ear?'

Riley stuck out his jaw, and scratched it. 'Not yet. But not looking good, is it?'

'And you've taken this to Ben Hogan. And for whatever reason he's not helping you ...'

'That prick. The amount of cash I shovel him. Reckons there's nothing he can do about it until they break a law. Doesn't care there's gonna be blood running in the streets. It's war, man, until we force those black bastards back to New Zealand.'

'Which leads me to the obvious question, Gus. Perth's a long way from New Zealand. What are they doing here?'

'In New Zealand, a gram of speed goes for fifty bucks. Here, because of the boom, the number of blokes into the goey, a gram sells for a hundred.'

Swann whistled. It was true there had always been an unofficial locals-only bike club policy, something that kept the Eastern States clubs at bay. But now a Kiwi club had leapfrogged the Bandidos, Comancheros and Angels to get a nose in the trough. He was genuinely surprised that the CIB wasn't enforcing the longstanding five-club policy the usual way: harassment of the newcomers, confiscations, red stickers on the bikes, some appropriate loading of drugs or stolen property, as had always been done in the past.

Was Ben Hogan, and the rest of the Purple Circle who now controlled the CIB, waiting until the arrival of the new commissioner before they cracked some Kiwi heads, or something else?

'The thing is, Swanny. Outlaw Mob's a national organisation, unlike us. They've got serious money behind them, not to mention muscle. They can afford to pay over the odds to operate here. More than we can pay, or have been.'

Swann steepled his fingers. Almost certainly, Riley was right. But if he wanted a war, it would have happened. Riley had no idea how many Maori bikies were living anonymously in the community, waiting for a call to arms.

'What did you want from Heenan?'

'I wanted to tell the fat prick to tell the premier there's going to be a war, and that the local coppers are going to stand by and watch, to see who comes out on top. Guessing he won't want that, in his first weeks ...'

'You're probably right.'

Riley leant forward, and a humourless mirth showed in his eyes.

Here it comes, Swann thought. He put up a hand. 'Two thousand?'

Riley's laugh like a depth charge made the young man at the next desk flinch. 'Fuck eh? Good news travels fast. But I heard two thousand and a taste.'

'A taste of what?'

'Whatever comes next. Access, for information, Swann. Currency of spies, dogs and women. The reason I'm here, talking to you. But if the hat fits ...'

'I appreciate you sharing, Gus. But back to your problem with our brothers across the ditch.' Swann inclined his head, to give the impression that he'd given it thought. 'I reckon you need to get organised. Put aside your grievances with the Barbarians and the Bad Breed, the Dingo Jacks, the Junkyard Dogs. David versus Goliath and all that. WA bikies versus the rest. The devil you know.'

'Like a union, you mean.'

'Yes, Gus, a union. Pool your resources. Go to the media and appeal to the West Australian in us all. Stand at the head of St Georges Terrace, under the Barracks Arch, on a soapbox, and warn of the foreign peril. You little West-Aussie battlers.'

Swann stood, and Riley stood, and they looked across at the staff, some staring like roos in the headlights. They shook hands. 'In the meantime,

Gus, I'll see what I can do with the premier.'

'Thanks Swanny. You do your bit, and I'll do mine. Like old times.'

Riley strode off, lighting a cigar with blunt puffs, deep in thought. The secretary broke out of the nearest group and headed towards the atrium by the lifts. The others remained quiet against the walls. It occurred to Swann that none of them had any idea what his role was. They only knew that two of the state's most notorious criminals had visited him, cap in hand. And that there were more supplicants waiting.

Access, for information ...

Swann didn't want to know what the others wanted, or had over him. He slipped his enamel mug into his Gladstone bag, slid out the Statesman keys and headed for the stairs.

He went ten flights down and two more to the basement, carrying the heavy bag over his shoulder. By the time he reached the basement, one of his knees had begun to ache and the urge for a cigarette had passed. He went back up the stairs and exited into the ground-floor lobby, then went back down. There was no security between the street and the communications system that operated across this building and the nearby public service buildings.

Swann entered through the cheap veneer door, reinforced with metal plating, that he'd been instructed led to the telecommunications room. In a narrow corridor that smelt dry and musty he could see the exposed wiring that carried the massed telephone and fax lines up into the higher reaches of the building, again unprotected by conduit or any kind of piping; something else that would have to be remedied.

At the end of a corridor was a solid wooden door that opened onto a room that was completely dark. A warm electronic heat and the sound of buzzing. There were banks of red and green lights, but otherwise Swann couldn't see anything. He reached his hand along the wall adjacent to the door and found a switch, tripped it. There in the centre of the room, hunched over the vast console, was the telephonist.

'Norman!'

The telephonist turned, lifted off his headphones and mike. 'Recognise that voice. Fremantle Station – Charlie sixty-six. That you, Frank? Frank Swann? I was warned you'd be coming down. Though by the smell of you, you've changed your brand of cigarettes. What's that – Craven A to Peter Jackson?'

'Close. Peter Stuyvesant.'

'Fair play to me, Swann. That's my own brand – invisible to my delicate nose.'

Norman Gorman was a legend in the police service. He was blind, which accounted for the darkened room, but had been the police force telephonist for as long as Swann could remember. Swann had heard that Norm retired, but clearly retirement hadn't suited the famously dapper man who got about with a steel cane that doubled as a fencer's foil.

'Couldn't stand the bloody silence out in the suburbs, Frank. Stopped looking after myself. Need the ritual of getting dressed and getting on the bus, getting off the bus, getting stuck into some work. The coppers didn't want me back, so here I am.'

Swann went and stood next to Norm, put a hand on his shoulder. He was looking good, except for his regular nightclub tan. Even as a younger man, seated at his desk underneath Central, dressed in a double-breasted suit and satin shirt, always a folded hankie and perfectly matching silk tie, his thin brown hair perfectly combed in a centre part, he'd often resembled a wax model of an Edwardian gentleman. And the thing was that Norman dressed himself.

As the telephonist for the police force, Norm was always treated with a deal of respect. He put through calls and took messages, but the rumours were that he also listened to everything. Nobody knew this for sure, because there was no way to know, but Norm had helped Swann with information on a couple of occasions when colleagues had been gunning for him. Swann never asked where Norm had heard the threats and the plans.

'Talk me through your system here, Norm.'

Swann listened while Norm described the internal communications network installed during the tenure of the previous government, and which linked eight local buildings and dozens of departments, with Norm as the focal point.

'And the premier's office – is that routed through here?'

Norm shook his head. 'They have a separate operator up there, a woman by the name of Lapin. French for rabbit.'

'You trust her?'

Norm wobbled his hand.

'Can we get the lines to the premier's office run through here? That doable? I've got to put some remedial measures in place outside your room too, because it's wide open to bugs, but in here it looks secure. In the meantime ...'

One of Norman's eyebrows lifted, but only for a moment. If he was curious about Swann's motivations for allowing him access to all of the premier's telephone conversations, it wasn't in his voice. 'Sure, Frank. Anything's possible.'

7.

Des Foley slumped in the bucket seat of the stolen Fairlane. He'd parked the chugging four-litre sedan across the road from the real estate agent, and cut the idle. It was only a few streets from where he'd stolen Old Tom's car, but he doubted the man would look for it here, at the bottom of Hay Street. Since the sixties, many of the previous residents of the East Perth tenements, slum-shacks and worn-out lodging homes had migrated to the public housing satellite cities of Mirrabooka, Balga and Nollamara. They had their own gangs up there now, but some still returned to their old haunts to steal, knowing all the backstreets and means of escape. It was fair to assume that Old Tom would write his car off as stolen by blacks, a thing to be thrashed and cannibalised. Foley had no respect for Old Tom and his dobbing ways, but he'd checked the car's glove box first, to make sure that Tom had insurance. He wouldn't steal it otherwise.

Foley watched the estate agent's building for twenty minutes, shifting only to slump deeper into his bucket seat when a car passed and its headlights strafed the row of double-storey shopfronts before turning left towards the Gloucester Park raceway. Foley was only a few hundred metres from the Central Police Station, and a couple of marked Falcons had cruised past, as well as some unmarked Commodores belonging to detectives. All of them were headed back to the station at the end of a shift, and none of them looked too closely.

Foley didn't drink much, and then only beer, and he didn't smoke. He'd learnt to avoid dependency while in prison, where it made you weak. In his line of work, anything that made a man twitchy was to be avoided. Foley had good focus, disciplined to analyse the job at hand, to problem-solve and anticipate complications. Anything else was a potentially dangerous distraction.

His only weakness was a love of adrenalin, but he was experienced enough to tamp that down, too, and use it as fuel, rather than make it the thing itself.

Foley could feel the embers of a familiar nervous glow awaken in his belly, radiate into his limbs. He took a deep breath, and then another. Applying oxygen to the embers, but only enough to keep them alive. He needed his mind clear. It was only a break-and-enter, but one mistake and he was back in jail, for twenty to thirty. Or shot dead in the street. He was parked in the middle of the one police jurisdiction where his fake ID wouldn't cut it.

When the street was clear, he opened the Fairlane door and stepped onto the footpath, still warm after the day's sun. He wasn't surprised that the branch office of Lefroy Realty was in this part of Perth. A few minutes away from East Perth by foot, there were no blackfellas or bog hoons or poor old immigrants on this street. It was all graphic designers and politicians' offices, real estate agents and gourmet sandwich bars. And then the looming Central Police Station, looking south across the Causeway.

Foley walked the block to gain access to the dirt alley that ran behind the street fronts. He'd B&E'd all of the shops down the terrace row when he was a kid, and years later there was nothing spruce about the rear of the shops. He peeled away a cack-handed effort at fencing with rusted tin and star pickets and slipped inside. He counted down the buildings that rose with the gentle incline towards the city lights, knelt before the rear security door and got to work with his picks.

It was an old lock and only took a couple of tweaks before he felt the tumbler snip. The crappy wooden door inside, loose on its hinges, gave him even less trouble. He closed the door behind him and reached for his torch. It was heavy and doubled as a weapon. He'd taped a brown paper bag over the nose, to diminish the light, but it was sufficient.

The files would be kept in the manager's office, which was unlocked. A single filing cabinet beside an unadorned desk with an electronic typewriter. He slipped the tray labelled M–S and found the Mostel file. It was fat. He shone the torch over photographs of properties and land deeds and council applications and rental agreements, all neatly numbered and too many to count. At the front was an index, linking property addresses. There were eighty-three in total, most of them addresses in the inner city, with a few down High Street in Fremantle.

Foley whistled. Eighty-three properties. That was a significant amount of rental income, every week. It only took a few seconds, but Foley's plan changed from the simple standover of a single landlord to something else. He didn't know what yet, except that it felt right. The bastard owned half the local area and yet there he was, bullying Foley's mother, making it personal.

Foley recited it back to himself. *Making it personal.*

Exactly what he would do.

He turned before he heard the sound. A car door slamming, the boot of a station wagon. He stood at the office door and looked into the street, recognising the face from the flyers throughout the office. It was Timothy Lefroy, the business owner. Foley had plenty of time to withdraw through the office and return to the alley. Nobody would know of his visit.

Except that remnant burn of anger, and the knowledge that the Mostel file would only reveal so much.

Lefroy was carrying a swag and a sleeping bag over his shoulder, a pillow in each hand. He unlocked the front door and held it open with his foot, threw in the swag and sleeping bag, the pillows, let the door close as he returned to his car.

Foley waited for Lefroy; this time he was carrying takeaway in a heat-sagging plastic bag, and a bottle of wine. Lefroy unlocked the door and entered, kicking the sleeping materials towards the nearest desk.

When Lefroy approached his office, Foley stepped into the hall and punched him in the face. Lefroy stood there, hands by his sides, still holding onto the wine and food, so Foley punched him again, watched his knees buckle, the light go out in his eyes.

Foley caught the estate agent as he fell, and dragged him into the office. When a man is knocked out it's impossible to gauge the length of his spell – could be a few seconds, could be a few minutes. Could be forever. Foley sat on the edge of the desk and fished around in the takeaway bag, drew out a paper wrapper containing four spring rolls, began to munch. There was no need to hurry. The real estate agent was aiming to sleep in his own office. Meant a break-up, or a divorce, and he smelt of booze. Nobody would be looking for him tonight.

When Foley finished the spring rolls, he was still hungry. He opened one of the foil trays and began to shovel fried rice into his mouth with his fingers, pausing every few mouthfuls to flick rice onto Lefroy's face. Finally, the man began to stir. Foley put down the tray of rice in preparation. As he expected, once Lefroy's eyes opened he was immediately lucid. Fear will do that, and the next thing. Lefroy began to shout. Foley pinched Lefroy's nose, forced his jaw shut. Knelt on his chest, and pushed. Lefroy nodded, unblinking. He'd recognised Foley, and that was a good thing. Cut out all of the unnecessary. The need to hurt him further, or explain his purpose. Lefroy knew.

But whether it was guilt or shame behind that look of understanding, or just plain fear, would make all the difference.

8.

Swann hung his towel on the veranda railing and went to the garden hose. He stood under the mottled shadow of the tuart tree and let the sun-heated water in the length of hose run out over his head, the colder water coming through onto his belly and legs. He stripped off his shorts and wrung them out and stood naked under the cold water, gazing up at the tracer-lines of pink and amethyst and orange streaked across the western sky. He hosed the beach sand off his feet and padded over to the jarrah porch, wrapped the towel around his waist and eased into his old canvas deckchair, to watch the sunset fade. On the upturned milk crate beside him was a bottle of Captain Morgan rum, and he poured himself a couple of fingers into a patterned glass that his children had once used to drink milk. The glass had somehow managed to avoid the carnage of twenty-two years of accidents and more than a few tantrums. He added cold water from a plastic jug and took a sip, added some more. He ignored the cigarettes on the floor beside his chair. He'd just swum a kilometre down at South Beach, a hundred metres or so offshore, weathering the small chop and stingers until he couldn't swim anymore.

Swann sipped on the rum and closed his eyes and felt the last rays of sunshine leave the yard. Some wattlebirds were fighting in the nearby callistemon over the first red flowers. In another tree up the street he could hear a party of red-tailed black cockatoos, their laughter loud across the neighbourhood.

Swann never thought he'd say it, but it felt good to have a nine-to-five, to not have to linger in parking lots overnight doing surveillance, or stalk company CEOs across town while they lived the high life, from Coco's to Clouds to the clubs in Northbridge – them drinking champagne and eating oysters, Swann drinking lukewarm thermos tea and pissing in a bottle.

He heard the screen door swing open, and listened for the sounds of Marion's padding feet. She'd been over at their second daughter Sarah's house in White Gum Valley, babysitting Neve and Jock, their first two grandchildren. Sarah had her first child at eighteen, soon followed by another. She was finishing high school at the nearby TAFE, and Swann and Marion were often called to help.

Swann had just turned forty-five. He felt young to be a grandfather, but there it was.

'Frank, come here. I've got a surprise.'

Swann grinned at the pleasure in Marion's voice. It hadn't always been like that. When the kids were young and Swann was drinking, the stress of his job had taken them close to divorce. And then he'd lost them all at one point, for the sake of another woman, who wasn't worth the pain it caused Marion and his kids. He rewound the towel over his waist and wandered into the kitchen. There on the table was a banana box. Inside the banana box was a pair of eyes, brown and wet, and an even wetter muzzle. He looked to Marion, who laughed, lifted off the box's lid to reveal a puppy, between two and three months old. 'She's a staffy-kelpie cross. Sarah's neighbours had one left, and it was headed for the pound. Couldn't let that happen.'

Marion kissed Swann and stroked his neck, watching his reaction. The kids had various pets growing up, including a feral cat called Colonel Charles Custard who'd wandered over from the nearby quarry and, most recently, a wiry mongrel called Clarry who bit Swann on the feet whenever he was hungry. In every case the strays had adopted the family, rather than the other way around, wandering into the yard and refusing to leave.

Swann picked up the dog and held it before him. She licked his hand and piddled down his arm, a warm yellow stream, her trusting eyes staring into his.

'Don't tell me that wasn't planned.'

Swann placed her back on the table and scratched her ears. He put his dry arm around Marion and they watched the dog circle the edge of the table, looking for a way down. Swann didn't need to say anything. He felt like he understood. The quiet in the house, the absence of children, it was a relief, but it was also hard.

Marion worked as a home-care nurse, tending to the palliative needs of dying men and women, the drug problems of those too screwed up to attend clinics, the clap treatments of the prostitutes in the nearby area, and the various ailments of the street people around Fremantle. She was nobody's fool, but also tender by nature. It was draining work, and she didn't get much in return. She'd always loved animals for that reason. They loved her right back, even Clarry, who'd never once bitten her.

The phone rang. Swann washed the dog pee off his arm under the kitchen sink. As a PI, he hadn't been able to afford an office, and his clients called him at home. One or two had called over the past days, offering him work that he'd been glad to turn down, and no doubt they would keep ringing. Marion took the pooch out back while he lifted the receiver.

'Swann?'

An unmistakable voice. Chocolate and whisky. Heenan.

'Swann? Turn on your TV at seven, check the leading story. Something to think about. I'd like to meet with you about it, first thing tomorrow. In the meantime, I want to hear how today went. The people who came to see you. We've got to keep a hygienic distance between us and some of these jokers. But they do need to be heard, for reasons of keeping an ear out. Sure you understand, Frank.'

Swann recounted, in detail, his conversations with Corvo and Riley. He kept waiting for the Heenan to stop him, to say that he didn't want to hear, but he never did. Instead, he had the impression Heenan was writing it all down, taking notes, and he kept prodding Swann for further details. Did he think Corvo really believed that a casino was on the cards, or was he just fishing? When Swann replied that he seemed pretty sure, Heenan became angry. Ludicrous, that was. What a stupid idea. Someone was white-anting the premier already. Most likely Sullivan, the ex-minister of police and recently retired leader of the Liberal opposition, who the premier had thrashed at the election. Bent bastard. Long history with the worst coppers. Could even say he'd learnt strategy from them. Whatever means necessary.

Heenan was ranting. Sounded a little drunk. Swann looked at the clock above the fridge and saw that it was nearly seven.

But then Heenan's voice changed, became coy, suddenly choosing his words carefully. 'Swann, I see this as part of your job, to ... I don't know, cultivate these people. Feel free to ... do them favours, if you think it useful to us. You know what I mean.'

'They're in our debt.'

'Precisely. But don't forget that it goes both ways. They offer you something, do a favour for you, for us, then ...'

'I understand. Heenan, it's seven. You want me to hang up?'

Heenan grunted. In the background, Swann heard the ABC news start up, the symphonic strains familiar to millions: marching music on the road to truth.

Heenan hung up, and Swann replaced the receiver. He turned on their small TV, already tuned to the ABC. The vision was of the Old Swan Brewery, the announcer getting in a punning headline before the morning papers, stealing some sub-editor's fun – 'Trouble brewing on the banks of the Swan'. Aboriginal protesters had set up camp by Kennedy's Fountain to protest the government's plan to redevelop the Brewery into a hotel complex. The Brewery was built on a sacred site. There were images of police clashing with angry men and women, Nyungar elders in the background, arm in arm.

9.

Blake Tracker crouched in the dark shadow of a flowering wattle, sweet air scenting his head. He'd scouted down the back alley to check for dogs, peering between the sheets of rusted tin that did for a back fence. It was a warm night but in the rear yard the southerly carried the caustic stench of the Kwinana refinery, something like burnt rubber and the sweat of hot metal. It was better in the front yard, out of the wind. He still had on the shorts, tee-shirt and sandshoes he'd worn during his escape. He'd managed to stay warm by walking through the dark hours, keeping to the bush that followed the foothills south, sometimes running over well-lit open ground when there was no other way. To avoid the main roads he'd waded across farmers' creeks that trickled down from the higher ground on the scarp and fed into the Canning River, avoiding the lights of Gosnells, Kelmscott, Armadale. He followed the South Western Highway in the early hours, sleeping in the bush when he got near Mundijong, the sun rising over the forested hills behind him, wedging himself into the gap between two granite boulders.

He slept a few hours with his tee-shirt over his face and had woken hot and dehydrated, his feet sore and his legs heavy. His ribs were still bruised and it hurt when he yawned, and his wrist was still swollen. To loosen up he shadow-boxed, rolled his shoulders and cracked his knuckles then began to head west across the bush and sparsely populated farmland that would take him to the southern edges of suburban Perth. He was hungry and thirsty but it felt good to walk. It was the long way round, but it was better than being caught. No way was he going back inside. Those guards were going to kill him, for real.

When the sun broke, he slept the next day inside a drainage culvert until the darkness came. It took another night's walking before he hit

Stock Road, which ran north–south, where he'd camped for a few hours in the banksia swampland by Beeliar Lake, waiting for the shadows of late afternoon. As soon as the sun dipped behind the dunes to the west he'd turned north, cross-country again, but always staying near the highway that took him into Coolbellup, the blue-collar suburb where his father lived.

His father and his father's mates were drinking in the kitchen, as always. He heard his father's laugh like thunderheads in the darkness. His uncle Dennis, who always had that wheezy laugh. A woman whose voice he didn't recognise. Might be white, might be black. In the front room the television blared through the uncurtained windows past the ripped-up couch and plastic chairs on the front porch, a yard of dried weeds and the odd stem of lemongrass. Behind the open front door was his father's bedroom. It was dark in there, smelt of Champion Ruby and goon wine, sweaty leather boots and engine oil – a cave that his father only entered to sleep.

It was good that his father's dog was missing. Betty was a pig dog with bitten ears and a misty eye. She would smell him from a mile off, and get to barking. The three of them had made the journey down from Laverton to Perth four years ago, Blake and Betty in the swag on the ground at night, his father with some old mission blankets on the truck's flatbed tray, afraid of snakes. The old Datsun banger had a busted head gasket and a dud radiator, and pissed out steam every fifty k. But the Datsun was his father's pride and joy, still had the same faded yellow panels with bogged patches and rusty sills, and was now parked beneath the fibro shack's front porch, as close to his father's bed as possible. His father slept with an axe handle next to his pillow, and could be out the door in seconds.

The run-down workers cottage belonged to his father outright, paid for in cash. Blake had never asked where the money came from. His father was old-school about things like that. He'd made his mistakes and had served his time in Freo prison. Two long stretches before and after Blake was born. It was only after Blake's mother died of pneumonia that his father came back into his life. Had come out to the desert to collect him. What he thought was the right thing to do.

That was Blake's father for you. He'd say half of something and it was up to you to figure out the rest. He'd been through the Law, however, and that counted for something, even in the city.

It was all – a man does *this* – a man does *that*. What a man is, and isn't. What a man should *do*. What a man should never do.

But they were just words. Even Blake could see that. And Blake had seen at his trial how words meant nothing on their own. How they could be twisted and turned to mean something else.

In the mouth of a witness. In the mouth of a lawyer. In the mouth of a judge.

In the mouth of a father, too.

Blake sucked the bitter juice out of another stalk of lemongrass. Dogs had probably pissed on it, but no matter. The drinkers in his father's kitchen had gone quiet. Rolling out their swags against the eastern fence in the grey dirt backyard, shaded from the morning sun.

He heard a water hammer bang through the old pipes that clad the western side of the house. Last drink of water before hitting the sack. Last piss. Last fart. Last spit.

The television went off, and so did all the lights. The front door slammed shut. Goodnight, Pops.

10.

Swann was asleep when the phone started to ring. He looked at the clock on his bedside table. Two am. He rolled onto an elbow, flipped his bare feet onto the floorboards. Paused, hoping the phone would ring out, except that it didn't.

He made the kitchen and hefted the receiver. 'Yeah?'

'Swann, it's Heenan again. Sorry about the time. But it's important.'

Heenan always spoke in short sentences, which had a lot to do with his weight and lack of puff, but now it was exaggerated, sounded winded. 'I spoke to you earlier about favours. We've been asked. A close friend of the premier, on a delicate matter. Total discretion. Can't have the coppers involved.'

Swann scratched his belly, yawned. Whatever he'd been dreaming about, it had been good. He wanted to go back there. Out of reflex, he flicked a switch on a black box spliced with a joiner into his phone line. In his line of work, threatening phone calls were part of the job, but he always made sure to record them. The key word that made him reach for the switch now was *discretion*.

'Have you had any dealings with Mr Le?'

'Jesus, Heenan, get on with it. You mean Charlie Le?'

Swann knew the answer. Big wheel in the Chinese community. Owned a couple of restaurants, ran illegal card games, was into the thoroughbreds, but only if they raced in Hong Kong.

'He's been taken for half a million cash. A card game gone wrong. Reckons he was put under a "black spell", though I reckon he was drugged. His head still isn't right. Keeps falling asleep. Heavenly Swindlers, he calls them. They're Triad.'

'Le is good mates with Tommaso Adamo. Why did he call *you*? If these jokers are Triad, why doesn't he let the Italians help him? I assume he wants them tracked down, cash returned, et cetera.'

'There's your answer. He wants the cash returned. All of it. It isn't his, strictly speaking.'

Swann sighed. He was awake now. There'd be no getting back to sleep. 'Whose is it?'

'He borrowed it, at short notice, from Larry Conlan. Or Conlan's bank, Harrowgate, to be precise.'

Which made sense to Swann – Harrowgate the only bank that would hand over half a million cash to a Chinese businessman for the purposes of a card game.

'Swann? I understand how it looks. I know Harrowgate money's behind some of the people you've been … looking at lately. But quite frankly …'

'None of my business, I get it.'

Larry Conlan was an old-school racetrack shark and property developer who'd started his own bank four years ago. At the time, Swann like most people thought it was a joke. He'd taken a bankrupt local footwear company called Harrow's and changed its name to Harrowgate Investment Bank. Credit was cheap internationally, and he'd been able to borrow heavily, and find borrowers of his own. Against expectations, the bank had become a major player in the local scene. On the back of his brother's cheap credit, Larry Conlan's brother Maitland had become the city's biggest tycoon.

'But why doesn't Le want the coppers involved?' Swann asked. 'Ok, stupid question. Same answer.'

'Precisely. It's complicated. The premier would take it as a personal favour if you could drop everything else, track these men down. There are four of them; that's all I know. They're Chinese, a range of ages, they posed as high rollers, the reason Le brought so much cash. He'll lose face in his community, not to mention the monetary loss.'

'We scratch Le's back, he brings his community vote for evermore.'

'Something like that. These are clever people, Swann. But we have one advantage. Le explained it to me. They won't expect anyone to come after them. They know that Le doesn't want it in the papers, that he won't report it.'

Because Swann was recording the conversation, he asked the question.

'That's all fine, but what if I need to get heavy? There's four of them, and they won't just hand it over ...'

Heenan attempted a laugh. 'You've been watching too many Bruce Lee movies. These guys are grifters, not muscle. You'll be ok. We've got someone looking at the airport, and the bus station. They'll call you if they see anything. Whatever you need to do, Swann. Hire who you need to hire. I'll reimburse any expenses. But we're wasting time ...'

Swann hung up, watched the red light on the receiver box glimmer and fade. The receiver automatically sent the conversation wirelessly to a hidden recorder in the roof-space, just in case the house was burgled. You couldn't be too careful.

*

Swann drove east through the sleeping city, thinking about the Heavenly Swindlers. Despite himself, he'd always admired a good con-artist, part of a breed common enough during his childhood, operating mainly out of the racetracks. The kind of set-up that had conned Charlie Le took patience and nerve – each of the four men would hold down a role, and get it right like a trained actor. There was the added anxiety of prison time, or worse if they were discovered early on.

He crossed the Swan River at Canning Bridge, alone on the road, only the pale shapes of sleeping pelicans on the river pylons for company.

Swann doubted that the Heavenly Swindlers would flee by car. There was two thousand kilometres of wheat stubble and desert until they hit the next city. Being the world's most isolated metropolis had its advantages. The men were a chance to exit from the Fremantle port, although the Swindlers would almost certainly have flown in.

More likely they'd hide out in a motel near the airport. There were dozens clustered along the Great Eastern Highway leading into the city.

He thought of calling the night desks of each of the motels, but that would take time. Set a thief to catch a thief. The men would be wired after their success. Adrenalin would keep them awake. They could take the edge off with drink, but there was something better, and therefore more likely. Swann dialled as he drove, punching in the numbers of the escort agencies he kept in his notebook. Prossies were always good for a bit of information, madams even better. They were predisposed to help Swann after he'd ruined his career trying to find brothel madam Ruby Devine's killer. Many of the city's working girls also knew Marion, who saw them at their workplaces. If the Heavenly Swindlers were calling down women, Swann would get the information.

Swann parked near the Ascot racetrack, on a dark street by the river. A streetlight leading to a nearby jetty was engulfed in thousands of moths, swirling in and out of the yellow haze. He lit a cigarette and scrolled down the driver's window, felt the night chill on his bare arm. He held the car phone in his other hand, while he waited for the madam of Magenta Escorts, Sally Sargent, to check her books. The Swindlers wouldn't go out to a brothel and leave the cash unattended. And they wouldn't want Asian girls – it might get back to Le. The chances were good they'd opt for busty blonde Aussie women, or a variation on the type, ordered by the motel night desk, for a finder's fee.

The phone clicked. 'Swann? Yeah, we sent one girl out to the Raceway Motor Hotel, Candice, about two hours ago. Hired for the night. But that's about it.'

Swann considered, but it didn't sound likely. 'No parties tonight?'

'Nah, all single punters. Mostly regulars. Average Tuesday night. That's the only one to a highway motel.'

It wasn't impossible. Cheap, to order one woman for four men. Cheap and nasty, but not impossible.

'The night desk – what's his name.'

'That'd be Derek.'

Swann hung up, and punched in the numbers. The phone rang and was answered immediately. Smoker's voice, scratchy and worn. Not much to do between midnight and dawn except smoke. Tinny radio in the background.

Swann introduced himself to Derek, and told him what he wanted. Derek's delayed reaction confirmed Swann's suspicions.

'Nup, nah, can't help you mate. What our clients do in their rooms, their business. And besides, no Chogies here, mate ...'

'Yeah, alright. What I want to know is how much the four Chinese gentlemen are paying you to keep your mouth shut. To keep their room off the books. To tell people like me to mind their own business.'

Swann waited while Derek, he assumed, tried to double whatever he was being paid. Obviously not good at maths. Took him near ten seconds.

'One thou. Cash. And I'm fucken keepin' it.'

'I want you to keep it, Derek. And I also want to double it. All you got to do is tell me which room the gentlemen are in, turn off all the corridor lights, leave out the key and take the phone off the hook. Reckon you can do that?'

Didn't take Derek long to think about Swann's offer. Swann asked him what the men had been drinking, and how much. Derek had delivered them two bottles of Dewar's and three buckets of ice, about two hours ago. Derek told Swann the room, and hung up.

*

Just as Derek had promised, he'd cut the lights to the motel parking lot, forecourt and quadrangle around which were clustered the mostly single room apartments. Even double-storey fleabags like the Raceway, made of salmon-brick and orange terracotta, usually had a couple of self-catering rooms for larger groups or a family. Down the end of the darkened row was number sixty-three. Without Derek's help he would have found it. Dawn wasn't far away, and sixty-three was the only room lit. Swann took out his .22 pistol and checked the safety. It was a Beretta 87 Target. The gun wasn't registered – Swann had two pistols at home that were legal – but it suited his purposes. If things went south he could ditch it. He had the advantage of surprise, but no knowledge of the men on the other side of the shitty veneer door.

He wiped spit onto the key before he inserted it, in case the lock was tight. He felt the lock give. He didn't know whether the doorway was visible from the lounge room, but he guessed that it was – the sound of murmuring was loud. He opened the door and sighted the pistol and strode into the brightly lit and overheated lounge. All of the fluoros and two lamps were on, and for a reason. While one older man, who looked like Buddha with hair, sat on the couch and had his dick sucked by Candice, another younger man was mounted on her back, pumping away like a Chihuahua riding a Great Dane. The other two were sprawled across the carpet, looking up at the show, stroking themselves through white briefs. It couldn't have been better – their other hands were busy with whisky and cigarettes.

Candice was a big unit, and she didn't flinch. Swann still looked cop, and she knew the drill. She shrugged off the bareback rider and reached for a towel.

The silence remained, until Swann broke it. 'You been paid?'

'Yes, hon. I took quite a bit of convincing to let this happen. I'll be on my way.'

Swann stood back and let Candice gather her pumps and frock, her knickers and sequinned handbag. She left in a cloud of sex and cheap perfume, quietly shutting the door behind her.

'Righto. Who's the boss?'

Swann was met with three empty stares, and one of piercing hatred. The two men on the ground, and the fat man on the couch were glassy-eyed and reeked of whisky sweat. Their chubbies hadn't faded, which was a good thing. In all his years, Swann had never seen a man with a stiffie throw a punch.

But the young man who'd been riding Candice was sober, which at least showed a degree of smarts. He'd be the one to wake them, get them packed and onto the next plane. His nodded his chin to a matching pair of white briefs on the couch, and Swann waved the gun, yes. This was where it could get tricky. That much money, they might have stashed it nearby; outside in the garden, an air-conditioning vent, a roof-space. Swann would have to play the game. They would have to believe that he'd torture it out of them, even if that wasn't the plan.

'Where is it?'

The younger man smirked. 'You know who we're with?' American accent, but all the vowels kicked out.

Swann looked the man up and down, chicken legs and wings, belly like a soft-boiled egg, white undies pulled high. He too was acting a part.

Swann didn't have cuffs, or rope, so he waved the gun again, pointed at the bare space of carpet where Candice had been. 'You, get on your back. Lie down.'

The young man complied, folding himself into a spider's crouch, energy poised for a moment, the fierce hatred in his eyes and mocking smile never leaving his face, before he unfurled on the carpet. Swann kicked the fat man on the leg. 'Get on top of him. Facedown.'

There was blood in the young man's face, pinned by the weight of the older man. 'Now you, on your back, on his back.'

The man on the bottom had to translate, and when the third man looked reluctant, Swann pointed the gun at his tackle. He rose to his feet, and draped himself over the fat man, facing up, grunting with the effort.

Swann directed the last man to take his place on top of the pile, looking down into his mate's eyes, his toes gripping the carpet.

'Don't look so unhappy. People pay good money for that. Don't move an inch.'

The three matching pairs of jocks, the fat man's flaccid tackle, a sweaty pile of angry, incapacitated men. Swann finished the tower with an ice bucket on the final man's back into which he stuffed the empty bottle of Dewar's and three nearby glasses. If the men moved, it was going to tip off.

He rummaged through the empty cupboards in the kitchen, the oven, the fridge, but he needn't have bothered. The youngest man on the bottom of the pile was struggling to breathe. The smug look had gone. He looked stricken.

'In the leather suitcase. The Louis Vuitton ... bedroom, on bed.'

It was there as he promised. Swann kept an eye on the four sets of feet, one of them trembling to hold the pyramid together, and opened the latch. All of the luggage was matching leather, and expensive, as you'd expect from a theatrical troupe impersonating high rollers. The cash was banded in packets of ten thousand, stuffed into cotton bags stamped with the cheesy faux-imperial logo of Conlan's Harrowgate Investment Bank. All present and accounted for. Swann did a scout looking for weapons in the suits hanging in the wardrobe and in the other suitcases; he found nothing more offensive than cheap aftershave and dirty jocks.

He snapped the suitcase shut and walked into the lounge. Not a drop of the ice-water had been spilt. He moved to the door but changed his mind. He went back into the bedroom and took the four passports, sealed in a plastic bag, and their Cathay Pacific tickets, leaving their wallets and loose change. The men could make their way out of Perth overland, or hide out and wait for more forged passports. None of his concern. He was no friend of Charlie Le's, but the young man's arrogance had pissed him off. Their adventure in a foreign land was only just beginning.

'Wait. No. I tell you something.'

The man on the bottom of the pile, pinned down, only one hand free. He used it to wave Swann back towards him. 'I tell you something good.'

Swann laughed. 'I don't want any of the money, mate. It's not mine, it's not yours, it isn't even Charlie fucking Le's. You feel blue-balled now, but you'll be right after a cold shower.'

'We don't want the money either.'

There was something in the man's voice. 'Good, then everyone's happy.'

'Give us passports back, I tell you something. Charlie Le.'

Swann walked to the pile of reddening flesh and toppled them over, stood back. 'Go on then ...'

The young man crawled away from his colleagues, straightened his skewiff undies, cracked his wrists. The others crawled over to sit alongside him, leaning back against the couch, four in a row, their faces strangely earnest.

'Charlie Le, we didn't come to take his money. We work for a different company ...'

Triad, he meant, but Swann wasn't about to correct him. 'Go on.'

'Charlie Le, he buys from Hong Kong. We are from Singapore.'

'Buys what?'

The man looked at him strangely. 'You are not police?'

Swann laughed. 'No, I am not.'

The young man muttered in Chinese to his colleagues, who looked at each other, then looked at their feet.

'Heroin. I am surprised you do not know this. He is become one of Australia's biggest buyers.'

'Ok, how does he get it in?'

'The port. Merchant sailors. All Chinese. They walk off the ship. Like that.'

'And you wanted a cut of his business. You counted on him losing big, so you could own him.'

'That is correct. But he fears Hong Kong too much. He refused to join us.'

Swann looked at the bag in his hand, the money. The men looked sheepish, refused to meet his eye. Taking the money wasn't the plan. The men weren't killers, he could see that. That would come next, perhaps, involving other men. But in the meantime, the bag of cash, the look on the men's faces ...

'You weren't planning on telling your bosses about this, were you?'

Swann held it up, just long enough to catch their eyes, let it fall.

It made sense. There were two young Western Australian men on death row in Malaysia, waiting for the noose. Italian money was behind that. As a result, using mules was on the nose, for the time being. The arrest of Clifford and Welsh had seen to that. But Swann hadn't heard which opportunist had stepped in to fill the void.

Charlie Le.

'Start talking. Everything about Le. Then you might get your passports back.'

The young man spoke for ten minutes. Swann heard about the officer at customs Le owned, a fellow gambler, a big loser. The quantities and quality. And then the familiar name, the one he was waiting for. Benjamin Hogan, Chief of the CIB. Some of his fellow officers. There to smooth things over, to gather intel from within the force, to keep the Feds at bay, to take their cut. The kind of friends that strangers couldn't buy. The reason the Singaporeans needed Le, and needed him alive. For the time being.

Swann tossed the young man the bag of passports, their tickets. Getting back to their masters, on time, to deliver Le's response, was more important than the money they'd taken. The young man said nothing, but the other three thanked him, in Chinese, their red drunken faces breaking into smiles, grateful that he was taking the money away, and with it the temptation to ruin their lives. Swann guessed that the youngest man had talked them into it, and he added a wink to his goodbye.

11.

Swann drove along Great Eastern Highway, towards the city that glittered under the first rays of dawn. The river was calm and slick under the Causeway. He dialled Heenan and gave him the word. Heenan didn't want the money, and he didn't want it returned to Charlie Le either. 'The man's a degenerate gambler. I've organised for Conlan's bank to take it back. Go and have a coffee at Bernie's, and call me in twenty.'

Swann did as suggested, if only because he hadn't seen Bernie for months. The fry-up shack at the foot of Mt Eliza was an institution, and he'd eaten there for most of his life. Bernie was at his grill, frying eggs and bacon, gammon rounds and slices of minute steak, with tomatoes and onions bubbling in pans beside. He was old now, shrunken inside his leather apron. His blue eyes brightened when he saw Swann, and took his order of coffee and a cheese and tomato toasted sandwich. Swann chatted to Bernie, whose hair had long ago turned the colour of smoke. He was a Tobruk Rat, deaf in one ear from an explosion, and he angled his face to listen. They talked about the coming footy season. Bernie was a Cardinals man, and Swann backed South. They both agreed that since the Krakouer brothers' departure for Victoria, Claremont was ready to be taken. When Swann's order was ready he thanked Bernie and went out to the Statesman, drove around Mill Point Road and up into Kings Park. He sat the car beneath lemon-scented gums and watched the sun rise over the corrugated ridge of the Darling Scarp. After he'd finished his toasted sandwich he placed the coffee between his legs, lit a cigarette and dialled Heenan on the car phone.

'Don't worry, there'll be someone to meet you, at the rear entrance. Backs onto the alley between Murray and Wellington.'

Swann answered Heenan's next question in the negative. He hadn't seen the protest site at the Old Swan Brewery, around the corner on Riverside Drive, when he'd gone to Bernie's. His mind had been on breakfast. Heenan apologised for keeping Swann up all night, and congratulated him on retrieving the money. But Heenan still wanted Swann to accompany him when he visited the protestors in about an hour.

Swann cruised the Holden down from the higher ground of Kings Park into the city, past the remnant gates of the old Barracks, marooned above the vast moat of the Mitchell Freeway, streaming with morning traffic. Looking down St Georges Terrace he could see cranes across the horizon. The old buildings of his childhood had been torn down as the corporations moved in and the people moved out.

The building that housed Harrowgate Investment Bank was a case in point. Built to replace the weatherboard tenement slums at the top of Murray Street, the long row of two-storey brick bunkers were beautified only with a coat of white paint, long since stained with soot. Harrow's Footwear had been one of the first tenants, and for whatever reason, upon converting the retail enterprise into an investment bank, Larry Conlan had chosen to stay in the original building. He'd tarted it up with new aluminium window frames and a brass nameplate above its doors, and had fitted out the interior to resemble a modern office, including a vast steel safe imported from the US, but it didn't look much different from the era when the building housed brogues, boots, loafers and golf shoes.

Conlan had the money to move to the exclusive Terrace, but the barely renovated building was part of the joke, as far as Swann could tell. Whose expense the joke was on depended upon who you asked. The Conlan brothers were either local boys done good, loyal to their working-class roots, or smart-arse shonks, playing fast and loose with other people's money.

Swann knew the stories, and had seen firsthand how Conlan's money was used to inflate the worth of stockmarket scammers and their penny dreadfuls, not to mention inveterate Chinese gamblers. He turned the Statesman down the narrow brick lane that ran beside the bank, and into the carpark at the rear of the building.

Ringed by asbestos fencing, the carpark had been laid with new macadam. Wild oats grew in the spaces between the fence and the car bays, and blocky fluoro graffiti covered the face of the red-brick building across the alley.

Swann parked as close to the heavy steel door of the bank as possible, which was the only place in the carpark not in shadow. He noted how little security there appeared to be, beyond motion-detecting lights and a lone security camera, precariously hanging on a rusted frame. He rolled down the car windows and let the sunshine warm his face. He must have dozed off because when he awoke a long black Bentley had entered the carpark. It gleamed in the sunlight, making guzzling sounds as the engine idled. Swann had expected that a bank worker would meet him, or more likely the bank manager, but it was Larry Conlan himself who stepped out of the chauffeured car, still in his pyjamas and slippers, snug in a white terry-towelling dressing gown. He too looked like he'd just woken, rubbing his eyes in the morning glare. Conlan didn't approach Swann; instead he leaned against the Bentley and yawned.

Swann got out of the car and popped the boot and removed the cash, which he'd transferred into a garbage bag. The flash suitcase that he'd taken off the Chinamen would make a nice present to one of his daughters. The black plastic sagged and stretched as he lugged the cash over to Conlan, now joined by his chauffer, who Swann recognised as Pete Griswald, a local jockey whose career had ended in a three-year prison sentence for carnal knowledge. Swann was amused to see a bulge in the armpit of Griswald's black suit jacket.

Larry Conlan didn't recognise Swann, although Griswald did, and he caught the bemused look on Swann's face.

'Boss, this is Frank Swann. Y'know, the ex-copper. Just fucked Trevor Dragic in the arse.'

Conlan's jowls shaped his face into a doughy circle, his skin the colour of batter. His eyes tightened, and he smiled. 'Superintendent Frank Swann. How the mighty have fallen. Count it.'

The words were directed at Swann, so he dropped the bag. Packets of cash spilled out. Griswald reached over by Swann's legs and scooped up the packets, hefted the bag. 'No need to count it, Boss. Swann's not like that.'

Which to Griswald was no compliment. Not to Conlan either, judging by the little sniff and shrug, adjusting his balls in his striped silk pyjama pants. He looked Swann up and down, taking his measure. Griswald tossed the bag of cash through the Bentley's window onto the driver's seat.

'You aren't going to bank that?' Swann asked.

Conlan laughed. 'What, in there? Nah. Don't think so. None of your business anyway.'

It was Swann's turn to stare at Conlan, weighing it up. He could smell the piss on Conlan's silk pyjama pants, which meant that he leaked at night. He thought about making a comment, but decided against it.

Swann turned, and walked to the Statesman, aware of their eyes on his back. Conlan was right, it wasn't Swann's business, but there was more to it. Conlan's need to standover Swann was familiar. Swann had met plenty of men like Conlan, although none had risen so high. Swann had brought some of them down, if only a peg or two. He'd delivered some of them to prison, had even broken one or two with his bare hands.

It was a sign of the times that men like the Conlan brothers were lauded in the media, mentioned in the same sentence as the premier. Larry Conlan, after all, hadn't tried to milk Swann for information. He didn't need access to the premier, like Corvo, Riley and the others. That prize was already his. Never mind the premier doing personal favours for a Chinese businessman who traded in smack. Swann doubted the premier knew about this latter fact, but either way, it didn't matter. Swann decided that he wasn't going to tell Heenan about Le's heroin, or about Conlan taking personal delivery of the cash. That was the reason he walked away from Griswald and Conlan, and their sneering eyes. He didn't want to show his hand. Instinct and experience told him that it was better to be underestimated.

12.

Mostel was an easy man to follow. He drove a silver Porsche 911. The air-cooled two-door had a small hole in its muffler and roared under acceleration. And yet Mostel was a cautious driver, something that made him easy to tail.

Going on the address supplied by the real estate agent, Foley started his day in bushland near Kings Park. Mostel lived in a tall apartment complex that looked out over Crawley Bay, the wide stretch of river at the base of the park. It was pleasant hiding among the grevilleas, flowering banksias and blackboys, with the wattlebirds and pink-and-grey galahs, honeyeaters and magpies loud through the bush. The place reminded him of the swamps by the river where he'd grown up; setting fires and building cubbies, where the local schoolkids had their daily prearranged fights; got his first root there too, when he was older, aged twelve.

He smiled at the memory, his cockiness at that age a product of his anxiety, not knowing what to do, or where to put his thing. He couldn't remember the girl's name, except that she was black, and older and more experienced. She'd been stoic while he poked away, the half-bottle of green ginger wine retarding his orgasm.

The clothes in the bag owned by the real estate agent were a good fit, as were the leather-soled loafers. Foley was deep enough in the bush to avoid the eyes of passers-by. He'd heard some leaves rustling, and had been pleasantly surprised to see a western brown bandicoot doing its business on a nearby trail, until it saw him and darted off. A large feral cat passed along the bandicoot's trail minutes later, nose to the ground. Foley reached for his pistol, and without thinking shot the animal in the side, making it jump vertically before scampering off, looking behind for its attacker. The sound of the .22 pistol wasn't too bad, and he knew that the bullet had passed through the beast. It took more than a .22 at close range to stop a wildcat, but he didn't regret it. The noise hadn't alerted anyone, and it would remove the cat from the area. Most likely, it would die alone in the bush, just as it had lived. He felt sympathy for it – living as he too had become accustomed to living – hated by some and admired by others.

Mostel, on the other hand, was a different kind of animal, and Foley had no respect for him. The old saying of a wolf in sheep's clothing. Mostel fitted in among the flock, invisible, useful even. There were reasons for that, and they weren't a credit to the man.

Foley recognised Mostel for what he was. He had known some of Australia's hardest men, had lived by their code.

That code was about respect.

Hustlers in suits preyed on the weak, and retreated behind the law when threatened, used the law and lawyers to do their dirty work, to break people financially.

Hustlers like Mostel – well, he doubted his mother's advice, that the man couldn't be stood over. Foley doubted that Mostel had ever been truly alone, or knew what that meant. For sure, he'd never been hungry, or hunted, or afraid.

Foley turned off the voice in his head. He recognised it as the voice that kept him alive in prison, building up his motivation to lay a surprise attack, or strategising on how to outwit an adversary. But on the streets, obsession was dangerous if unchecked. He might do something foolish, miss something on the periphery, and there was no margin for error.

*

At first, it felt good to drive around the city on Mostel's tail. The sun was hot and the Fairlane's air-conditioning was frosty. He even saw some familiar faces on the street, although he couldn't stop to reminisce. His disguise was sufficient, as long as he kept moving.

The one exception was when, out of curiosity, he'd parked the Ford and followed Mostel into a shop. Foley checked the addresses off as he went, on the estate agent's file. He didn't know why Mostel was visiting his rental properties, instead of attending his accountancy firm offices, and they weren't linked by location. Some were in North Perth, some in West and East Perth, until he saw the common factor. In every case the lease had nearly expired; the same as with Foley's mother's lease. When he understood this, Foley wanted to get close.

He entered the florist's on Outram Street in West Perth a minute after Mostel, drifted to the back of the shop, paused in front of a display of funeral wreaths, a mirror panel before him. He stroked the petals of a white lily and looked into the mirror.

Mostel was surprisingly small up close. He was in his late forties, his hair dyed black, the back of his neck pockmarked by acne scars. He dressed well, smart but casual, and moved like an athlete. His voice was deep and powerful, and his words seemed to hang in the air.

Which didn't make sense. The real estate agent had told Foley about how successful Mostel was, did the books for both the Conlan brothers, and more recently had moved into property development. Had some big projects in the pipeline; was a friend to the new money entrepreneurs like the Conlans who were doing so well; could even be counted among their number.

And yet here was Mostel berating a mousey florist, with her rounded shoulders and cheap print dress, with a thudding bass voice that was building towards something.

Even if Foley wasn't casing Mostel, he would have felt like intervening. Mostel was accusing the woman of ducking her responsibilities, of trying to cheat him. He demanded that she paint the front of the shop, replace the aluminium window frames, and the plasterboard ceiling. The wiring would need re-doing throughout the shop. The tin roof was rusted, and needed replacing.

When the woman tried to point out that this wasn't part of her contract, that all she had to do was leave the place in the condition she'd found it, that her business was already failing, that doing what Mostel requested would bankrupt her, Mostel twisted the knife, as Foley knew he would. Mostel threatened to take her to court, to recover the full costs of fixing the place up. Either she could do it herself, using contractors of her choice, or he would do it and recover the costs. And he'd win. He knew all the judges.

He named a figure, and the woman braced herself against the register. The figure was a bad joke, even Foley knew that – probably more than the woman turned over in three years. She was shocked into silence, and Foley felt his fists clench. He looked into the mirror to calm himself, his crisp blue eyes, sunburned face and scruffy beard out of kilter with the staid check shirt he'd taken from the estate agent, tucked into cream chinos and a thin leather belt. Mr Suburban.

When he'd settled his breathing, Foley started to think clearly. Now he understood why Mostel did the rounds of his tenants in person, rather than leaving it to his property manager. No estate agent would act like this. Extortion wasn't their game. If this was Mostel's approach, and it was successful, he'd probably leeched more money out of his tenants this morning than most businessmen earned in a year.

But there was something else that interested Foley: the need behind the strategy, its cruelty. In everything Mostel said to the woman there was distrust and disdain. Not just a business strategy, but a part of his nature – a reflex. And yet, as Foley's mother had said, old Schloime Mostel had been a good man. Gentle and funny, and generous to the urchins who gathered in the nearby streets, Foley among them, always up to no good. He knew that were Schloime alive, he wouldn't be proud of his son.

The woman was in tears now, as Mostel took her outside and began pointing at other things that needed doing. Foley left the shop as well, and for a moment their eyes met, Mostel not pausing his cataloguing but watching Foley leave. His eyes were dark and vigilant, burning with mock outrage.

For a moment, Foley hoped that Mostel would recognise him, so that he could end it there. But Foley turned the voice off. There were better ways, he just had to figure them. And he'd left the shop with a new understanding of the man he was stalking.

As he suspected, Mostel had no code beyond *fuck them before they fuck you.* It was him against everyone else. This had worked for him until now, but it was also a point of weakness. Once the shit hit the fan, nobody would cover for a man like Mostel, not his business associates, not his friends and, Foley suspected, perhaps not even his family. It was a character flaw that Foley could exploit and, as he ambled towards the parked Fairlane in his ugly clothes, he began to think on how.

13.

Swann parked the Statesman a block from Parliament House on a hill running down Hay Street. Heenan hadn't asked for the Statesman keys back, but Swann knew that it was a matter of time, especially when he saw the peach Commodore assigned to him parked where he'd left it, in the parliamentary car bays, dusty and covered with purple jacaranda blossoms.

He waited there as instructed, standing as far from the Commodore as possible. He was tired now, and his eyes burned despite the coffee. He was still dressed for the raid on the Chinese gamblers, utilitarian blue work trousers and a faded denim shirt, boots and a peaked cap, sunglasses to hide from the glare. The posse of premier's men who emerged from the parliament were all in the regulation dark suits and shiny black shoes. Heenan's shirt was untucked where his belly fought against his belt. He too hadn't slept, but then again, as he'd confided in Swann, he rarely slept. He indicated that Swann should follow the seven men, some of whom Swann recognised from the premier's office, towards two black Ford LTDs shaded beneath the muscular arms of a Moreton Bay fig. Three of the men who'd been talking to the premier peeled off when they reached the first car, which the premier entered alone. Heenan shook Swann's hand, and opened the door of the second car for Swann. The car was the long wheelbase model, but with five grown men inside it felt small, leather creaking and the air stuffy, soon smelling of the mints that Heenan sucked. Both the driver and the man on Swann's left were compact and efficient in their movements, clearly ex-army.

Heenan didn't mention the Chinese gambler, but Swann expected that. As the Ford circled Kings Park back into the city, taking the

Riverside Drive exit beside the Narrows Bridge, Heenan leaned into his corner like an exhausted boxer, and talked.

'According to the CIB, there isn't much to go on. The consorters have been taking photographs, but many of the faces aren't names. We need to nip this before it gets out of hand ...' He paused to look down the sweep of river to where the Old Brewery stood, ruined, on its retained banks like a medieval castle, uniformed police directing traffic and hundreds of protesters waving placards and banners. 'Fucking land rights protest, right in the middle of a capital city. The Libs are going to eat this up. We need to be proactive. A solution needs to be found.'

'What do you want from me?' Swann asked, a question he understood was going to become commonplace. He hadn't followed orders for years, and the asking didn't come easy.

'Line of communication, Frank. The peelers aren't giving me anything ...'

Heenan let the statement hang there. It didn't need to be said, what both of them knew – the premier's looking interstate for a new police commissioner, part of his pre-election promise to clean up the force, was coming back to bite him.

'We didn't see this coming, Frank. We can't have it. It's on the front pages of the papers over East, the ABC news is leading with it nationally. And I'm not getting any clear picture of what these people want. There doesn't appear to be any spokesman. Find out who has the authority to speak, so we can start a dialogue. You wander around and watch, Frank. Speak to whoever you think might be useful. The premier's been invited for a cuppa, apparently, by some of the old ones. I'll mingle with the journos, see what's what.'

Swann nodded as the Ford pulled into the siding to let him out early. The police had blocked off a lane with a string of witches hats, and the premier's LTD drove as close to the protesters as possible, sequestered from the road by a line of uniformed police linking arms. The driver didn't get out, and kept the engine running, in case they needed to U-turn fast.

Swann crossed the four lanes of traffic so that he could join the protest and distance himself from the premier's group. The limestone bluff of Mt Eliza was hard against his right, zamia palm and acacia scrub growing down to the narrow thread of verge grass. He cut behind the first wall of protesters, looking for a familiar face. The chants of *Always was, always will be, Aboriginal Land* increased with the arrival of the premier, but the tone wasn't angry. The antagonistic relationship that the Libs had with Aboriginal people, who they perceived as standing in the way of progress over the past twenty years, was something that the premier had promised to remedy. It was the Commies and Labor who had agitated against the draconian laws directed against the Aborigines over the past century, and the premier had positioned himself as their natural friend.

Swann knew this, but he didn't know much about the protest, or the people involved.

When Swann was a boy, a black man needed a dog tag to justify his presence in the city. Aborigines lived in fringe-dweller camps in the dunes south, and some of the bush around Coolbellup. It had always been like that. And white boys like Swann always fought with black boys.

It was a Yamatji kid who'd ended Swann's boxing career, but he wasn't bitter about that. Swann had been street fighting for small stakes on behalf of his stepfather since he was thirteen. It was the early 1950s, and Brian saw it as an easy way to make money. Brian would organise the fights in the sailor bars down by the port, boasting that he had a kid no foreigner could beat, and if the goading worked, and he had a taker, the crowd would follow him out into the alley to find Swann waiting there, stripped down to his jeans, still a skinny kid. It was bare knuckles and no rules, and on one occasion lasted for a gruelling blood-soaked hour. If the sailor was drunk, Swann was lucky. Brian and his mates organised the betting, took the money and called the odds. It was up to Swann to take down the inevitably larger and older man. He had fitness and a few tricks to wear them down; a relentless rabbit punch and a few dozen kidney blows usually did the trick. He copped some terrible hidings but he learnt from those. And Brian always bet against him if he thought Swann was a guaranteed loser.

He'd taken to the amateur boxing circuit in the RSL halls and Italian clubs and PCYCs around the city, but when he fought a black kid the same age in a scout hall in Armadale he learnt the hard way that he was merely a brawler, and no boxer.

Bloodied and bruised, Swann saw out the fight but the other boy was a clear winner. He'd never forgotten the other kid's name – Gerry Tracker. For most of the past twenty years Tracker had a mechanics workshop in Spearwood, and Swann went to him from time to time, looking for parts.

It was no surprise to see him at the protest now, still fit and strong and warlike, sporting a beard and a red-and-white Bulldogs beanie.

Swann approached Tracker from the side, his eyes never leaving the man's profile. Tracker's posture said comfortable, leaning down to listen to the older white woman beside him, but then Tracker sensed his observation and turned.

They shook hands, and Tracker introduced Swann to the older woman, an Anglican nun.

'Never picked you for a ratbag, Swann. What you doing here?'

Tracker laughed when Swann told him. 'True? You're on the gravy train? They lookin' for a handsome black man to play Tonto?'

'Your skills, Gerry, they translate. But I don't see you wearing orders from the Boss.'

Tracker had done time in Fremantle Prison after the armed robbery of an armoured vehicle, a crime unusual for a black man, and he'd worked standover inside. But after ten years of *Yes Boss* this, *Yes Boss* that, released men like Tracker usually preferred self-employment in all its varieties, legal or illegal, to having a white superior standing over them.

Tracker laughed again and clapped a hand over Swann's shoulder. The gesture was friendly, but his eyes were watchful as the pitch of the chanting increasing for the benefit of a panning TV camera.

'Never been one for crowds, meself,' he said. 'Make me jumpy.'

'Same here. Always associate it with holding the line.'

Swann looked to Gerry, who was turning away every time the camera swept over them. 'So you know I'm on the clock. Going to help me out?'

Tracker shrugged. 'Not for me to say. I'm Yamatji, and this is Nyungar business. I'm here to support the cause, but I'm not going to speak for anyone else.'

The older white woman had no such reluctance. She looked with distaste at the navy-blue police truck that now arrived, bearing a dozen reinforcements. Riverside Drive was blocked, and the traffic was banking away from them in both directions.

'Say what you want, just don't mess with commuter traffic. Bad for productivity.'

Swann was surprised by the nun's working-class drawl. When she spoke, he listened.

'The Brewery was built near a sacred site. Where the Wagyl, or creator water serpent, passed through. Now they're going to flog the Brewery off to the highest bidder. The Nyungar elders want the place returned to them.'

Swann nodded. 'Can you see that happening?'

The nun grunted. 'The last site we pointed out to a council, over there in Bassendean – a woman's birthing place on the upper Swan, they immediately built a toilet block over it.'

Tracker shook his head. 'Can see *somethin'* happening, Swann. Can see it happening till we get some justice.'

'How many here have the authority to make a decision?'

'Take me to your leader, you mean?'

'Something like that.'

'Man, you don't know much, after all these years. It ain't like that – never was. Only the people from here, and I mean right *here*, got the right to speak for here.'

There was a hint of sarcasm in Tracker's voice as he watched an angry young man in jeans and a cowboy shirt turning on a megaphone. At the first warped sounds of the megaphone the dozens of journalists in attendance began to rush and jostle. Swann looked around at the black faces. Many of them shared Tracker's bemused expression, arms folded.

Swann didn't want to hear a speech, and he put out his hand, which Tracker shook. 'Anything I can do to help, let me know.'

'You just sayin' that, or you mean it?'

Swann's answer was drowned out by the crackle and tearing sound of the young man's voice smashing through the speaker. He winced, as did everyone else, moving back a step but locked in.

14.

Foley slid the Fairlane into a park opposite Parliament House. The heat of the day was broken, the sun gone behind the limestone hill to the west. He rolled down the front windows and sucked in the air, heard the drone of traffic low in the moat of the Mitchell Freeway – all the worker ants heading home. Mostel was idling the Porsche in the parliamentary carpark, cigarette smoke curling from his limp wrist on the sill. Foley looked over the parliament. The building held no interest for him, except for the fact that he'd considered bombing it on his last visit. The pigs had been close, and blowing up a bin or a postbox in the centre of power would turn them away. As it turned out, the bombing hadn't been necessary – the Ds weren't smart enough to dig him out.

Foley had a regular place to hide that nobody expected, where nobody bothered to look.

A fat man with his shirt-tails hanging out huffed out of the parliament building and lit a cigarette as he walked, eyes scanning the carpark. The Porsche sank on its springs when he entered shotgun, pulled away with less than its usual enthusiasm. Foley followed at a distance until the Porsche reached Kings Park, drove along the parapet of lemon-scented gums, around the war memorial and the view east over the CBD, then took a bay near the botanical gardens. Now the view was south over Melville Waters, but when the two men exited the car they were looking down rather than across. At their feet, by the bottom of the limestone cliff, was the Old Brewery. Mostel pointed at the Brewery and at the man, getting his finger under the fat man's chin. They argued for a while, both of them smoking. Then Mostel did something Foley hadn't seen coming. He took the fat man by the forearm and turned him, pointed directly at Foley, and his Fairlane. Made a show of pointing him out, keeping eye contact.

At some point during the day, Mostel had made the tail. Credit where it's due, although the real estate agent must have shopped him.

The two men didn't approach, but this changed everything. The fat man had emerged from Parliament House. No politician would want it known that Foley was back in town but, depending on what happened next, Foley could expect a few thousand coppers to drop everything to hunt him down. The word would be leaked to the media, and then the fun would really start. Mostel was obviously well connected, and had called in a favour. Now it was Foley who had to show his hand. He could either run, or finish what he came for.

It didn't take long to think on it. Funny how things work out. The little coincidences that you feel aren't coincidences. Feel like messages from the part of you that never sleeps. Foley would need that hide-out now, where nobody would think to look. Not because it was well hidden, but because it was where nobody liked to look, among people nobody bothered to look at.

15.

Marion's Datsun was in the driveway so Swann parked on the street. The sea breeze was gusting from the south, whipping the heads of the eucalypts in his front yard, carrying the smell of salt and seaweed and the aluminium refinery down at Kwinana. A spray of red needles lay over the drive, dropped by the flowering bottlebrush either side of the letterbox. Swann reached to cut the engine just as the phone in the console began to trill.

'Swann, two things. Firstly, the arrival of the commissioner's been delayed. Reckon about a month. Health reasons.' Heenan ploughed on, not wanting Swann to get a word in. 'Second, and fucken Murphy's Law, Des Foley is back in town. He's been stalking a local businessman, and –'

Swann cut Heenan off, or he'd never get a chance. He was tired and needed a drink. 'I missed out on a night's sleep, Heenan, to troubleshoot a problem for you. Problem solved. Des Foley is no problem of mine. With the new commissioner being delayed, yes, the local CIB are going to make you squirm, remind you of their power to make you look soft on crime, exact a bit of payback until you kiss some blue arse. But when it comes to arresting Des Foley – that's not an arrest they'll back away from. That's a career-making arrest, for the right D with an ambitious mindset. You don't need me to –'

Now it was Heenan's turn to talk over Swann. 'No, Swann. It's not that. I'm just keeping you in the loop. This … businessman, he doesn't want me to take this to the coppers. He's putting it on the street. Giving it to Adamo, Leo Ajello, maybe some of the bikie clubs. Says his family have been threatened.'

'Why's he telling you this? He stupid?'

'No, Swanny, he's real smart. A major player in the Conlan empire.

I didn't want to hear it, but he didn't give me a choice. He's an up-and-comer. Irons in the fire.'

'One of the premier's new breed.'

'Exactly. Now I'm complicit in anything that goes down.'

'That's as good as blackmail.'

'I know it. How he operates.'

'Now I'm complicit too, is that what you want?'

'No, I want you to ... jam it up. Get to the potential shooters. Let them know we don't want that.'

'Heenan, money talks. This fella ... I don't even want to know his name, he pays right, they'll take it. They might not do the job, but they'll take his advance.'

'Good. Tell them to do that. Rip him off, whatever it takes, but don't do the job. I'm going to leak Foley's presence to the media tonight, and bring the coppers into it.'

'This bloke – he'll know the leak came from you.'

'I can live with that. I've got to protect the premier. Tell me you'll help.'

'Sure, but I'm keeping the Statesman.'

Heenan laughed, and Swann hung up. He locked the Holden and stepped into the darkness. He heard someone approach from behind and watched his neighbour, Salvatore Picirilli, lay down his hose on the grass verge. The hose wasn't turned on, and Salvatore was dressed in his regular garb of black stubbies and blue singlet, barefoot. A pot-bellied man with a shaved head and translucent jug ears, in the shadows Sal looked like a baby bear. He sidled up to Swann and put a hand on his forearm, peered into his yard. 'He's still there. I bin keepin' an eye on him, don't you worry Frank. But better you go.'

Swann looked through the hedge of tangled jasmine and Hardenbergia but couldn't see who Salvatore was pointing at with furtive, underhand movements, pushing him towards the drive.

'Behind the frangipani. A big black *buck*. Better you go.'

Swann thanked him and pocketed his keys, walked down the drive. On the porch, behind the stooping branches and thick leaves of the frangipani, seated on a rattan chair out of the wind next to Marion, was Gerry Tracker. They were both smoking, and holding glasses of rum and ice. Marion smiled as Swann kissed her on the forehead. She smelt of pine needles and Ponds, her forehead shiny.

Gerry stood and thrust out a hand. He smelt of diesel and grease, and his overalls were smudged with oil. He was a big man, and seemed larger in the dark, thick at the waist and barrel-chested, his bare arms muscular and tattooed. Long black hair with greying roots pulled behind his ears. A strong grip, just like always.

He got straight to the point. 'Swann, like I just been explaining to Marion. Something I didn't want to say in front of Sister Prue, good lady that she is.'

'Had the feeling there was something you wanted to say. Give me a second. Top-up? Marion?'

They both nodded, and Swann went inside and fixed himself a drink. The house was quiet. No record on the player, or conversation at the kitchen table, or daughters chatting on the phone.

Swann tossed some extra ice cubes in his glass and carried the bottle of Captain Morgan outside.

On the porch, Swann saw the look on Marion's face; he turned and there was Salvatore, watching from the rose bushes, not looking where he hosed. Swann shook his head and Salvatore nodded, and stepped away. Gerry laughed, and stared down into his glass. Being a black man in the city, he was used to the scrutiny.

'What's on your mind, Gerry?'

Gerry Tracker exhaled smoke through his nostrils. 'Didn't want to mention it at the Brewery, polite company and all that, but as I was just telling Marion, my boy, Blake ... he's done a bolt from Longmore. Blakey was a week shy of being transferred out of juvie into Freo Prison. Went over the wall a few nights ago. Nobody's heard from 'im since.'

Gerry's voice was matter-of-fact, but his eyes were soft. Confusion and hurt in there.

'I *know* what everybody's thinkin'. Blakey doesn't want to do hard time – real adult time. Don't reckon he can cut it. But they don't know him like me ... He did a man's crime, got to do a man's time. Coppers 'ave been around night an' day, but I haven't heard from the boy.'

There it was. Not the fact that Blake Tracker had gone over the borstal wall, like so many boys before him, but that he hadn't made contact.

'It's only been a few days, Gerry,' said Marion. 'Maybe he just wants some time, before handing himself in.'

Gerry looked at her and nodded. 'P'raps. But I doubt it. He's been around my place. The other night, while I was asleep. Knows where I keep the spare key. Nicked that and took himself some food and money, some of his clothes. A sleeping bag.'

Swann lit a cigarette and topped up Gerry and Marion's glasses, and his own. Sure now where this was leading. 'There's miles of bush out your way. You looked around?'

'Yeah, I walked the whole southern swampland yesterday. All the lakes right over to Murdoch. Nothing. But when I find him ...'

'I can do that for you Gerry. No problem. But the sooner you get him back, the easier it'll be.'

Marion looked to Swann and Gerry, didn't understand. She would know that Blake Tracker was in for stealing cars and assault on a police officer, but that was only part of the story. The detective that Blake had beaten up and disarmed after a car chase through Como and Melville had been humiliated by the ordeal. A thirty-five-year-old detective sergeant had been beaten up by a fifteen-year-old Aboriginal youth, who'd then stolen the detective's .38 handgun and turned it against him, threatening him with it before fleeing, leading to disciplinary action. That D and his mates would very likely love to get their hands on Blake Tracker. The gun itself had never been recovered, part of the reason Blake's sentence had been so severe – four years – to be served in juvie until Blake reached a majority, then the rest to be served at Freo jail, with the general population. So they would be looking for an Aboriginal youth with access to a handgun. They would call Blake Tracker an armed suspect. The boy would have to turn himself in eventually, but after what happened last time, who he handed himself over to might mean the difference between life and death.

'I'm not giving him to any bloke except you. I know you're out, but Blakey's a man now. And that copper he done over, since his demotion back into uniform he's a turnkey at East Perth Lockup ... I been askin' around. He's there alright, on the night shift.'

'Blake didn't leave a message, anything? This is just between us.'

Gerry Tracker shook his head. Swann had seen Gerry fight, had learnt the hard way how tough an opponent Gerry Tracker was. He'd stand alongside his son. Trouble for Blake spelt trouble for Gerry, and potentially another long stretch inside.

Gerry tipped his glass and crushed the last shards of ice in his teeth. He stood and shook Swann's hand, then Marion's. Marion and Swann both stood and watched him leave, his bulky figure ducking beneath the branches of the bottlebrush that hung over the drive, fists thrust deep in his overall pockets, long hair bouncing off his shoulders.

Swann sank into his cane chair, let his neck loll, sucked on ice and felt the booze in his limbs. The moon was rising to the east, and the garden was cast with a satin sheen. Marion sighed, sipped on her rum. 'You think the boy is in real danger?'

'Yeah, he is. They'll call the TRG at the first sight of him. Shoot him down. Unless he hands himself in to someone sympathetic, or we get hold of the gun somehow.'

'Nothing you can do though, is there?'

He heard the concern in her voice, picking up on his exhaustion. 'Not at the minute, no ...'

Swann felt a weight in his lap, knew that it was one of Marion's feet. He put down his rum and took her foot by the ankle, started to rub with his other hand, gently knuckling the inner sole like she preferred. Marion lifted his legs from the floor, one after the other, and took off his shoes and socks, caressed the tops of his feet, began to stab her nails into the sole around the toes, just as he liked.

'Dinner at the Capri?' she asked. Whenever Swann rubbed her feet, caressed the silky skin of her calf, Marion's voice thickened. There was a time when this cue meant they had to wait, to get the girls asleep, or out of the house, but no longer. Marion's fingers made his skin tingle. It would be nice, exhausted as he was, to make love beneath the ceiling fan in their bedroom. His mind was quiet but his senses were awakened, and there was no hurry, already on the feathered edge of sleep. In the meantime, a bottle of house red and whatever looked good at the Capri. A cold shower and change of clothes. He felt the weight lift from his lap and followed Marion with his eyes. She was smiling too, tweaked his ear as she brushed past his chair, her bare legs catching his hand.

16.

He awoke groggy with sleep, relaxed but for his aching jaw, where he'd been grinding. It was minutes after sun-up but the day was already hot. An easterly was blowing off the desert. Swann rolled out of the low bed and scratched his shins, his belly. He still wasn't used to the early mornings, wasn't getting to sleep any earlier. He padded down the empty corridor past the empty rooms and put the kettle on, stared blankly into the backyard and began thinking about the morning and the tasks ahead. The premier's office, followed by a visit to some of the heavy-hitters likely to field a call from a disgruntled businessman offering a contract to kill. The list wasn't long, but few of the men would be easy to find.

The Statesman put her nose down. He accelerated off the Canning Bridge ramp onto the freeway, began weaving between the smaller sedans while heading towards a convoy of trucks returning from the Burswood site near the city. The trucks had been plying the same route now for weeks, hundreds of them, mostly at night. He assumed this was to avoid traffic, although he had no idea where the infill was coming from. He looked at the drivers as he passed them at speed. They all wore the same grey truckies cap and grey work shirt, but the trucks were unmarked by any company logo. With the buckets on the tray empty, the wind rang against the steel hulls and whipped at the remnant soil and Swann changed lanes to avoid the spray of sand that burned on his forearm. He had passed a dozen trucks and there were dozens more ahead. Soon the Burswood site would be levelled and re-contoured and the tendering stage would begin. When he'd passed all the trucks Swann wound down his window again, smelt the baking limestone and stewing algae on the easterly, watched the pennants on the South Perth foreshore batting the hot air.

He took the opportunity to dial the central Perth police station,

Homicide desk, and ask for Terry Accardi. It'd been a few days since Swann checked in with Terry, although Swann had mentored Accardi ever since he was a tough neighbourhood kid. He'd continued that role when Accardi joined the force, although by then Swann had been publically disgraced and their meetings took place in secret. Lately, the arrangement was of mutual benefit. As a young detective, Accardi was a good source of information about matters in the force. Ambitious and capable but smart enough to fly beneath the radar, Accardi didn't belong to any of the cliques. Acting on Swann's advice, Accardi knew which door to listen at, which hand to shake and which men to avoid. The fact that he'd not only survived but thrived in the tough political world of the force showed how shrewd he'd become.

Accardi picked up the phone. He sounded tired and harassed, but his voice sharpened when he heard that it was Swann, going with his agreed alias of Peter Drake. Swann gave him his number and waited for Accardi to call back from a secure line. Swann's phone rang, and he launched into telling Accardi about the Good Morning Bandit, Des Foley, and the fact that the man Foley was stalking wanted him dead, not arrested.

Swann had nothing against Foley, but if the country's most wanted man was stupid enough to return to Perth and get himself arrested, he wanted Terry Accardi to be the one to bring him in. Terry was Homicide, but because of the threat of murder he could work the case. Swann wasn't able to give Terry any information on the businessman who'd put the contract on the street, but every cop in WA knew about Foley. If the bikies and the Italians were hunting him, there was every chance of bodies in the streets. If they got Foley first, he'd be disappeared, but if Foley fought them off he'd make the corpses public, as a warning to others. This alone would be enough to guarantee police resources sufficient to the case, compounded by the inevitable media circus – something that happened every time Foley was rumoured to be home.

Swann told Terry the word about the new commissioner being delayed, which was old news to Accardi. The new commissioner was supposed to be coming to clean up the force, but according to Terry the rumour was that his delay was more about giving them time to clean shop. Files were disappearing everywhere. Work orders the same. Threats were being made to potential informants, on the street and in jail. All coordinated by the head of the CIB – Ben Hogan. By the time the new commissioner arrived there'd be nothing to investigate. Heenan and the premier would be disappointed, but Swann should have guessed.

There was nothing else to report to Accardi, and Swann hung up and pulled the Statesman into the parliamentary parking lot, beside the sad-looking Commodore with its layer of dust and purple flowers. Swann took up his staff lanyard and bag of tools, made his way through a platoon of magpies working the perimeter of the parliamentary lawn.

17.

The premier's office was dark and smelt of tung oil and filtered coffee, and the heavy door muffled the sounds in the corridor. Swann knelt with the wireless meter and wafted it across the wooden desk. The premier was on a call and so Swann couldn't check the phone just yet. He worked the wand across the walls, over the paintings that had become familiar, all gin-soaked faces and mutton-chop sideburns and oily eyes, along the architraves and window frames. Heenan wasn't in yet, or was out doing the premier's bidding, and the premier didn't seem to mind Swann listening as he went about his business. Whoever he was talking to, the premier was on a charm offensive, laying on the flattery with a trowel, though his eyes told Swann his heart wasn't in it.

Farrell Jnr sounded sincere as he talked his way through a list of the benefits that would accrue to his interlocutor, namely the prestige of being associated with such a project, and finally the satisfaction of doing something good for the state. Swann caught Farrell's eye, who winked. Whoever was on the other end of the line was being invited to eat a shit sandwich, but Farrell got his way, hung up the phone, jotted something in a black notebook that he filed away in the top drawer of his desk. Farrell watched Swann work the wand over the light fittings last of all, then took the black notebook out of his desk and opened it again. 'Frank ... I can call you Frank right? But Heenan tells me you prefer Swann ...'

Swann raised a thumbs-up over his shoulder, and the premier continued. 'Your wife, *Marion*, Heenan tells me that she works with ... community nursing outreach. Is that correct?'

Swann turned off the electronic device that looked like a cross between a coathanger and a TV aerial, folded its arms and placed it in his

Gladstone bag. He turned to Farrell and nodded. 'Yes, that's correct. It's a good program. Really makes a difference.'

Farrell tented his fingers, gave Swann a shrewd stare. 'Must be useful to you, given your line of work. Needing to keep an ear to the ground and all that. She'd have a pretty good idea of what's going on in the criminal community, wouldn't she?'

It was a strange line of questioning. 'Sure enough.'

'And what about you, Frank? You've spent a lifetime with criminals, enough to form an opinion. I'm curious as to your impression, as this affects our current discussions around the policy on law and order. We're always under pressure from the community, to lock 'em up and throw away the key. Like there's no point rehabilitating. So, what's your opinion – nature or nurture? If it's the former, well, I guess there's little that we *can* do except take criminals off the streets. If it's the latter, well, there's always hope ...'

The look in Farrell's eyes was genuine interest, and his hands were motionless on the leather blotter of the old jarrah desk. But it wasn't the kind of question asked by someone who'd grown up among 'the people'. Rather, someone who'd been cosseted in Catholic boys schools, been on the school debating team, gone into law straight after school.

'My experience of crims,' Swann began, 'most of the ones locked up at least, is that they're either stupid, unlucky or they're lashing out. Most of them aren't dangerous. The ones that are, sure, they belong in jail.'

'Not worthy adversaries for an intelligent detective, then ...'

Swann ignored the statement, didn't like the look of complicity in Farrell's eyes. Farrell wanted something from him.

'But with the men you've been chasing recently,' Farrell said, 'is it the hunt that motivates you, the money, or both? After all, it can't be as satisfying bringing down a company director, as compared to locking up a bank robber?'

'I wouldn't agree with that, having seen the damage they've done.'

A line of muscle tightened in the premier's jaw. 'I'm surprised to hear that from an ex-copper. So forgiving of thieves, hoons, violent criminals, and so cynical about the wealth generators of this economy. The men who build companies and create jobs ...'

The premier was on his feet now, looking for an explanation. But just as suddenly he sat, smoothed his hair, looked at Swann and smiled. It wasn't a friendly smile, but there was no heat in it either.

'Sorry, Frank. I'm tired. Didn't sleep at all last night. Got another hard day, hard years ahead.'

'What do you want me to do?'

The premier leaned back on his plush chair, ran his fingers over his hair. 'Very perceptive, Frank. To the matter at hand then – I never thanked you for seeing to my father the other day. And what I wanted to ask was ... Marion, your wife, would she be able to look in on him? In her capacity as a community nurse, of course. He refuses to go to the "sick-house", as he calls it. Although he's clearly dying. Doesn't look after himself. I'd take it as a personal favour.'

Swann buckled the Gladstone and hefted it. 'Stormie ... your father, he isn't really in her jurisdiction, but I'll ask her.'

As Swann reached for the door, the handle turned and Heenan barged inside, his face red. 'Jaysus. Premier, you have to see this. Swann, you're going to want to see it too. Better still, head down to the Barracks Arch and try to head it off ...'

Heenan strode over to the bay window with a view east over the city, pulled back the heavy drapes. Both Swann and the premier winced at the burst of light. Heenan shook his head, peering over at the red-brick Barracks Arch, a couple of hundred metres to the south and across the freeway. Swann joined him, saw the television vans and gathering of interested onlookers and journalists, and massed in a wall before them, four bikies, dressed in denim and leathers, the cameras snapping them. He remembered what he'd advised Gus Riley. 'Oh, shit,' he muttered.

'You *know* something about this?' Heenan asked.

'No, I just noticed that they're wearing their colours. That's the club presidents of the Nongs, the Bad Breed, the Barbarians and Dingo Jacks – only mob missing are the Junkyard Dogs. Standing next to one another, without killing each other. I'll get down there and take a look.'

18.

It took a few minutes to walk the bridge over the freeway, and join the crowd at the Barracks Arch. Swann was old enough to remember when the Arch had fronted the Pensioner Barracks, a vast martial structure built by convicts in the 1850s for the men and their families sent to guard them. The barracks had been torn down to make way for the freeway, but the Arch still looked like the remnants of a castle wall.

Swann jostled his way through the tourists that thronged around a bus parked near the Arch, taking holiday snaps of the four riders of the apocalypse, the four bikie presidents, fists by their sides. Film cameras from the three local stations were rolling, while telecasters did pieces to camera, and newspapermen knelt and took angled photos to magnify the height of the four already gigantic men, the great brick structure overhead. Gus Riley stood forward and nodded to the others, saw Swann in the crowd and winked, saluted. He didn't need a microphone. Years of shouting over the strafe of Harley Davidson motorcycles had given him a good voice for theatre. And he was enjoying the moment, the attention. He tossed the ginger fringe out of his eyes and repeated himself. 'THANKYOU EVERYONE. Thankyou. I'm not going to bugger around here and waste everybody's time. I know you've got less important things to do. So I'll get to the point. My brothers here, we live the outlaw life. You don't have to like us, or respect us, but hopefully you at least *fear* us ...' Riley's grin was off-colour, and caused some nervous laughs from a couple of journalists. 'So be it. I'm not going to give you the old line: "We're really misunderstood men who do good deeds and give to charity and give a shit about you and your mug lives." Fuck. That. Shit. We live the outlaw life without apology and we have a code. You keep out of our business and we'll keep out of yours. But there are always gonna be times when our interests are the same. And this is one of those times ...'

Riley paused for effect, turned to each of the men standing beside him, who nodded for him to continue. 'My brothers here; and all of our brothers. We're from here. Born and raised. We were born into the same communities that you were born into. We all have family who are civilians, ordinary West Aussies like you. Sisters and daughters and mothers. So when I say to you that a new mob of bikies, not from over East but even worse, from across the fucken ditch, is muscling into Perth, a mob so low and cowardly that they make *rape* a compulsory part of their initiation, who unlike *us* don't care if their mob use the needle, who peddle smack and who're only a couple of generations away from bein' fucken cannibals – I'm warning you that the fight that we're about to take to these animals is in *your* name as well as ours. And I'm tellin' you this because the local coppers, who're supposed to be protecting you, who know all about this, aren't doing a fucking thing about it. Why not? You might want to ask yourself the same question. Or, you might want to ask me now, in private, off the record ...'

Riley grinned at Swann. To cement the message he stepped back into the embrace of the other club presidents. They stood arm in arm, chins high and bellies sucked in, imperiously ignoring the shouted questions. Swann moved to the wings of the crowd and waited. He had to admit, it was an effective stunt, and would bring plenty of pressure to bear. Riley had handled it well. The four bikies now shook hands and prepared to depart on the four Harleys parked beneath the Arch, Riley's own Knucklehead the lowest, leanest and most highly polished of the four.

Some of the journalists around Swann paused their pointless question-throwing and cocked their heads, becoming stiff and aware, like a family of meerkats. Swann turned. A lone Ford LTD with a flashing roof beacon, siren off, nudged its way up the Terrace through the tourists and the gathered businessmen and pulled alongside the Harleys. Four doors cracked at the same time. Out of the driver's door climbed CIB Chief Benjamin Hogan, dressed in a black linen suit with high padded shoulders and pushed-up sleeves. He ran a hand over his side part, smoothed down his golden hair, adjusted his aviator sunglasses and strode over to the journalists. The rest of the detectives, all Hogan lieutenants, still wore the long hair and beige and grey sports jackets and leisure suits of the seventies. They gathered behind Hogan as he prepared to speak, all of the journalists and television crews having abandoned the bikies and clustered before the detectives.

'What a disgrace! What a bloody disgrace!'

Hogan's words silenced the chatter and gossip. Riley and the other bikies nodded to one another, pushed through the crowd and around the Ford, took to their bikes, cranked the ignition and revved loudly. Hogan's face flushed red, hiding his anger beneath a smirk, and a casual gesture with his hand that said *let the children play*. The revving grew in volume; rolling thunder, clouds of exhaust and dust. The four bikies dropped clutches and rode up Malcolm Street, towards Kings Park, their middle fingers raised.

Hogan shook his head patiently, waiting for the noise to clear. He looked across each of the faces in the crowd, finally settling on Swann. His eyes turned to slits, his posture stiffened. Hogan stared at Swann for so long that the journalists began to notice, turning to him, until Hogan saw this and made an oily little grimace that he replaced with a look of mock indignation. Swann knew that look – it was the look that every station sergeant cultivated when there was arse-kicking to be done.

'A bloody disgrace. Good thing my colleague Jeffrey here had his radio on. Gave us time to get here, to set this story straight. Because what I have to tell you is that the media stunt you just witnessed, complete with libellous allegations of police incompetence, has not only ruined an ongoing investigation into the activities of the aforementioned and aptly named Outlaws, but also put the lives of two of our undercover operatives at risk. So we've had to proceed hastily against the targets of Operation Golliwog, before we've had time to properly make the case for prosecution. A raid is in progress as we speak, and we hope to make arrests, but because of the charade you've just witnessed, and yes, because of the part you've played here too, my guess is that only minor violations will be recorded against these interlopers from across the ocean. I hope that some of you feel ashamed for the part you've played today, which has severely weakened our operational capacity to protect this city. That is all. No questions.'

Hogan replaced his sunglasses and stared confidently into the television cameras. Journalists had begun shouting out questions, but he waved them away. One question repeated by all of them, eager for the next thing: 'Where is the raid taking place?'

Swann lit a cigarette and shuffled his feet. There was no raid taking place. There was no operation, or undercover operatives. But Hogan had convinced them otherwise, and Swann had to admit – it was a performance that would please the bosses, not to mention the premier. What did the journalist in *The Man Who Shot Liberty Valance* say, after tearing up his notes? 'This is the West ... when the legend becomes fact, print the legend.'

Swann's beeper began to pulse its insistent chirp. He didn't need to look – he knew it was Heenan, wanting the low-down.

19.

Swann parked on James Street, in front of the Greek café whose tables were crowded with musicians in leather jackets and old men in fedoras playing cards. A dero crouched in the nearby doorway of a nightclub, keeping as far from the fierce light as possible. Swann bent and passed him a dollar note, told him to keep an eye on the car. He lit two cigarettes and passed one over and watched a group of teenage Nyungars make their way down the street towards the train station. He looked for Blake Tracker among the kids dressed in jeans and tight tee-shirts and flannel but he wasn't likely to wander along the most highly policed street in the state, even during daylight hours.

Swann inhaled deeper on his cigarette, blocking out the sour smells of chip oil and griddle fat from the burger joints. He said hello to a few faces as he walked towards Corvo Snr's gambling den on the corner, quietly cursing Heenan under his breath. It was Heenan who'd tipped Hogan to Riley's antics, and there was something in the telling that made Swann wonder – how much did Heenan know about Hogan's relationship with Riley? It was Heenan's advice to the CIB Chief to not only front the media pack but also deflect blame from the premier and the police service by mentioning the imaginary investigation.

Either way, there was the job at hand. Stormie Farrell. Swann saw the Thunderbird angled across two parking spaces. The convertible's roof was up, and he peered inside, noticed the rabbit and the rooster looking near-dead on the back seat. He opened the door and wound down the windows, let in some air.

The floorboards in the darkened corridor that led to Corvo Snr's casino – the grandly named Mediterranean Club – were freshly washed, and smelt of Pine O Cleen and mouldy mop. He climbed the creaking stairs to the second floor and knocked on the anteroom beside the frosted glass doors of the casino floor. Gregory Corvo answered, and let Swann in. He didn't look particularly happy, waving a hand at the couch where Stormie Farrell sat drinking from the neck of a carafe of red. By way of greeting, Farrell Snr burped and wiped his mouth with his hand, blinked and grinned.

There were dirty ashtrays stacked on a table, a bag of wine-stained tablecloths next to the bucket and filthy mop, the bottle of Pine O Cleen, but the room smelt only of Stormie Farrell. He was wearing the same safari suit, and his feet were still bare.

Corvo grunted. 'He slept on the couch. My ... partners wanted to drag him out the back and give him a hiding, set him on fire was one suggestion, but when I heard who he is ...'

'Thanks Greg, you did the right thing.'

'If you're wondering why he's got a black eye, he urinated on one of my bouncer's legs. We wouldn't let him in. He's got bare feet.'

'I'm a fucking Muslim convert! I've got a religious dispensation.'

Swann ignored Farrell Snr, took Corvo by the arm, led him out into the hall.

'What was the other thing?'

'Oh yeah. It's bad enough we got to make payments to the CIB, the council. But twice this week – an old bloke who claims he represents your boss, and the ALP, has tried to shake us down. Came in at closing with a big brown envelope. Said he'd be back in the morning to collect it, and that it'd better be full, if we want to keep operating. Said it's a donation to the party.'

'He have ID?'

'Nope.'

There was a loud bang from inside the room, the sound of Stormie Farrell trying to stand and hitting the drywall.

'I can hear youse, ya mugs. You lock me up here, Swann, you work for my son, but you don't even recognise my little brother? Graham, the fucken bad son? The sperm that crawled off the street and got into my ma?'

Farrell took the sides of the doorway and made a frame for himself. 'The bastard have dyed hair? 'Bout a decade younger than me? Gut like a bag of footies?'

Corvo looked Farrell up and down. 'Hard to tell how old you are, mate. Look like one of those fuckin' ... mummies.'

Farrell laughed. 'If wit was shit, you'd be bloody constipated, son. Answer me question, playboy. He look like Barry fucken McKenzie after a six-day bender? Suit like he'd just been demobbed? Built like fifty pounds of shit in a twenty-pound bag? Slicker than snail-snot?'

Corvo waved away Farrell, hadn't understood a word. 'Was about seventy, I reckon. Fat bastard. Had a big gold ring.'

'Ha, yair, that's Graham. Grae's ring. You want his advice, you gotta kiss it.'

Corvo turned his back on Farrell, made an unpleasant face. 'What do you reckon we should do? My father said to ask you.'

'Sounds like he might be legit. I'll find out. Meanwhile, do me a favour and ask around, see if he's been hitting up anybody else on the street.'

'Do I pay him?'

'Leave it with me. And thanks for not laying into Stormie – he's not well.'

Corvo nodded and went through to the casino floor. Swann helped Stormie down the stairs and out into the blazing sunshine. He stood Stormie up against the shopfront of a tattoo parlour, popped the bonnet of the T-bird and looked under the distributor cap. The thing was still disabled.

Stormie gave him a look of triumph, followed by the forked fingers.

'How'd you do it, Stormie?'

'Rack off.'

Swann dropped the bonnet and the car shook. The driver's side wing mirror slumped and the steel front fender slipped.

Swann looked at his watch. 'No hard feelings, Stormie. Could leave you here, of course. Or I could buy you a beer, while you tell me how you managed to get the Yank tank halfway across the city?'

Stormie's eyes lit up. 'Cool as the other side of a pillow, you are, Swann. A beer would make for a suitable dessert.'

'What about your rabbit and rooster, Stormie? Can't just leave them here.'

'Them? Eh? Stop having a lend. Figments of my imagination, they are. That's what the old trick-cyclist told me. I'll send them home with the car.'

'Are you going to tell me?'

'The RAC, mate. I'm a premium member. I'm entitled to five free tows a year. I told them I live at this address.'

Swann shook his head. 'We'll call them from the pub, get you towed back home.'

The promise of a drink smoothed the kinks out of Stormie's bent frame. He stood tall, spat on his hand and rubbed it over his hair.

'The Great Western, eh?' he said, indicating the gold-rush pub across the road. 'You know I'm barred from there. Told the manager he had a face like a bulldog licking piss off a nettle. Didn't know who I was, of course. Nobody in this town remembers anything. Total fucking amnesia.'

Swann guided Stormie in the side entrance of the darkened pub, sat him at a back table where his bare feet couldn't be seen. He ordered two beers at the wood and dialled the RAC to come get Stormie's Thunderbird.

20.

Swann dialled Heenan as he crossed the traffic bridge over the Swan River and entered Fremantle. The docks were crowded with container ships and tankers and ships covered with new white fleet vehicles destined for the mines. Swann had left Stormie Farrell in the company of two of his old friends from Kalgoorlie, celebrating a big win. The partners made a living out of watching the lease books of the local gold mines. When a lease expired, often an oversight, they pegged it and bought it for nothing. Yesterday they'd pegged a lease belonging to a major player, on land containing real gold. They were in negotiations with the mine to sell back the lease for a small fortune.

Swann was clearly in the wrong game. He'd confirmed with Heenan that the premier's uncle, Graham Farrell – Stormie's little brother and a man who'd dabbled in real estate, importing luxury launches and selling gold to the Middle East – was now working full-time actively fundraising for the party. When Swann had described Graham Farrell's modus operandi to Heenan – standing over standover merchants like Corvo – Heenan seemed unconcerned. Swann needn't worry, it was all above board and properly documented. Graham could be a little overzealous, to be sure, but then again he was a terrific fundraiser. Raising investment capital was his expertise and the party was lucky to have him on the team. Swann had to ask, however, because Graham Farrell didn't sound the type. What was in it for the premier's uncle? The answer was a commission of twenty-five percent on every dollar he raised.

Swann had pulled into his street in South Fremantle when Heenan finally got to the point. 'Forget the surveillance cameras project for the time being. I don't know what you said to the premier this morning, but he's requested your time on something.'

Swann cruised the Statesman to a stop beneath the hanging arms of the flowering bottlebrush, a carpet of red across the street.

'Go on.' Swann turned off the ignition. Leant back in the seat. He was thinking about the beach. Marion's Datsun 120Y was in the drive, and the sun on his face and arms was fierce. He cracked the door to get some air and waited.

'Basically, those tenders for the Burswood development – they're in. The premier wants your oversight on the tendering process.'

'I thought the public service did that – arms-length, et cetera.'

'True, but he doesn't fully trust the public service. Most of them have links to the Libs, one way or another, which means links to the companies putting the tenders forward. I'm sure it'll all be above board, but just in case, he wants you to look into the companies – make sure we're getting the best value for our money.'

It was almost too good to be true. Swann had imagined it would take him months, even years, to get this close, to garner this level of access and trust. He wanted to say yes immediately, but didn't want to appear too keen. 'And the seven am sweep of the offices for bugs? Does that continue?'

'Yes, it does.'

'Surprised the tenders are in already. Should take months for such a big project.'

'Don't be naive, Frank. To get in power, we had to bring along the big end of town. We let them know about this development, off the record, nearly a year ago, warned them to get ready, to get in before the Eastern Staters and overseas mobs got wind. Nothing dubious about it. We got them onside, and some of them, I won't tell you who, they donated big to our campaign. All the staff you need, Frank. Whatever you need ... but complete discretion.'

'Understood.'

'And there's an invitation to a barbie, the premier wanted me to pass on. The weekend – I'm not sure which day, but I'll let you know.'

'Don't usually work on the weekends, Heenan. That's for something called life. You might remember it, back in the days of short pants.'

Heenan wheezed out a laugh. 'Not work, Frank. Play.'

'For you, maybe. I'll think about it.'

But again, Swann was foxing. The very thing he'd been looking for had landed in his lap.

He hung up and entered through the front gate. The black puppy slinked and wagged her way out of the shadows, began to nip at Swann's shoes, licking his hands. He knelt and scratched her head, looked up and saw Marion on the porch, already wearing her bikini. She held his faded old footy shorts at arm's length, and dropped them onto the towel at her feet. But she looked perplexed.

'What's wrong?' he asked.

'Oh, nothing's *wrong*, exactly. I've been promoted. Promoted and transferred to a job I didn't apply for. You wouldn't know anything about that, would you?'

'Let me guess. To South Metropolitan.'

'So you *do* know.'

The premier had gone and moved Marion without running it by her, just so she could minister to Stormie Farrell's needs. Swann asked hopefully, 'Is it a good promotion?'

Marion shook her head, although she didn't look displeased. 'Administrator. Office-bound. Completely unqualified for it. But the pay's good.'

'You going to take it?'

'Tell me about it first – how it came about.'

*

The beach was crowded for a weekday. Swann and Marion lay at the base of the dunes, Swann in his old footy shorts and Marion in her purple bikini, while their daughter Sarah and her toddler, Jock, nosed around the shallows near the reef, picking up pieces of coral for Jock's shell garden. In the rock pools where Swann had taught her and his other daughters how to snorkel, a new generation of children, too young for school, were doing the same, tossing seaweed at one another, duck-diving and letting the swell wash over them. Swann elbowed Marion, and she opened her eyes, looked over the top of her sunglasses. Jock was still hunting and gathering, according to Sarah's precise instructions, but Sarah had struck up a conversation with some of the children, and one of the young mothers at the base of the reef. The woman rubbed her swollen belly in answer to Sarah's questions, smiling down at Jock. Marion groaned. 'Grandparents already. God help us.'

Swann rolled over and took her hand, placed it on his hip. He kissed her on the nose, on the lips. 'Sneak into the dunes with me, Granny?'

Marion kissed him on the nose, tweaked his nipple hard. She climbed to her feet and wandered down to the shoreline, knowing that Swann was watching her, that little lilt in her step. She paddled out beyond the first low waves and turned on her back, watching him. When they were young lovers they'd lacked for places to be alone. Out in the water was one place, at night.

South Beach was on the edge of the port city, but to Swann it felt like any of the thousands of remote beaches up and down the coastline. The sunshine and horizon were good for his nerves, and made the anxiety about the new opportunity fall away. He hadn't expected the news from Heenan about the tenders, and although the news was good, his guts were a mess of excitement. Marion was the only person who knew about Swann's role as Accardi's sniffer dog, and Accardi's role as forward scout for the Feds. To everyone else, Swann was back working a day job.

Marion didn't want the job promotion, or the relocation. Marion wanted what he wanted: enough money to live quietly, maybe down the coast. Look after their three kids, the grandchildren coming through. Swann rolled onto his back and closed his eyes to the sun, but he wasn't able to sleep.

21.

Blake Tracker knelt in the darkness by his father's Datsun truck. He ran his hands beneath the chassis, where the rear bushes of the suspension locked into the frame. His father always kept a spare key taped to the chassis, but it wasn't there. So his pops knew, and expected him.

Blake had waited until after midnight to walk the five kilometres from his camp in the banksia scrub near the Beeliar swamps. During the day he slept in the shade of two flowering banksia trees that had become entwined, bent and weighted in their struggle with one another, like two brothers fighting. He made no fire and ate cold food. He waited. He could tolerate being alone in the scrub during the day, but couldn't bear it at night. The balga trees, with their spears. The banksia nuts, rattling in the wind. The smell of the swamp, like a grave. The moonlight, shimmering around the clouds, dancing on the grey sand. Foxes and cats hunting, their eyes inflamed with dark. The sounds of rabbits caught and screaming. The scent of campfires past, snatches of song on the wind. It was too much, and so at night he walked. The quiet roads through the bush, keeping to the white lines in the middle, ready to run. Entering the bush when a car passed. Walking up into the suburbs, prowling the moonlit yards, afraid of dogs, afraid of guns, afraid of the police.

He took food from the bins out the back of supermarkets: tomatoes, stale bread, bruised fruit. He stole coin from the dash of parked cars. He rested in the playgrounds of suburban schools. The stars wheeled about the sky, marking the time. Before dawn he walked back to his sleeping-bag beneath the banksias. He pulled his shirt over his face, and slept.

On the third night he had gone and dug up the gun. It was still wrapped in the canvas tarp he'd cut from a trailer. It was buried deep, and he'd hoped he wouldn't find it, that it had been found, handed in. But it was there. A revolver, still loaded. He cracked the chamber and tipped out the two shells. They didn't appear rusted. He put them back in. The gun was heavier than he remembered. He had to carry it in his hand. It weighed down the elastic in his tracksuit pants, slipped out. He walked through the bush with the gun pointed at the ground. He'd never fired a gun, had never wanted a gun. But there it was, in his hand.

He hadn't spoken to anyone since leaving the borstal. He talked to himself, in whispers, but even that sounded loud. He sang songs that his mother had sung to him; he couldn't remember all the words. He hummed, and the pitch of the hum disturbed him, didn't sound right.

He wanted to speak to his father, then. But he wasn't ready. Maybe never be ready. When he heard himself humming so high and weird he thought of his father and the humming stopped, but nothing came in its place.

Blake Tracker went down the back of the house, where two of his uncles were sleeping. He took a deep breath and edged the sash window by the back door higher, leaned in and slid out the door bolt. It was dark and quiet inside the house. He could hear his heart beating, sure that his father would hear it in his dreams. He found his father's wallet on top of the fridge, as always, out of reach of any kids. His keys to the truck, and his business, and his house there too, all on the one ring, splayed out like silver petals. He carefully lifted the keys, helped himself to the cash in the wallet, and left the way he came in.

He sat behind the wheel of the Datsun, the door open. He knew from experience, had been chased enough times, that it was the sound of a car door shutting that woke people. He slid in the ignition key and turned it one step, saw the dash lights come on, plenty of diesel in the gauge. He waited for the diesel light to switch off, as his father had taught him, then cranked it round. The radio blared a Charlie Pride song but the engine didn't take, not even the starter motor. He turned his head and saw a man with a gun pointed at him. The man was quiet and moved swiftly to cut the radio, yank out the keys. He looked at Blake strangely, and then Blake recognised him.

The lights on the front porch came on, and his father stood there, axe handle loose in his fingers, long hair over his shoulders. He made a movement with his other hand, and the man whose name Blake remembered now, Des Foley, a name that his father made Blake promise to never mention, took Blake by the wrist and guided him out of the truck. The man saw the S&W revolver that Blake had placed on the bench seat and slipped it into the pocket of his denim jacket.

Blake's father walked the stubbled lawn and embraced Blake, which took him by surprise. 'Welcome home, son. But you can't be here.'

Blake's father led the way down the side of the house, with Des Foley following Blake, so that he was crowded between them. He could smell his father – port and tobacco – and it was a good smell. The man behind was a silent presence; it was the same feeling as walking before a screw, knowing their eyes were on you. Blake's dad prised away four jarrah fence palings leading into the next house, and bowed and climbed through, waited for Blake on the other side. The moonlight dappled the sweat on Blake's arms, glimmered over the age-silvered weatherboards and tin roof of the house next door. Blake stood in the darkness while Des Foley patted back the palings and indicated for Blake to follow his father, who headed quietly over to the house. Two joined weatherboards had been prised off, and Blake noticed the steel handle affixed across them. Blake's father crawled into the floorspace beneath the house and disappeared. Des Foley indicated with his gun that Blake should follow. The cold dirt and the smell of creosote. The old jarrah bones of the house – giant stumps and the dusty underside of floorboards. Behind him the moonlight disappeared as Foley replaced the cover. Blake's father turned on a torch and slipped over an embankment, his head bobbing up and showing Blake the way. Blake joined him in the cellar dug out of limestone. The rubble had been used to build up the embankment, so that it'd be invisible to anyone peering under the house. A shovel and pick rested in a corner of the dugout, and a mattress and sleeping bag, kerosene stove and box of canned food, candle in a stubby.

When Blake was a boy, Des Foley had lived with them on occasion, in the sleep-out, and sometimes shared Blake's room in winter. He wasn't a friendly man, but was a good mate to his father. They'd met in Fremantle Prison. Blake didn't know more than this, except that Des Foley was wanted by police, and that Blake could never speak of it, even to his best friends. Blake had visited his pops in prison as a boy. It was a frightening place that stunk. Some of their uncles had died there, and Blake's dad told him that if Blake ever mentioned it to anyone, Foley would go back inside for life. There was a big reward on Foley's head, and the world was full of dobbers, fizzes and loudmouths. Blake had seen what an eight-year stretch had done to his father.

Beyond that, the two men always treated it as a bit of a joke. The coppers turning over every rock looking for Foley, never thinking to look at what was under their noses. Didn't occur to them to look for a white man at a black man's camp.

So why the hole in the ground, beneath the neighbour's house? It was Blake's fault. They were looking for *him*. And the neighbour was white – old Tom Pickett – a war veteran and ex-prisoner who got along with Pops. He'd hide Foley under his house for the odd carton of beer.

Blake's dad took him by the upper arms, squeezed hard. 'You're staying here, from now on. Till we talk. I've gotta get back. The *munatj* were here about twenty minutes ago, gave the house a tossing. Not good if they come again, and I'm out. See you in the morning, son. Till then, do what Des says.'

Blake let his pops embrace him, his warm and sour smell and the hot blunt force of his hands pressed into Blake's shoulders. Des Foley followed his pops over to the loose weatherboard while Blake looked around the dugout. There was only one mattress, but enough room for both of them to sleep. He sat down on the rough limestone floor, leaned into the corner, felt sand run down his back and arms. Didn't matter, tired as he was.

22.

Swann parked at Parliament House beside the peach Commodore, now streaky with dust and purple pulp and bird shit. He looked up into the branches of the jacaranda and saw cockatoos and reversed the Statesman into another park. He lit a cigarette and dialled the payphone at the roadhouse in South Australia, just as his watch ticked over 6.45. Dennis Gould answered on the first ring.

'Frank, seriously mate, get me out of here. I'm done with baked beans and Chiko Rolls. Last night, I was even dreaming of a pig on the spit. Laying there in my scratchy rags, a lucid dream, watching myself watch the pig as it roasted – the juices, the glaze, the smell. Then I woke up. My neighbour was boiling another pot of King George whiting. That's how these Croweaters cook their fish – boiled in saltwater. You believe that?'

'Doesn't sound too bad. King George is a sweet fish.'

'Until you start to smell like one. What's the news?'

'You wanted me to get you out of there – the news is I need your help. It's the new job – more work than I can handle. Get into Adelaide, onto the next flight. We'll keep it quiet. Nobody needs to know you're back. I'll pick you up. We'll get a feed. Call me from the airport.'

Swann watched Heenan, struggling under the weight of two shoulder bags and a couple of boxes, make his way across the concrete apron leading into the building. Swann dialled Terry Accardi at Central, and was put through to the CIB under the pseudonym of Peter Drake.

'Mr Drake, what can I do to help?'

'We need to meet. Usual place, in an hour.'

Swann hung up, hefted his Gladstone, climbed out of the Statesman. The time had just ticked past seven and already the sun was brutal, shearing off the glass canyons of the city and catching the thermal heat rising out of the concrete gorge of the freeway. The corridors of power were cool by comparison and the hall echoed to the squeak of his rubber-soled boots over the polished parquet floor. He showed his pass to the guard at the entrance to the ministerial rooms and found the premier pacing the carpet behind his vast bureau desk, smoking while listening to someone on the speakerphone. The voice was Maitland Conlan's, all bluff and swagger. Swann showed the premier his wireless detector and the premier nodded, took a deep drag on his cigarette and put a shoe up onto the desk. Swann got down to work while he listened to Conlan tell a story about a liquid lunch he'd shared recently with a Japanese company director, involving the best champagne and sushi served on the belly of a hooker named Sal. Conlan lingered on the details and painted the picture of a reluctant investor won over by the power of booze and pussy, the moral of the story being the adage of every man has his price. A quick glance at the premier told Swann that Conlan's thuggish charm was working its magic, which was a surprise. He could understand how the Conlan brothers might seem a breath of fresh air in boardrooms full of corporate functionaries; how the working-class humour would be useful disarming middle-class businessmen used to politeness and formality, but he couldn't credit the look of rapt attention on the premier's face. Surprised because his father was Stormie Farrell. By comparison, Maitland Conlan had lived a shifty life – he had the buccaneer stories, and Swann could see that the premier wanted it for himself. He chuckled and wiped a tear from his eye, rearranged his tackle and didn't care when his cigarette ashed on the carpet.

Swann worked the wand over the same configurations he followed every morning: the skirts, architraves, light fittings and window frames. He made a desultory pass of the wand over the telephone and was surprised to hear it beep. He caught the premier's eye and passed the wand over the telephone again. Again it beeped. He laid down the wand and turned over the phone. No sign of any tampering to the plate beneath. Conlan continued to speak, unaware of the look on the premier's face – somewhere between hurt and fascination. Conlan was building up to his pitch. It was delivered while Swann used a Phillips head to unscrew the plate and peer into the wiring. The bug was spliced into the phone line – a professional job. He gave the premier a look: did he want to hang up the line? The premier shook his head. Conlan was suggesting a play for the Swan River Electric and Gas Company – he knew the director and could get a price. Did the premier want him to proceed?

Swann stood back and waited. The premier replied, 'Yes, look into it. Gotta go, Maitland.'

Swann killed the call. He heard Heenan's wheeze behind him and stood away. The sight of the phone's wiring splayed out on the desk stopped Heenan in his tracks. He looked from the premier to Swann. The premier was about to speak when Swann put up a hand. He reached into his Gladstone and took out some pliers and snipped the wire either side of the bug, the size of a five-cent piece, and dropped it onto the desk. He pointed to the door, and the two men followed him out. He held the door open for them and shut it.

'There might be fingerprints on it – unlikely but possible. It's an expensive piece of work, and professionally done.'

The premier had his hands on his hips, looking up at Swann in the cramped corridor. His breath smelt like egg sandwiches and stale tobacco, and his skin was damp with perspiration, despite the chilled air. 'Leave it with us, Frank. We'll deal with it.' His glance at Heenan was fierce enough to keep him quiet.

'You don't want to know how it works? What you need to do to find the recorder?'

'Go on.'

'That wireless receiver has a range of about fifty metres. Means that the recorder is somewhere in this building, or nearby outside. I can trace it.'

The premier shook his head, scuffed his shoes. 'No, if it's in one of the ministerial offices of the other parties we'll need warrants, won't we?'

'Probably. Unless there's someone you particularly suspect. You might also want to contact the police. You should.'

The premier was acting strangely enough for Swann to challenge him, but the premier avoided his eyes. 'No. It'll get out to the media. Leave it to us. But good work. Well done. How do I get rid of the thing?'

'Flush it down the toilet. But that receiver wasn't there yesterday. How long was the room left empty last night? And it's locked, right? To install it ... about ten minutes. I'll need to talk to the building's security – cleaners and the like.'

The premier grunted. 'We will, Frank. We will. Heenan, that's for you, but softly softly. No harm done, is there? You caught it early, Frank.'

Heenan and the premier conferred in the corridor while Swann retrieved his bag. Heenan pretended to appear concerned, but Swann wasn't buying it. He was almost out of the corridor when Heenan shouted, 'Frank, the files, they'll be on your desk at ten. They're being photocopied.'

Swann nodded and turned the corner.

*

The sun beat down on the bronzed river, flat and wide to the city. Swann parked the Statesman beside Accardi's new model Falcon. Accardi got out of the plain white car and tossed a burger wrapper into a nearby bin. Each of the hundred gulls on the South Perth foreshore edged closer. The small carpark near the grove of paperbarks was a junkie hangout, and there were two men on the nod in the front seat of an HK station wagon two car bays along, and another carload of kids in a kombi looking nervously over at Swann and Accardi, while scouting the street behind them for the arrival of their dealer.

Accardi sat next to Swann and got himself comfortable on the deep leather seat. He wore a plain blue tailored wool suit and ankle-high leather boots and yellow socks, all Italian-made. He took out a pouch of Drum and set about rolling himself a cigarette.

'You hear the news?' he asked, but didn't wait for an answer. 'Clifford and Welsh, their final appeal failed. They're going to hang next week.'

'I heard.'

A seagull landed on the bonnet of the Statesman, and Swann beeped the horn. The junkies next door woke up, panicked for a moment, then went back to sleep. Across the river the city shone. A cloud passed over the sun and the light took on an eerie clarity. The vista looked unreal, like a dream city and a dream river.

Then the cloud passed and Swann's arms began to burn.

'There's your front page, editorial and letters to the editor for the next week. Should take the pressure off the Des Foley story.'

Swann remembered young Clifford, who'd gone to the same school as his youngest, Blonny. John Curtin High. A smart kid, but a little wild. Just like Swann at that age. And now he was going to hang. Swann wondered whether he'd spill, now that there was no chance of clemency, now there was no point to his not-guilty plea. Tommaso Adamo and Leo Ajello and his boys would be spending a nervous week, hoping that Clifford and

Welsh went quietly. None of the local papers or television coverage thus far had asked the obvious question – who the heroin was for. Neither of the men had the profile to deal that quantity. It was a matter of time before a local journo formally raised the question.

Swann lit a cigarette and told Accardi about Heenan's offer to have Swann scrutinise the Burswood development tenders. He told Accardi about the bug on the premier's phone and the fact that Dennis Gould was flying in, to help him search through the tenders. Accardi seemed pleased, as Swann expected.

'I'll get you a copy of the files,' said Swann. 'I'll probably need some help from the stock exchange. Until then, anything to report on Foley, and the guy he's stalking?'

Accardi bit a string of tobacco and pulled it from his teeth, flicked it out the window. 'We're watching all the roads in, the usual places. Can't figure out the guy's attraction to Foley. It doesn't make any sense. Mostel's an accountant and Foley's an armed robber. It's got to be personal in some way. And there's no corroboration of the lawyer's suspicion that Foley's after him. You get that word out?'

'I put it to Greg Corvo that it'd be unwise to take the Mostel contract – that he's being watched. I'm speaking to Gus Riley this afternoon, about another matter.'

'Good. I hear anything from the boss, I'll let you know.'

Accardi wasn't married and he didn't have children. He was nearly thirty but Swann still thought of him as the kid he'd helped raise. Not yet thirty and already a Homicide cop – the boy was headed places. Playing the middle was never a long-term option, but if Accardi gathered useful intelligence on the links between local police, organised crime and legitimate business then he was set with the Federals. It would be proof that he'd outgrown the small, murky pond of WA CIB. But it could go terribly wrong. Swann was involved for his own reasons, but foremost among them was keeping an eye on Accardi, doing the legwork where it might save Accardi from scrutiny, from being outed as a rat. It was work that Swann was familiar with: looking at the people he was accustomed to watching. His bread-and-butter.

'Look at this joker,' said Accardi, packing away his Drum and opening the door. Swann looked at the HK station wagon. The nearest junkie was slumped with his face against the passenger window, his finger up his nose.

Accardi patted Swann's shoulder and left the car. He walked up to the junkie and leant down to the window and shouted, 'Pick a winner, mate!' The junkie started, eyes wide.

*

Swann waited by the pond with two black swans paddling around in the dirty water. They didn't appear to mind the sound of the jet engines blasting air across the tarmac. He watched the line of wind-buffeted passengers disembark the TAA Boeing down the mobile steps. Dennis Gould was noticeable because of his marked limp, the result of having one of his kneecaps shattered with a ballpein hammer. That and his mufti disguise of bucket hat, Hawaiian shirt and brown polyester shorts and thongs, obviously bought at a Nullarbor roadhouse.

The joy of returning home was written all over Gould's sunburnt face. He tossed the bucket hat in the nearest bin and hobbled over and shook Swann's hand and tilted his head back and let the sun kiss his smile. He was even happier when he saw the Statesman – took out a hipflask and toasted the car and fell in the passenger side.

Swann needed to put food in Gould's belly, and he lifted the centre console and showed Gould the telephone, suggesting he call Bernie's on the number taped to the phone and order them lunch. Gould ordered five steak sandwiches 'with no rabbit food', and one for Swann with everything.

Gould lived on the top floor of an old deco block of flats in Subiaco, its pink stucco faded by the sun and bore-water stains like dried blood along its base. He hadn't been joking about his hunger – he'd already finished the steak sandwiches by the time they arrived at his home. His gammy leg was stronger than it had once been but Swann carried the box-files up the four flights. The smell of Gould's apartment nearly bowled him over – soured milk left on the galley bench and an unflushed toilet. He waited for Gould to open the door to the small balcony and the windows in the kitchen. The sea breeze began to flow through the apartment. Swann sat on the old couch and lit a cigarette and heard the toilet flush, and waited. He laid out the six tenders on the coffee table in the numerical pattern established by Heenan, stamped by the public servants from the Ministry of Development, starting with the lowest, and assumed best bid, and finishing with the highest and least preferred bid.

Having thrown some water over his peeling face, Gould returned. He made a point of placing the empty hip flask in the sink. There would be no more booze in the apartment until he'd made some headway with the files. On previous investigations he'd been known to work sixty hours straight. He missed nothing, and drove himself on with coffee and cigarettes.

Gould burped and looked satisfied. 'So, the state's biggest urban development and the premier doesn't trust his own ministry to get it right? Nice. But we'll get it right.'

Swann nodded. 'We're looking for the usual. Dragic is overseas, but his money might be in this, so look for any phoenixing from him or others. Any faces that don't fit. It's heroin money the Feds are interested in, a la Clifford and Welsh, and links to the CIB, but we can go wider, and deeper.'

'Jesus Christ, it's good to be back in the old dump. Everything a fella could need!' Gould swung his arms about, the proud homeowner of a box with a view of a hospital wall. A bed, a roof over his head, booze and cigarettes. And work. The man was set.

Swann left him clearing the floor, pushing the couches against the wall, making space for the loose sheets of the first tender on the dusty brown carpet. He'd already forgotten Swann was there.

*

Swann sat at Gus Riley's kitchen table and sipped on a coffee made with an imported espresso machine and served in a miniature glass mug. Riley lived in a semi-detached on the edge of Chinatown. The thick limestone walls and high ceilings of the Federation building meant the room was nicely cool and dark. Riley smoked a cigar and necked his espresso, then leant over the mirror and snorted another line of cocaine through a fifty-dollar note. 'Fark, love this shit. Though enough is never enough. It's a fucken tease, just like Karen there. I plough into her too, but can't never get enough, eh Karen?'

Karen had been introduced to Swann as Riley's secretary in the home-office set up in a front room with a computer, a fax machine, a printer, jukebox and a pinball machine. Karen, in her mid-twenties and dressed in a pencil skirt and jacket with enormous shoulders, gave Riley the finger and continued sorting through a sheaf of papers that she slid into a leather case. She pointed to her watch, plumped her big peroxide perm, blew Riley a kiss and left the room.

She looked familiar to Swann, and he tried to remember from where.

'No, Swanny, she's not a prossie from one of the William Street knocking shops, she's a chartered fucken accountant. Does my books and things. And my thing, yeah.'

The cocaine made Riley stare. 'Life is fucken sweet, yeah. Sold the panelbeating business to my mate Snotty. You might have heard, I'm going into construction now. Ok, demolition. And cartage. Got a contract on the East Perth housing precinct. The boys are pulling through. Most of 'em never done a hard day's work but the money's sweet.'

Swann let Riley's drivel wash over him, let the cocaine do the talking. They had a long history, dating back to the early sixties when Riley reinvented himself from bodgie hoon to bikie legend. He was pretty for a bikie, but as the Nongs' public face he'd developed a reputation for murderous rage and rat cunning – enough to negotiate his club through the shoals and reefs of drug dealing, standover, contract beatings and worse – while keeping in good with the CIB. Riley talked like a mug, but that was just him cracking dumb.

'The other part belonging to that ear, it get found?' Swann asked.

Riley grunted, looking for mockery in Swann's eyes. Finding none, he nodded. 'Old Stiggs, yeah, they let him go when the cops raided. Turns out, and get this, it wasn't even Stiggsie's ear. They brought *a bag of ears* over with them, for just that purpose. Cunning fuckers.'

'Resourceful. Where do you reckon they got a bag of human ears from? Funeral homes? Robbing graves?'

'Apparently, for a while there it was an initiation thing. They had to get an ear from one of the other bikie mobs. Black Power, Hell's Angels, et cetera. When that got too hectic they started taking ears off civilians who owed them money, as punishment.'

'They told all this to Stiggs while he was captive?'

'Captive's one word for it, Swanny. Kept him pissed and stoned and sucked-dick happy most of the time. Dickhead even told me, "Good fellas, those brown boys." Nothing personal in it. Anyway, those Kiwis have gone underground now. Went and had a squiz at their clubhouse myself. Looks like the set of a B-Western. Fucken tumbleweeds blowin' through.'

'So Stiggs won't be helping the police in their inquiries, I take it.'

'What inquiries? They knocked those Maori boys around a bit, trying to get at why they were here.'

'I thought you said they were here for the drugs?'

'There's that, but that ain't it, Swanny. According to Hogan, they were here to patch over the Junkyard Dogs.'

'Why'd anyone want to patch over the Junkyard Dogs? There's only a couple dozen of them. Hardly got a street presence anymore.'

Riley looked evasive. 'Beats me. Old news now. Balance has been restored – thanks to you.'

Swann let it go, though the look in Riley's eyes suggested he knew more than he was saying.

'On that matter. You owing me one,' Swann replied. 'I've got a question for you. One of my ... associates. He asked a few inconvenient questions at a shareholder's meeting for one of Trevor Dragic's companies, before we closed the bastard down. Got picked up later that night, driven out into the forest, handed a shovel, if you get me.'

'I heard about that. Poor bastard. Hang on, how do you know all this, about where and how?'

'How do you know about it?'

'Loose talk, Swanny. Wasn't one of my mob, if that's what you're asking. Not even a freelance job. We keep a good discipline – any bashings, especially any killings, it'd have to come through me.'

'You say that with such pride.'

'Proud of the discipline, Swanny. Don't like your tone either. Thought we had one of those ... whaddya call it ... non-judgemental relationships?'

Swann finished his coffee, tapped out another cigarette from the soft packet, lit and took a deep, deep drag.

'Jesus. Hurts my lungs just watchin' you smoke, Swann. You should give the cigars a go. Can see you're rattled, which ain't like you. Was he a good mate, the dearly departed?'

So Riley didn't know that Dennis Gould was alive. 'Which mob were the bastards from? That's all I'm asking.'

'Well, on this occasion, I don't mind telling you. Since they're already on today's minutes. The Junkyard Dogs, of course. They might be few in number, but that's just because they've weeded out the non-heavy riders – very particular about their novices too. I heard it was them who did your boy in.'

'You didn't think to tell me that earlier?'

'You didn't ask. Otherwise, none of my business. And I've told you, right, so we're square ...'

Swann took another deep drag that nearly killed the ciggie. 'Any names?'

'Nope, just that it was them.'

Swann got up to leave, stubbed out his cigarette. 'One last thing. You would have heard about a contract to knock Des Foley, put on the street yesterday. Don't touch it. Take the money, whatever, but the bloke who's offering is being watched. You'll get nailed. Understood?'

'Wouldn't anyway. Des was a mate of mine, from way back. I've instructed the boys.'

'Your organisational discipline. I forgot.'

Riley pretended to look hurt. 'No need for that, Swann. Though I wouldn't want to be in Des' shoes. That bloke who put the contract on, he's got deep pockets from what I heard. He's the Conlan brothers' personal accountant. Going places on his own, too. Plenty who'll want to help him out, is my guess.'

'You hear anything, you let me know.'

Riley laughed. 'We got that kind of relationship, Swann? I hear things; I let you know?'

'It'll be worth your while.'

'I know. You got *the man's* ear.' Riley picked up the rolled fifty. 'But that's enough about fucking ears. Feed the nose, that's the ticket.'

Swann walked the cool dark corridor towards the doorway of blazing light, felt the heat on his face.

23.

Des Foley cracked his neck and rolled his shoulders, put his face into the southerly wind and inhaled jasmine and cut grass and grilled meat and stewing garbage from the nearby shops. His legs were stiff and his back ached but he was ready. The kid was in the dugout, reading comics by torchlight. The old coot who lived above them was an insomniac, walked the creaking floorboards all night, room to room with his .303 rifle, checking the perimeter. Foley thought that he was guarding them but Gerry Tracker told him that old man Pickett did that every night. Another old soldier who couldn't shake it off – knocked himself out with booze every morning and slept through the day.

Gerry's boy, Blake, had been good about sharing a camp with an older bloke he hardly knew, but Des didn't know how much longer the kid would last. Word had got out that he'd escaped, and last night some of his friends had come past, parking on the verge and calling out to Gerry for Blake to join them, the sound of music and girls in the back seat laughing making the kid edgy. Between them and the coppers, coming round day and night, poor Gerry was getting cranky. He didn't need the hassle, and hopefully Des would be able to deliver some hurt to Mostel soon, get the hell out of the city, the state, maybe even the country. In the meantime, Gerry Tracker would never give him up, or ask him to leave. By way of thanks for hiding him in the past, Des had contributed a sizeable chunk to Gerry's payment on the house. They'd done armed robs together for a while, back before Gerry had taken charge of the boy. Now he was on the straight and narrow, for the sake of his boy, and Des admired that.

Des shook the limestone dust off his trousers. He'd eaten the best part of a tank loaf hollowed out and filled with cold canned steak 'n' onions for dinner; the kid had eaten the rest. Des was used to laying low – he'd once spent eight days and nights in a roof-space at a primary school, all day listening to the chatter and sing-song voices of the kids, and nights trying to sleep. That time he'd lived off peanuts and dried apricots, and a Zane Grey western that he reread twenty times. He pissed into a bucket and shat in a Ziplock plastic bag. Amazing how he could let his mind float during such times, so that the days seemed to drift by, the heat and smell and loneliness not affecting him at all. And it'd been worth it. By the time he broke his cover the papers had dropped his photo and the roads out of town were clear of pigs.

The stolen Falcon was where he'd left it, parked in the driveway of an abandoned fibro house. Foley crouched in the shadows of a peppermint gum and watched before approaching. He re-hotwired the ignition and reversed onto the quiet street and headed north of the river.

*

Foley hid in the wattle scrub beside Mostel's apartment building and looked for a way in. He could see the river shining under moonlight down the hill, the lights of prawners in Crawley Bay, and their voices carried in soft flutters on the wind. It was a twenty-storey block with each floor broken into four apartments. Each apartment was framed by a large concrete balcony, with no spaces between. The front door was well secured and covered by a security camera. This visit he wanted to enter and depart without being clocked.

An apartment on the second floor was dark, whereas the rest were illuminated. He could see the shadows of their inhabitants pass across the high glass windows and doors. Foley worked out which apartment it was and checked the carpark – the bay for apartment seven was empty. Very quietly, he stayed in shadow until he returned to the garden bed beneath the first balcony. If he stood on the ground-floor balcony he could just touch the base of the second. He reached a hand into a rainwater drain-hole and made sure there was circumference enough for him to turn his wrist. He walked his feet up the building wall until he was horizontal with the base of the second-floor balcony. The pressure on his trapped wrist was tremendous – he took one more step sideways and now all of his weight was on his forearm. He slung a leg over the balcony and withdrew his wrist and pushed himself over the lip and onto the cool slate floor of the second storey. As he'd expected, the sliding door leading on to the balcony was unlocked. He pushed it back, slipped inside the heavy drapes and moved to the front door.

It had been a guess, but a good one. Exiting the emergency stairwell onto Mostel's fifteenth floor, he saw the sisal-plaster tiles of the corridor ceiling laid in large square blocks, resting on painted steel framework. The building had ducted air-conditioning, which necessitated access to a roof-space – something he counted on in most of his bank robberies. There wasn't anything handy in the corridor for him to climb on. He tested his weight on the brass box containing the buttons to operate the lift, and it held. With one foot on the brass box he pushed up the nearest sisal tile and climbed into the dark. Remembering the floorplan of the second-storey apartment he'd entered, he clambered along the framework until he crossed onto a concrete load-bearing wall that took him directly above Mostel's apartment. The bearing wall was dusty and the space was two-foot high, but sufficient for him to crawl on hands and knees over to the wall closest to the balcony. The wall was thicker than those separating the rooms, and farthest from the bedrooms and kitchen. Below him, he could hear the sounds of jazz music and canned laughter. The occasional murmur. Foley looked at his watch. It was just gone midnight. He lay on his back and rested.

Foley woke at the first sound of morning voices. He was dehydrated and cold but that didn't matter. He made sure to drink as little as possible before a job – there was nothing worse than a painful bladder, and the cold kept him from sleeping too long.

The voices below him were harsh. A man abusing a woman. A woman nagging two teenage children, one boy and one girl, to get ready for school. Everything the woman asked of them, the children said no, or swore about. The woman shouted and the man shouted. Sometimes all four of them were shouting at once. Foley couldn't help compare Mostel's family with his own dear ma and her uncontrollable sons, each of whom out of agreement at least pretended that their mother had the final say.

Foley looked at the luminous dial on his watch as the last voice left the apartment. He rolled onto his knees and crawled across the bearing wall onto the framework fixing to the plasterboard ceiling, moved stiffly over the wires and aluminium ducts towards the ceiling manhole. It was hinged and lockable, but the lock wasn't set. Foley felt around the edges of the cover with his hands, brushed his knuckles on something leather. From his pocket he took out his torch and grunted with satisfaction at the sight of the leather satchel, just to one side of the cover. He put the torch in his teeth and opened the satchel. Traveller's cheques. A passport – Mostel's face but a different name. More fake ID. A Harrowgate Bank safety deposit box key. A little velvet bag that he could feel contained diamonds. And cash, paper-banded, denominations of fifty and twenty – looked like thousands. Foley put the lot back into the satchel and clicked back the manhole cover and dropped his head and shoulders down into the room, peering like a reverse periscope until he was sure the lounge room was clear. He dropped the satchel onto the leather couch below and spat on his hands and wiped them of dirt – he didn't want smudges on the manhole. Very carefully, trying to keep the dust down, he slipped his legs through the manhole and, with his clean fingers, rested the manhole on his shoulder, dropped the twelve feet onto the couch, and heard the manhole click shut above him.

Foley ignored the small terrier that raced in from the balcony, began yapping at his heels. He checked that the manhole looked clean and that no dust had followed him onto the couch. He checked his watch and smiled. He was hungry, and needed the toilet, maybe even a shower. Foley didn't know what kind of shit Mostel was into, but no man who made an honest living ever had a false passport and diamonds in a get-out-of-town bag, ready to run. There would be a safe here somewhere too, he was sure of it. He didn't have the tools to break it open, but would try his luck on the tumbler combination. But first, a feed. No doubt Mostel kept a well-stocked kitchen. Foley wanted to leave no trace of his visit, but that wouldn't stop him filling his belly and getting cleaned up. The dog was now nuzzling his leg. He knelt down and scratched its ears, saw that it was called Ruth. The dog followed him over to the kitchen, a hopeful look in its eyes.

24.

The morning had gone smoothly. Neither the premier nor Heenan had mentioned yesterday's surveillance device, and Swann hadn't raised it either. The premier had agreed with the arrangement Swann proposed, setting Stormie Farrell up with a full-time carer. Marion had a young woman called Janey Simpson in mind. Janey was a resident of the battered women's sanctuary on Pakenham Street in Fremantle, but her ex-boyfriend was still in the picture, and Janey didn't feel secure there. Swann had gilded the lily – failing to mention that Janey had finished only the first year of her nursing traineeship. Her main role was to keep Stormie out of trouble, and to call Swann if anything brewed. Swann had a feeling that the two would get on well. He promised the premier that he'd drop Janey around to Stormie that evening, get her settled in.

In the meantime, Dennis Gould had called him at the crack, the first arrows of light piercing the faded curtains. Gould had found something of interest, deep into the first tender. Something worth a look at.

Swann let himself in with his key, and found Gould pacing his apartment, listening to loud classical music as he smoked and scratched his belly. His only concession to sleep or relaxation since Swann last saw him had been to remove his trousers. His pale hairless legs glowed in the semi-dark, the same off-white as his undies. He saw Swann standing in the doorway and waved, nearly tripping over a coffee mug.

Swann sat at the kitchenette and waited for the onslaught of staccato sentences and bad breath. 'The first tender, Exetar, is Maitland Conlan's largest company, acquired two years ago. Very solid history, prior to that. Projects delivered on time and on budget. They did the harbour at Port Hedland and pretty much built the mining towns of the Pilbara. Had their first big break constructing the infrastructure around the Kwinana aluminium refinery, then two of the office blocks on the Terrace, but this would be the biggest undertaken so far.'

Swann had leaned so far back against the kitchenette that he was wedged in a corner. Gould's eyes were wild and over-focused, dried spittle at the edges of his mouth, breath foul. Swann put a hand on Gould's forearm to stop the younger man crowding him further. 'So far so predictable. And yet?'

'The contractors they've identified are proven performers, and mostly from companies recently bought by Conlan for Exetar. Which has allowed him to cut costs – simplifying admin and project managers, et cetera. Prior to Conlan buying them, all of the companies were well established, so no evidence there's phoenixing, although I haven't looked at the recent financials yet. Most of the company managers look solid too – in fact I've met most of them personally, back when I was broking. Mostly local. Nobody too suspicious. I've run backgrounds on them all, no bankrupts, no convictions. A few have been major donors to the Liberal Party, but a few have also donated large to the current mob. Hedging their bets ...'

'And?'

'*And yet*. When we get down to the level of subcontractors. The itty bitty jobs – suppliers of porta-dunnies, safety officers, crane hire, donga hire, site fencing, liquid waste removal, et cetera – there was a name that you'll remember – running a small outfit that does site security. Might have no bearing on the value of the tender, but ... Gary Quinlivan.'

Swann had no space to shrink in surprise, but he made the right face. 'I thought he was dead.'

'We all did. Want a coffee?'

Swann nodded.

Gary Quinlivan. Smack dealer and smuggler, flew the route that Clifford and Welsh were now getting hanged for flying. Son of a judge. Best schools, millionaire then bankrupt at twenty-one. Part of a gold consortium run by bent cops, dodgy bookies and Northbridge identities Leo Ajello and Tommaso Adamo, that ended in a gunfight killing one cop and one bookie. Arrested at the scene and went missing from the East Perth Lockup. Was widely presumed to have been murdered by Benjamin Hogan, then a senior consorting detective, for the crime of knowing too much.

Four years had passed. 'We know where he's been?' Swann asked.

'No, but I'm dying to find out.'

The kettle boiled, a gust of wind bashed the curtains, collecting half of the papers lain in a grid across the floor, scattering cigarette ash from the tea-saucers.

'Me too, but we'll have to tread carefully.'

25.

Des Foley pulled the sliding door that led onto the second-floor balcony and waited until his eyes adjusted to the light. He wasn't alone in the apartment – a cleaner who'd left the front door ajar was vacuuming in the next room. He slipped out onto the balcony and looked over the gardens that rose to the edge of the native scrub fronting Kings Park. His backpack was crammed with food taken from Mostel's apartment – canned fish, pastrami, four types of cheese, different biscuits and dried fruit and nuts – good for a week's rations, and the best way to avoid spending time in shops where he'd be recognised. Leaning over, he dropped the backpack onto a woolly bush that sank upon impact. Foley followed the bag over and landed on the jarrah-bark mulch around the garden. He remained in a crouch until the pain in his ankles subsided and hoisted the backpack and headed towards the sheltering bush. It was then that he saw them – saw that they'd seen him too. A big man in leathers, perched over a trail bike too small for him, helmet on. And a young man in an Alpha Romeo sedan, sunglasses and pink shirt, parked up the street facing the river.

Not coppers.

Foley fingered the butt of his pistol and headed for the bush. He heard the dirt bike rev and kick into gear. The scrub was thick with wild oats and juvenile sheoak, creeping ground shrubs that he stepped over as he pushed himself deeper into the park. He'd watched the helicopter from Mostel's balcony, doing a grid search over the one thousand acres of the park – an obvious place to look for him, camped in the scrub. That the coppers were looking but not asking told him they'd forced a media ban on the local newspapers and stations – for how long he didn't know.

Foley made the crest of the hill and waited in a stand of bull banksia. He could hear the trail bike gunning up the path and looked around for something heavy. There weren't any rocks or branches so he took out his gun and clicked off the safety. When the bike was near he stepped towards the path and aimed, and when the bike turned the corner he stepped closer and shot the rider three times in the chest. The noise of the .22 was lost in the strafe of the two-stroke engine that died as the rider slid off the path and rolled into the grey dirt and was still. Foley knelt on the man's back and searched the sky for the chopper and looked down the path for the Alpha driver, who'd have to be on foot. With his pistol pressed into the man's neck, he searched his pockets and came up with a facsimile mugshot of himself, taken from his last stretch in Pentridge. Whoever got the photograph had connections. It was the most recent photo of Foley in existence, although two years old now. Had to have come from the police wire. The man regained consciousness and started to groan. Foley pulled off his helmet and turned him over. The bullets from the peashooter had lodged in the man's chest, done the .22 pinball inside his ribcage, hadn't exited. He might live or he might die, depending upon luck.

Foley was wild at himself for getting seen. That the coppers weren't watching the Mostel apartment meant that the bastards didn't know the connection – for now. The man beneath him was no kid – a bikie in his forties. Foley unzipped his leather jacket and saw the Junkyard Dogs patch on the denim vest inside and put two and two together. Mostel had put his name on the street. The young Ding in the Alpha was most likely a scout for someone like Leo Ajello – to put a tail on him until Foley led him to his hide-out, bring in the big guns to do the execution.

The leather satchel of diamonds, cash and passports. Putting money on the street. Whatever Mostel was up to, it was big.

The bigger the better – meant he had more to lose.

Foley began to strip the bikie of his leathers, his boots. The two men were roughly the same size. The bastard could crawl to the main road in his jocks, or die trying. Foley zipped himself up and put on his backpack and lifted the bike. He flipped the leather seat and saw the butt of a sawn-off .303. He gunned the bike and took off down the path, away from the Alpha driver and along the empty hiking trails that led over to the Subiaco side of Kings Park. He exited the park near Rokeby Road and slipped into the traffic headed to Karrakatta Cemetery, the army barracks and the coast road that would take him south to the river, and home to Coolbellup.

26.

Swann parked the Statesman in the cool shade of a peppermint tree. Apart from the line of verge trees planted down Royal Street, this part of East Perth was unrecognisable. Gone were the old tenements and coke-covered industrial buildings, the alleys of tin and weatherboard, the old paperbarks that fronted Claisebrook canal. The water itself was fenced off, too polluted for children to play in. The Exetar-run building site was vast and laser-levelled, the grey dust rising in flumes that hung in the air as trucks carried contaminated soil away from the demolished power station. Swann took out his binoculars and recognised the trucks belonging to the cartage haulers trucking up the freeway all night, delivering infill to the redevelopment site on Burswood Island. The trucks were unmarked but the drivers wore the same uniform of grey shirt and cap. Swann panned the binoculars across the building site and zeroed in on a shipping container perched on jarrah sleepers against the nearest fence. It was a site manager's office with the words SECURITY handpainted across each of the walls. An old Landrover was parked nearby under a jerry-rigged hoochie strung up on steel poles. The donga was air-conditioned and had phone lines attached and nobody had entered or departed in half an hour.

Swann lit a cigarette and climbed out of the Statesman and wandered over to the nearest fence, parted the wire and slipped onto the site. He stood outside the security office and listened. Inside, a man was talking on the telephone. The voice was posh Australian with a hint of Queen's English. The voice's owner was speaking to a stockbroker, that much was clear. The names of mining companies Swann had never heard of and quantities of shares.

Ten years ago, a site manager speaking to a stockbroker would have been unlikely – but everyone was on the bandwagon now. Just this morning Swann had waited in line at his local deli while Brendan, the deli owner, and an older man in a bus driver's uniform had discussed which shares were hot. It sounded to Swann like mug punters talking horses.

But the voice in the donga lacked the mug punter's excitability. It was him giving advice to the broker, rather than fielding tips. The quantities of shares were large.

Away to his left, Swann watched a Toyota utility with a flashing orange cab-beacon head towards him. He knocked on the flimsy door of the donga and stepped inside.

Gary Quinlivan. Even with his back turned, it was the same young man Swann had thought murdered: the same expensive clothes and freshly barbered neck, hair combed in a side part but quiffed and gelled, his leather-soled brogues up on the desk.

Quinlivan didn't turn around but raised a one-minute finger. 'Your time, close of London exchange … yes … that's local time ten pm. Fax me the orders if they hit five pence. Otherwise, we'll speak tomorrow. Thanks Benny.'

So Quinlivan was talking to a British broker about transactions involving tens of thousands of pounds on a shitty line sent out from a handpainted shipping container on a dusty Australian building site. You wouldn't know it from the look on his face. He clocked Swann, and there was a little flicker in his eyes, but the old confidence remained. He was wearing pinstripe suit trousers and red braces over a starched white business shirt, no tie. This was the man who, in his early twenties, carried kilos of smack strapped to his body from countries where the penalty for doing so was death. Became a dealer for Leo Ajello, selling to the rich kids in the western suburbs. Last seen being escorted out of the lockup by two uniformed police, into a divvy van driven by Ben Hogan.

'How can I help? Are you the man who called yesterday, complaining about allegedly toxic dust on your tomato crop? If so, I apologise – I was out of the … office.'

Said with a deal of charm, the mockery implicit. Swann heard the clump of boots, felt the presence of a large mammal at his shoulder. The mammal waited for a signal from Quinlivan, whose eyes were bright with good humour.

'Quit the smart-arse act, smart-arse. And tell your mate here to visit the vet, get his teeth cleaned.'

Quinlivan nodded. 'Very well ... Swann, isn't it? What do you want? You can see I'm busy.'

'I need a list of all your employees, past and current. And I need to know your whereabouts these past years.'

Quinlivan laughed. 'Very well, Mr Swann. Although, whether I can be bothered reaching over to that filing cabinet depends upon your having a warrant.'

'I'm employed by the premier's office. I can have a subpoena here within the hour, although I'm sure that won't be necessary. I'm sure the management of Exetar will want to know that you've been helpful. This is about their tender for the Burswood job.'

'Well, in that case ...'

Quinlivan pushed his chair, the casters rolling towards a filing cabinet in the corner. Without getting up he reached into the second drawer and pulled a file, slid back to his desk, handed it over.

'I'll need that back – it's my only copy.'

'You don't keep copies at head office?'

Quinlivan smiled. 'This is head office. We like to keep overheads low. Key to survival in a tough market.'

'Always a market for apes with truncheons. I look in this file, I'm not going to find men with criminal records for violence and theft, am I?'

'God forbid.'

'How did a half-arsed operation like this get in with a Conlan corporation?'

'There were building site thefts, damage to expensive materials, equipment, ongoing. The last operation couldn't control the situation. We've remedied that.'

'Bit of the old *create the problem, fix the problem*, eh? And you, how did you get involved?'

Quinlivan leaned back on his chair, which creaked, ran his fingers down his braces. 'You mean, where have I been these past years, when everyone thought I was dead? I was questioned about the double-murder you're familiar with, and released. I chose to leave the country. I've been in London, working as an analyst and consultant to various broking firms, specialising in Australian stocks. And before you ask – I've come home because of the same opportunities – to get in on the ground level of what's looking like a very promising –'

'And you couldn't get any more level with the ground than a building site office stiff. You're the manager – where can I find the company owner? Who I've been told is a Mr … Calhoun.'

'Ah, Mr Calhoun. He's on an extended holiday, I believe. If you leave me your details –'

'I'll find him myself, thanks.'

Swann stepped back into the midriff of the goon, let his elbow and shoulder turn with the contact. Heard a little grunt and looked into the eyes of a ginger-bearded thug with broken capillaries over his sunburnt face. Not a face he knew, beyond a faint resemblance. Swann tucked the file under his arm, leant further into the man and cleared his way to the door.

*

He drove out of the city across the Causeway into Victoria Park, weaving among the trucks carrying contaminated dirt out of the city. He flipped through Quinlivan's file as he drove, single sheets held up against the steering wheel, a cigarette burning at his lips. A *Who's Who* of local lowlife – rejects from the bikie clubs, thugs from the fishing fleets working the off-season, wannabe gangsters from the suburbs, and washed-up boxers and bouncers from the local circuit. Nobody too heavy, but Swann guessed most of them were in the wrong game – security staff weren't allowed to work with a criminal record. Only problem was the time it'd take to follow up. And another anomaly – most of the employees had signed on as recently as a month ago – although the security firm had worked the East Perth job for nearly six months. A big clean-out, or a big takeover – Swann would have to investigate which. He needed to find the founder of the agency, Calhoun.

If the other tenders were like this – Swann was looking at months of work, when he only had weeks. But first to put a full stop after the experience of babysitting Stormie Farrell. The street was quiet except for the gentle whispers in the casuarina trees, at least until he got to Farrell Snr's house. He parked at the foot of the drive and could see Stormie and Janey outside in the Thunderbird, the stereo playing rockabilly – Wanda Jackson's 'Funnel of Love'. It looked like Janey was painting Stormie's toes with nail polish, a goon of wine propped on the dash, sunglasses on – the two of them on an imaginary road trip, singing and giggling. Janey had been Marion's first suggestion as carer, and at first he'd laughed it off. An ex-prostitute looking after the premier's father didn't sound like the kind of arrangement that'd work for Heenan, despite her interest in nursing. A couple of months looking after an old man had sounded good to her, though, living in and making sure he ate, washed, cut down on the booze.

Swann didn't get out of the car. Now Janey was up on her seat dancing, her glad rags catching the setting sun. Stormie Farrell with one hand on the steering wheel, the other arm hanging loose outside the car, tapping rhythm on the driver's door, living out his rock-and-roll fantasy of a couple of kids on the road.

27.

A few houses from the derelict fibro shack, Des Foley killed the ignition of the Kawasaki, walked the bike along the edge of the house where he laid it on the concrete pavers in the backyard. He removed the sawn-off .303 and wiped the bike down then covered it with a plastic tarp. It was hot in the man's leathers, and he unzipped the jacket and found a place for the rifle in his backpack and started the hike over to Gerry Tracker's place. The night was cooling fast; the southerly scouring the empty streets, the smell of rissoles and prawns, cheap sausages and cabbage wafting from the quiet workers cottages. He rounded the corner of Tracker's street, keeping to the mound of verge rubbish – whitegoods, blocks of limestone and wheelbarrows, and bikes overgrown with weeds. He crouched and scoped the flat length of street, a gesture that was routine now, but he got a shock at the sight of the divvy van next to Gerry's Datsun truck. Its lights were cut but he saw a red point of fire that faded in the shadows, came back again as the smoker inhaled and exhaled, observing the Tracker house. Foley backtracked according to his routine and surveyed the dirt alley that backed onto the rear of each of the houses. The alley was strewn with fallen branches and homemade BMX ramps and jarrah offcuts, and under the moonlight he could see that it was empty.

Foley couldn't have been followed, because the divvy van was already there. It couldn't be a trap for him, either, because then the van would be hidden – the coppers would use unmarkeds. If they genuinely believed Des Foley was in the neighbourhood the place would be crawling with pigs – choppers would be overhead, the street would be burning with arc lights, the neighbours would be gathered outside a safe perimeter for when the shooting started.

It had to be the same coppers who'd come looking for the kid, one man outside and another tossing Gerry's house, yet again. The situation wasn't good, not for Foley. Too much heat. Too many things wrong. He thought of returning to the empty fibro house to sleep, but didn't know the neighbours, couldn't risk being observed breaking into the boarded-up building. Foley crept along the rusted tin and asbestos sheeting that made the back fences of the houses, listening for dogs, watching for torchlight. If he was careful, he'd be able to enter old man Pickett's yard and creep under his house. The media ban on reporting his presence in the city would be over soon, and then the coppers would be forced to look everywhere – abandoned houses, parks, swamps, the homes of former associates. The size of the reward for information leading to an arrest was significant enough to make even friends consider turning him in. Foley didn't know old man Pickett, but Gerry Tracker trusted him, and he was safe for now.

Foley entered Pickett's yard by prising back a sheet of tin, stepping into the dirt. He was halfway to the weatherboards when the shouting started next door. Gerry Tracker's voice, a couple of hard calls of defiance and then the sound of fists hitting meat, men banging into walls, plasterboard and glass breaking, the front door slamming and then the sound of truncheons on bone. Foley felt his fists tighten, thought of the armoury in his bag, dismissed the thought. Gerry wouldn't want that. He was protecting his boy. The thought of the kid brought Foley round. He saw the weatherboard sheet loosen, watched the kid clamber through, the .38 revolver in his hand. Foley got to him in a second, put a hand over his mouth and a lock on his gun hand, smothered him into the dirt, laid on top of him, held him there.

The sound of their breathing. A light above them. The shadow of old man Pickett cradling his .303, cast across the yard. The doors to the divvy van slammed, engine started, drove away.

The kid had tears in his eyes, his limbs trembling with adrenalin, unrealised violence. When his breathing settled Foley took the hand off his mouth – pointed to the entrance to the cave, their haven.

The boy nodded, gave up the gun.

28.

Swann sat across from Dennis Gould. The radio was off, but the words hung in the air, made the stuffy room even hotter. Swann knew from years of experience that stories of violence made Gould want to reach for the bottle. Sixty hours sober was easy, locked in his room. Swann's mistake had been to turn on the radio.

The leading story on the nine o'clock news described a near-naked man, shot three times in the chest and stomach, crawling out of the bush onto Riverside Drive, nearly run over by the driver who swerved, stopped, called an ambulance.

The man was at Charles Gairdner Hospital in a critical condition, sepsis in his blood, not expected to live. Had been identified by his tattoos as a member of the Junkyard Dogs Motorcycle Club. The club president, as always, was saying nothing.

'Chalk that one to Des Foley. The section of Riverside Drive the bikie crawled onto was near Mostel's apartment.'

No response from Gould, whose eyes were elsewhere, hands stuffed into his pockets – no drink to reach for. It was Junkyard Dogs bikies who'd made Gould dig his own grave, but it was the second story that'd spooked him. Swann described how, an hour ago, the site manager of Exetar's East Perth development had received a phone call, the voice on the line suggesting that he look out his front window. The manager thought it was a prank until his Mercedes W201 lifted off the ground on a cushion of fire that blew out his front windows and tore all the leaves off his trees and incinerated his cat asleep on the porch. The manager was also in Charlie Gairdner hospital in a critical condition. The shock wave from the explosion had caused haemorrhaging of internal organs, his skin shredded with glass darts. A call by Swann to Terry

Accardi had gleaned this information and the fact that the site manager couldn't explain the bombing. No warnings had been given. Accardi believed him.

'You'd have to say that Exetar's looking shaky.' Gould's voice was barely a whisper. 'Your copper mate Accardi should be pleased. An American construction manager having his car blown up, ostensibly for no reason, it's got to point towards crime gangs working inside the company, eating into the company from the bottom tier. If the message wasn't intended for the site manager, then it has to be for Maitland Conlan.'

Swann looked at his hands, felt the urge to drink too. Lit a cigarette instead, mulling over Gould's comment. 'Not to mention Gary Quinlivan. His presence on the building site also legitimates our interest in Exetar.'

'Not the usual front for money laundering, a company the size of Exetar. What exactly is Accardi looking at?'

'Material for some future royal commission. Organised crime, police and political corruption.'

'The tender then.'

'Possibly. Although he couldn't have predicted the election result, or the premier's rush to development.'

Swann stubbed out his cigarette, looked into the ashtray.

Dennis Gould had made calls to London, confirming Gary Quinlivan's employment as an analyst and broker of Australian stock, particularly mining stock. What Quinlivan hadn't revealed to Swann was his success. They were only rumours, but Gould was told by British friends in broking and banking that Quinlivan was now a very rich man. He had a part-share in a Namibian diamond enterprise that was drawing the attention of De Beers; he had several Swiss bank accounts, as well as recorded multiple daily share transactions of major quantities of stock going back years – he seemed to have the knack for riding the wave before it broke.

Not bad for an ex-junkie, bank robber and dealer from the world's remotest city. Quinlivan knew intimate details about Benjamin Hogan's criminal enterprises, and the minor business empires of Leo Ajello and Tommaso Adamo, each of whom he had outgrown financially. Swann doubted however that Quinlivan was free of them. For whatever reason, Hogan had allowed Quinlivan to live, despite his knowing too much about Hogan's scams and killings. Hogan was not a man known for clemency. That he had let Quinlivan go to prosper overseas suggested something else. Hogan still owned Quinlivan, and perhaps more. He needed to clean his money. There was only so much wealth Hogan could openly claim, as a chief of detectives; only so much wealth he could put in his wife's and his children's names.

Swann wondered. He saw Gould looking at him. 'You said Quinlivan claimed he'd returned to get early access, get in on the ground floor. He's just the kind of smart prick to tell the truth in your face, assuming you'll read it as lies. I think he's telling the truth.'

Swann nodded. 'I think you're right. We've got bipartisan support for state progress, foot-to-the-floor development. Quinlivan knows diamonds and gold, but that's all buy and sell. The way the mining boom's shaping up, the real money's going to be in construction. The whole North-West is going to open up. Iron ore. Rail and roads, towns. Service industries. Airlines. But mainly construction. They're talking billions of dollars of projects. The Japanese can't get enough. And now they're talking about China opening up to the West, building for the future. They're going to need steel. They're going to need iron.'

'So you think guys like Ajello, Adamo, Hogan – they're going legit?'

'In a sense. But they're all used to high-profit deals. Big drug mark-ups. There's more money in legitimate business over the longer term, but what they're after is the cream that's added to every construction deal. Higher tenders. Cost blowouts. Government subsidies.'

'And that's what he meant about getting in on the ground floor,' Gould said.

'Exactly. The process of awarding business contracts. That's where the cream comes from. The potentially huge profit. Corruption of process, or simple standover. Bribery or bashing. The lessons of the street carried into the boardrooms, into parliament. Because the government of the day gets some of that cream returned as legitimate political donation.' Swann lit a cigarette, couldn't help it any longer, pulled out the half-bottle of brandy in his jacket pocket, took a swig and passed it to Gould.

Gould drank, and wiped brandy from his three-day growth, flecks of ginger in the lamplight, eyes black and exhausted. 'Hogan's always been a close mate of the Conlan brothers, from back when they fixed races. Why is he trying to destabilise Exetar, by way of Quinlivan, when it's the premier's preferred tender?'

Gould passed the brandy back, his eyes following the bottle. Swann nodded that he should keep it. 'The Conlans got to where they are by looking after their mates. Now they've risen so high, perhaps they've forgotten that.'

Gould took another swig, the bottle nearly empty. He toasted, and necked the rest, eyes watering. 'There I was, sitting on the beach in South Australia, complaining about boiled fish.'

29.

Des Foley always knew there was something wrong. 'You're *different*, not wrong,' his mother always said, but Des knew. Fearless, and insensitive to pain. The sight of blood and someone else's agony moved him not at all. The worst he felt was nausea, in his guts and behind his eyes, but only when the tears started. It wasn't communion with another's suffering, just a kind of disgust.

Des Foley put a hand on the boy's shoulder, but it gave him the creeps. The kid sat in the dirt and wrapped himself up with his arms. His smell was strong, like hot smoke. His long hair fell over his face. There were wounds on his arm where he'd gouged himself, long stripes of red that resembled raindrops of blood, red barbed wire, when he'd thought that Foley was asleep.

Des Foley had snatched the blade and put it beneath his pillow. He put his hand out for the boy's gun, which the kid handed over. Spoke for the first time since the coppers had dragged his father away. 'You can fucken 'ave it. Brought me nothin' but trouble.'

'How's that?' Foley asked.

The boy told the story of beating up the detective sergeant and stealing his gun. Foley wanted to whoop with laughter, congratulate the kid, but thought of his friend Gerry Tracker. What being a father must be like – feeling one thing and saying another, lying to your children from day one, lying about who you really were and who they were likely to become.

'They're gonna charge him with somethin', aren't they?'

'For sure. But he didn't give you up.'

The tears started again. Foley saw that he'd been too honest, tried to soften his voice. 'Cuttin' yourself isn't gonna help. Your dad wouldn't want that.'

'You know it and I know it – I ain't worth the trouble.'

Foley didn't reply, let the boy feel sorry for himself. He was a staunch kid, had a clearly fractured wrist, swollen and blue, that he'd splinted himself with knives and a sock, and his ribs were bruised too, maybe broken. But there were tears, rolling out of his eyes like silver.

'Where's he bein' held, you reckon? Reckon I could bust 'im out? We got two guns.'

He meant it too, and Foley had to force back an admiring laugh. Just like he'd been at the same age. 'Nah, kid, that's what they want. This is a ... provocation ... means that they're calling you out.'

'Should I hand myself in?'

'Yeah, you should. But tell me why you busted out. I did my juvie time at Longmore; wasn't so bad.'

Foley listened to the boy's story, raised his eyebrows. The set-up made sense. Workable from the screws' point of view, but just ridiculous enough for them to deny it, should it ever go wrong, paint the bloke caught as a liar.

Target criminal families, just like Tracker's. One crim inside the walls of Freo Prison, the crim's family on the outer, forced to smuggle for the Purple Circle of screws that ran the jail black market. Better a crim's family take the risk of getting caught than one of the screws. And if they wanted to punish a crim, they just had to bust the family member. Good for keeping control.

'And you refused to get your dad involved? Mate, you've got a lot to learn. You'd be owned by the screws, sure, but there'd be favours granted. That screw system in the prison – you got to work with it. Ain't nobody gonna help you if you're on the out. People outside can't protect you. Can't protect yourself.'

'You're saying I shoulda –'

'Your dad would've understood. He's made hard choices before. Knows how things work.'

The tears had dried up. 'Just didn't wanna get him in trouble again. I remember as a kid ...'

'Son, your dad ... I know him like a brother. He's a survivor *because* he doesn't just look after number one. Can't be like that in prison, or in life. He's cunning and strategic, but most of all he's loyal. Son, don't you know? Most fathers are like that. They're *happy* to put themselves in harm's way, if it's for their people. Helping you help the screws would've been an opportunity for him to show that.'

'Your father or mine?'

'My father was a dog. Looked after number one. Why he ended up dying alone. Good fucken riddance.'

'I thought you were gonna tell me to run. But I'll do it – hand myself in. Show that I can make the sacrifice too, for him.'

'Good one. But hold yer horses. You've got to do it right. Your dad just bashed a copper. Chances are you hand yourself in, they'll lock both of you up. And he'll be taking his medicine tonight, either way – they'll be knockin' him from pillar to post as we speak.'

The kid's eyes flooded, but didn't spill. 'Fucken what then?'

'Money talks, son, your dad walks. You got to pay that sergeant you shamed, on top of returning the gun. And you got to pay those screws, make it right with them, before you hand yourself in. Otherwise, they're gonna make an example of you. The aggravation you caused by escaping – bad look for them. They'll neck you in your cell. I've seen it – they'll do it. You got to ... establish the trust again. Money's what they want – money's the only way.'

The boy nodded, wiped his eyes, gritted his jaw. 'I can help you rob a bank. I can be driver. Only give me enough for a bribe.'

Des Foley shook his head. 'No chance. I love your father like a brother, but I fear him too. He'd never forgive me. Besides, I work alone. Always.'

Foley reached for the leather satchel beside his pillow, worked at the buckle, tipped the lot onto his sleeping bag. He'd already hidden the diamonds in a rotted stump beneath the house. He picked up the passports and bank books and files and put them in the bag. He counted the money that remained. Four thousand, three hundred dollars in mixed Australian currency, two thousand more in US fifties. The Yank money was worthless to the kid – Foley replaced it in the satchel. He pared away thirteen hundred for his mother, took the paper bands off the remaining notes, gave two thousand bucks to the kid. 'That should be enough to make the sergeant happy. You have someone you can trust, to find out where he lives, drop the gun and this money off at his house?'

Blake Tracker shook his head, staring at the cash. 'Nope.'

'Well obviously I can't bloody do it myself. What about your father? He have any mates, uncles or aunts do the job for us? Think. Gotta be someone reliable. This is no ring the doorbell and run routine. It's got to get to the sergeant in person.'

Blake Tracker looked beaten, the exhaustion breaking over him. Foley shrugged. 'Ok, we need another stake for the screws anyway. You'll need a whole lot more than that. If we can get money to them, might be smart to hand yourself in to the sergeant. He'll beat three colours of shit out of you, but he'll keep the money, be able to claim that he retrieved the gun in the line of duty. Make him look good. What's wrong?'

Blake remembered the look on the detective's face, those years ago, just the two of them in the swamp. What he hadn't told the judge, or even his father. He hadn't knocked the copper out and then stolen the gun. The D had already drawn, was going to shoot Blake for sure. The sound of a woman calling her dog had interrupted him. Blake rushed him then, got in a lucky elbow, the gun fell his way. 'That guy's gonna kill me. Irish Pete, this screw at the home ... he heard things. Only thing stopped it happenin' already in Longmore is the fucker didn't have the money to pay. But he kept askin', how much? How much to neck the Abo kid?'

'Smart you didn't tell your father. He'd hunt him down.'

'I know it. What are we gonna do? I gotta get my pops out.'

'That ain't gonna happen, son. He's in for a time. They won't take him before the judge until his bruises heal. You best sleep. Thinkin' this tired leads to crazy moves. Sleep, and then we'll talk. I got an idea.'

Foley thought of Mostel's belongings in the satchel, the key to the safety deposit box in Harrowgate Bank. He had to get past thousands of coppers on the prowl. Some freelance killers. The Junkyard Dogs would want revenge for their mate. A fucking shitstorm. And the story of Foley's homecoming would hit the papers and TV today. The city banks would go into overnight lockdown, hire extra security, like always. His poor ma: the coppers and the papers would be all over her again.

30.

The return of Australia's most wanted, Des Foley, to the city had blown the soon-to-be-hanged Clifford and Welsh, their miserable pallid faces and hangdog postures, right off the front page. Replaced by the last known photograph of Foley, a mugshot released by Victorian police, the man looking bemused and optimistic, headed into a ten-year stretch at Jika Jika, the prison within the prison at Pentridge. He'd swallowed draino to get to the hospital, done a bunk from a third-floor window, his guts still burning.

Swann remembered Foley from when he started out in his chosen trade – did a couple of armed robs of local bank branches, two armoured-car heists, but soon outgrew the capacity of the city to support a crim with his smarts and ambition.

Swann finished his coffee, poured himself some more, glanced at his watch. Just gone six. The dawn chorus of magpies and honeyeaters was fading in the early sunlight, a sullen heat spreading into the house. He lit his first for the day, turned the page, expecting to see Clifford and Welsh. Instead, two images: one of the protest site at the Old Swan Brewery; the other of the premier and Sam Mostel, the latter with a pen in his hand, bent over a contract. The deal done. The Brewery sold to Mostel for an unnamed figure. His plans for the site, commercial in focus – a hotel, capitalising on the river views. Both Mostel and the premier looked pleased with themselves – the premier announcing that the funds secured would go to a development corporation, state owned and run, to facilitate further projects.

On the page opposite was a smaller piece about the bikie who'd been shot, 'Piggy' Taylor, owner of a bike shop that specialised in custom rides. Condition stable, after an operation to remove most of his stomach.

Claimed to have been going for a walk in Kings Park when someone shot him from behind a tree. Didn't see who it was. The journalist raising the spectre of a possible bikie war, links to Riley's speech beneath the Barracks Arch last week, the talk of interstate patch-overs.

Marion padded into the kitchen, scratched his head, leant down and kissed him on the cheek. 'Good news?'

Swann grunted, kissed her waiting mouth, taste of mint. 'Good news for a cartoonist. Any word from Janey?'

'All's well. She called late last night. Sounded drunk but happy. Said she'd got Stormie to eat some tinned asparagus soup and toast soldiers. She watered down his wine; the best she could manage to get some non-alcoholic liquids into him. He's a bit flirty, but nothing she can't handle.'

'Any sign of her ex at the shelter?'

'Nothing. That's two days now, he hasn't been pestering the other girls, or the shelter.'

'Hopefully that rumour worked. Hopefully the prick's broken down somewhere on the Nullarbor, drinking his radiator water.' Swann looked at his watch. 'Shit.' He ditched the paper in the bin, Des Foley's face peering out of a mess of cauliflower scraps.

*

Parliament wasn't sitting until the afternoon, and the absence of ministerial staffers and hangers-on gave the building a forlorn air, like the morning after a party. The premier's office was empty. Swann was followed to the office by a security guard, who looked like Lurch from the Addams Family, and who watched him go about his work. Swann went first to the telephone, which pinged immediately. The thing was still bugged. The security guard watched while Swann dismantled the cover and checked – it was the same bug. Swann wasn't about to remove it without checking with Heenan, but while he was replacing the cover he dropped the small Phillips head screwdriver into the deep carpet at his feet. He knelt to pick it up, saw the canvas tote bag stowed beneath the bureau. Pretending to check something beneath the desk, Swann opened the neck of the bag. It was stuffed with cash. There had to be one hundred grand there, easy. The bag itself carried no markers or labels. It wasn't a Conlan bag. Swann closed the neck and stood and finished his work, just in time to see Heenan huffing up the hall. Lurch stood aside and buttoned his jacket, gave a little bow.

'All good?' Heenan asked, looking deliberately at the phone. Swann caught the false chipper tone and the partially filled bag under Heenan's arm and shrugged. 'Sure. All good.'

'Kyle, leave us alone now,' Heenan said to Lurch, who nodded and left. 'That thing only records incoming calls, correct?'

'Correct.'

Heenan looked ready to collapse, his eyes bugged out and his forehead sweating. 'You know anything about stamps, Frank?'

Swann shook his head. 'Know I don't like the taste. Why?'

'Art? What about art? Or Persian fucking carpets? Vintage cars? The fucking reproduction rights to The Beatles fucking backlist?'

Swann let Heenan rant on. A meeting he'd just been to. Possible state investments in collectibles with long-term yields. Calls fielded from all over the world. Shysters and hustlers lining up to flog stuff. Swann stood away from the bureau while Heenan knelt and put more cash in the canvas bag, his voice wheedling and cynical in turn. He struggled to his feet and reached into the top drawer and pulled out a bottle of Jameson, cracked the cap of the new bottle and took a slug.

'Thought the premier quit the grog?'

'This is for me. I fucking need it. You ready?'

Swann blanked Heenan, who groaned. 'Didn't I tell you? In lieu of the weekend barbie that you're so reluctant to attend, we're both expected this morning on some bastard's launch, to celebrate the Brewery sale. We'll go in your car. I'm already too pissed to drive. Yeah, I know. You've got better things to do, you and me both. And you've got questions. Answers I don't have, but we can talk in the car.'

Swann latched the clasp on his Gladstone, put out a hand to steady Heenan, who buckled. 'Blood pressure. Goes up and down like a fucking barometer.'

*

Swann heard the first thwack of a bubbly cork from the yacht club carpark, followed by a cheer. Heenan winced, attempted to close his jacket, couldn't get the buttons round his gut, looked even more miserable. The morning sun lay upon the blue pan of the river and radiated in silver sheets across the white sands of Crawley Bay. The yachts of the rich and famous bobbed in their pens. The Royal Perth was the city's most exclusive, the grass freshly mown and the fences high, the clubrooms enfolded in dark glass. Swann followed Heenan as he navigated the concrete jetties towards the farthest mooring. Heenan waddled, and hitched his pants, and ran his hands through thinning hair, resembling a giant marine mammal thrown up by the river, at a disadvantage on the land. Beneath Swann's feet, hundreds of brown and white jellyfish floated in the still water; gobbleguts darted and trumpeter flashed among the pylons. Heenan had quieted on the drive over, had dozed off in the peaceful roads of Kings Park. In answer to Swann's question, he'd admitted that the bug was commissioned according to the premier's wishes – the recorder was in one of the bureau drawers. As to why, the answer was obvious – the premier's honeymoon period was coming to an end – there was pressure about the Brewery protest, pressure about Des Foley on the loose, discontent among the backbenchers about the new policy direction. There was pressure from some of his closest ministers, wanting to go freelance on brokering potentially lucrative deals. Lobbyists were going apeshit – demanding in-kind support for their support during the election. Information was a bankable commodity that appreciated with interest. Yes, the black book in the top drawer was a dirt file. For the time being, the MPs were calling the premier direct, as he wished, but that wouldn't last. Soon their calls would be among themselves, a supportive ear for their bitching and moaning. Many of them, the premier knew, were owned by some of the more aggressive lobbyists, and were under pressure to get results. If the premier needed to remind them of their arse-licking, compromised selves, the tapes would be there.

Heenan gave Swann a look that suggested he'd said too much, and then wouldn't be drawn on who had planted the bug. Most other PIs in the city shouldn't be trusted, Swann reminded him – ex-cops shunted out for being too obviously dirty, or volatile or violent, which was saying something. Heenan waved that away. Don't worry about it, Frank.

A young man dressed as an admiral in full whites and cap, golden epaulettes and gold-braid jacket piped them aboard. Heenan first, dropping down onto the back deck of the hundred-foot launch with a groan, Swann swinging behind. Twenty or so men sucking on beers and champagne in flute glasses. Swann clocked the Conlan brothers, Larry and Maitland, Feedledee and Feedledum, in full boatie regalia – polo shirts, white shorts and deck shoes, sunburnt legs – slouched against a rail with matching cigars, Swan Export cans in their mitts; Mostel the bookkeeper-turned-developer in earnest conversation with a man Swann didn't recognise; Coleman the building magnate chatting to Mattock the union heavy; Engle the High Court judge and Peter Spratt, the attorney general; and then the premier. He turned, saw Swann, little flicker in his eye and glance to Heenan before shaking Swann's hand, giving him the big welcome. Swann understood – there was never any invite from the premier, who wasn't happy to see him. The whistle blew and giggles followed at Swann's back, a broad murmur of appreciation from the men on deck. He turned, watched three sets of long legs and brown arms and white teeth and big hair, hookers in bright summer dresses climb down from the dock – girls from Dot Coulter's stable. The engine throbbed beneath them, another murmur of half-pissed anticipation and plenty of manly arms reaching out to steady the women lurching on high heels.

Swann took a rail beside Heenan, lit a cigarette. 'What are you up to, mate?'

Heenan's answer was drowned out in the roar of the inboards as the launch surged across the silent water, a mere five hundred metres round the bay along Riverside Drive, engines cut and coasting towards a mooring off the Old Brewery, toasts all round to Mostel, who grinned at the attention. On shore the hundreds of protestors must have heard the toasts. Heenan left Swann to shepherd the premier inside the wood-panelled cabin, in case there were cameras among the protestors, who began to jeer at the sight of the launch.

'Beer, Sir?'

Swann turned to the tray of drinks proffered by one of the women, summer dress shrugged off and now wearing a bikini. 'Cathy, isn't it?' he asked. Then watched over her shoulder as Heenan passed a stuffed envelope to Stormie Farrell's brother, reinvented as party bagman.

'Mr Swann? I didn't recognise you behind the sunnies. How's Marion?'

'She's good, Cathy. I'll tell her you asked. She'll like that. I'll let you go, there's thirsty men around. But perhaps we can chat another time.'

Cathy heard steps at her back and smiled false. 'Sure, I'll just check. I think we've only got white. But I'll check.'

A cordon sanitaire had opened up around Swann, backs turned to him as the outsider. Into the empty space Heenan staggered, sat his arse on the railing and crossed his arms, also an outsider. 'Every party like a business meeting, every business meeting like a party; that's the West Australian way.'

Swann didn't bother with a response, let the silence swell. Finally, Heenan uncrossed his arms, crossed them again. 'Come on, Frank. You work for me, right? I want you at my back. He's thinking of getting rid of me, I can tell. Just watch my back.'

As he said this, Heenan's eyes were glued to Cathy's arse. A look on his face. Not the usual hunger of an undesirable man. Something else. Swann wondered, before remembering the old man Mostel was chatting to, the Supreme Court judge that'd thrown the Dragic case out of court, hard to recognise without his powdered wig and gowns. His Honour Justice Roberts.

The barrister Swann's clients had hired was brought over from Melbourne; the evidence was compelling. The silk couldn't believe the not-guilty verdict, his ego offended. True that he'd done a great job on Dragic and his claims of bankruptcy – the money-trail Swann had uncovered there in black and white. But Justice Roberts had been unmoved. It wasn't until the case moved to the civil court that Swann's clients had a win, the burden of proof lessened and the younger judge willing to countenance fraud and criminal intent on Dragic's part. He had ordered the assets Swann uncovered to be seized. The look on Dragic's face was priceless. Bail set at a hundred thousand, pending an appeal. Dragic's skipping bail leading to the forfeiture of everything.

Swann caught it, the little nudge from Conlan, hand on Cathy's lower back, pushing her towards Justice Roberts. She looked at Swann at the same time Conlan did – his face a sneer. The launch throbbing to life. Some of the protesters on shore had begun swimming out, to cheers from their friends.

31.

As soon as Swann took out his car keys, the men emerged from the midday glare. Three detectives: two in the regulation trousers and boots and white shirt, tie askew and sleeves rolled; the other in a full cotton suit with ridiculously padded shoulders. It was the third man who badged Swann: narrow blue eyes, sunburnt nose, lips glistening in the brightness. 'Major Crimes. We'd like you to accompany us to Central. A little chat. Purely voluntary at this point.'

The detective was young for his rank, clearly a Hogan acolyte. Didn't move like a bash-artist, didn't have the eyes for it either. Nearly eight years since Swann had quit the force; a new generation coming through. This kid would have been in uniform back then – privy to the stories about Swann but not a player in the hunt.

'Undercover among the Pinocchio's crowd are you, son?'

The kid didn't bite. 'Like I say, purely voluntary at this point. We'll follow you.'

Swann was curious. A few years ago, a trip to the cells beneath Central would have been a death sentence. The detente of late – it was worth testing, although there was nobody to witness Swann's departure with the Ds.

'Alright, let's go.'

They followed in a cream unmarked Commodore; three big men in a small-nosed car. The first thing Swann did was call home on the car phone. Left a message for Marion on the answering machine, triggering the recorder in the roof-space. Told her what he was doing, gave the rego of the Holden, the name of the detective on the badge, description of the other two, made a show of letting the Commodore passengers see the phone.

He parked in the bays inside the complex, the concave building looming above, locked the Statesman and dropped the keys into the gap between windscreen and bonnet. If anything happened to him they would have to tow the car away, drawing attention.

Swann lit a cigarette, squared up and waited, the three men emerging from the underground carpark snapping on sunglasses, straightening ties and moving in a sleek wedge, cotton suit at the front.

He walked past Swann and signed in at the front desk while the other two stood away. Ten years ago Swann was superintendent of uniformed police, and this was his station, his little kingdom – a couple of hundred coppers answering to him alone. The young detectives would know this, everything else communicated from Hogan's point of view – Swann sticking his nose into the CIB's affairs after Ruby Devine's murder, putting at risk the lucrative kickbacks from the brothels, bookies and casinos, trusted drug dealers, green-lit bank robbers and car re-birthers – generating a total weekly income far in excess of a senior detective's yearly salary. Even when it was shared among a couple dozen Purple Circle Ds, it was still one of the best-paid jobs in the state. The crown had fallen into Benjamin Hogan's lap; for two years now he'd been head of the CIB.

Hogan emerged from the lift and ran a hand through his golden hair, pushed up the sleeves of his black linen suit – looked more like a French actor than a hard-nosed cop.

The old enmity there in Hogan's smirk, his easy posture. A wave of his hand towards the open office just inside the secure doors. Last year, a kid had blown the lobby apart, bombs strapped to a vest, his head found in the parking lot. The year before that, the TRG had been called to dispatch a kid in the lobby with a shotgun, a mental patient, gunning for death by cop, which is what he got – ninety-three bullets from eleven different handguns.

Hogan's choice of meeting room made Swann even more curious. It was deliberately public, the office beside the busy dispatch room. Not an interrogation room, but a security camera in the corner, a simple desk and plastic chairs. The other three detectives loitering outside, in case Swann went for Hogan, not the other way around.

Hogan sat at one end of the table and Swann parked himself at the other. Both of them lit cigarettes, stared. Hogan getting in first.

'Good job taking down Dragic. I always hated that ape. Too greedy, even by my standards.'

The inference: Hogan had let it happen. Swann waited for him to continue. 'You would have heard he's put money on the street. All the way from fucking Yugoslavia.'

'I heard. Obviously got the exchange rate wrong. Whatever the Macedonian currency is, two thou' Aussie, well ...'

Hogan grinned. 'We thought about doing a whip-around, put some cream on the biscuit.'

'But?'

'I don't know, Frank. Seems to me like things are working out. You're out there, doing your thing, got your fibro shack down there in Freo, livin' like a crab under a rock. I'm head of the company. Got more pressing concerns ...'

Hogan looked to his perfectly manicured nails, scuffed them on the palm of his hand. 'And you came, today. Of your own accord. Sign of maturity. Sign of things to come, I hope. You've positioned yourself well, under the premier's wing. I respect that in an adversary.'

Both of them trained interrogators, everything happening off the script. The false warmth in Hogan's voice, the easy posture.

Swann cut to it. 'What are you offering me? Before we get to the threats.'

Hogan laughed, genuine mirth in his eyes. 'Like I say, a worthy adversary. The answer – Dragic. A mutual foe. Shit under my shoe. Public nuisance. And the latest bloke to want you dead. But different to the others, I'm sure you'll agree.'

'You both hired mutts to do it.'

A moment of concern in Hogan's eyes, unsure whether his men had checked Swann for a wire. A measure of his imperiousness, the caution brushed off. 'I'm sure if Riley had really wanted you dead, that bomb would've done its job.'

'He tells you everything, doesn't he?'

'As you know, behind the smelly rags he's an A-grade snitch. I can forgive his moments of ... sentimentality. But Dragic, like I say, is a different kind of human stain. And those Albanians he's with. Nasty cunts. Which is why I called you in. Before this gets ... well ... Albanian.'

'Get on with it.'

Hogan sniffed. 'To business, then. What *I* want, is for you to leave young Gary Quinlivan alone. No more visits to the Exetar building site. That boy's going to make me very rich. Life is good, Frank, but you know the old Pommy saying – one does get so *tired* of the taste of champagne. I'm a man with ambitions, so keep your fucking nose out of my business.'

'And in return?'

'I let you in on a little secret. About the money on the street. The measly two thou. That's just a set-up, a line without a hook. You knew Dragic would come after you, and look how well a paltry figure put you at ease. In fact, the figure is far higher, as I understand it. In the order of fifty thousand, and it's not on the street. Those Slavs aren't like us, Frank. Basically, they're fucking animals. The money, the fifty thousand is for your wife, or one or more of your daughters. A real bash, rape and bury-deep job. So deep you'd never find them. Never know who, or how. Frank?'

The deal was on the table, and Hogan had no need to play the cop, offering Swann a way out of his fix. But Hogan was a trained liar, and Swann could see that the mockery in his eyes was genuine – the look you give a crim after he's been outsmarted, tricked into giving it up.

'Who's he given the job to?'

'Same bloke previously employed to snuff your mate, Dennis Gould. A patched Junkyard Dogs rider.'

So Hogan also didn't know that Gould had been spared. 'You got a name?'

Hogan sneered. 'Nup. And before you think it – you can't go around killing off a whole bikie club. Swann, I know you'd do it, but I won't allow it.'

'How do you know I'd do it?'

Hogan laughed. 'You crazy prick. You got away with killing my boss. You'll never be forgiven for that. Though it gave me the opportunity years before my time.'

So Hogan didn't know about that, either. Swann never pulled the trigger on Casey. He didn't know who did, and cared even less.

Hogan patted a hand on the desk, laying it out. 'But I can give you Dragic. That mutt's not in Macedonia. He's afraid of flying. Dumb bastard's in Wanneroo. He's waiting for the job to be done. And when it's done, when he's through watching you suffer, he'll move on you too. Don't look so surprised, Frank. You bankrupted him, after he'd gone semi-legit, after I told him to stay in the smack trade. Just when he had the sniff of a reputation, something to make his dad proud, you took it away from him. You know his dad made the poor cunt eat pigeons when he was a kid? When the other kids were down the park playing footy, poor little Dragic was down the swamp shooting pigeons for dinner. It's there on his juvie charge sheet, you should have a look at it sometime ... discharging a .22 rifle in a public place.'

Swann stood. 'Address.'

Hogan grinned. 'Just so happens, I've got it written, right here.'

'I don't want it written. Tell me.'

Hogan held up the slip of paper, the smile on his face like he was reading a joke from a Chinese cracker. 'Wattle Grove Smallholdings. It's a market garden on Wanneroo Road. Cabbages, caulis, broccoli and the like. The stupid prick's even planted dope in a tomato crop, to get himself going again. And watch the dobermans. They're hungry looking. And Swann: Gary Quinlivan and Exetar. Keep out of my fucking business.'

Swann nodded. The play was straight enough on the surface. But like the surface of Hogan's eyes, bright with reflected light, what lay beneath was a mess of shadow.

32.

Swann drove in a daze, the clear spring sunlight and the commuters going about their normal routines, the council workers lopping street trees and the children coming out of school. Hogan might be lying, or he might be telling the truth. One minute with Dragic, face to face, and he'd know which. The Statesman kept to a steady seventy, Swann not wanting to be pulled over, or delayed by anyone or anything. The throwaway pistol and his registered side-arm lay on the seat beside a box of shells. He smoked with the window down, playing the angles. Hogan obviously wanting him to kill Dragic, for reasons of his own. Hogan would then have the option of taking Swann down, or at the very least, owning him forever. Or maybe the threat against his family was a ruse; Hogan bringing Swann and Dragic together in a likely violent confrontation to further his own ends. The same result, assuming Swann came out on top: Swann down for murder, or owned by Hogan.

The cop in him was already drawing alibis, plausible denials, but his blood was too hot, pounding in his cheeks, the pressure of its circuit through his head audible above the engine, the street noise. Whatever the play, it was over. If it was true that Dragic had paid to kill Marion, or one of his daughters, then whatever happened next, Swann was out of the game. Corporate types hiring bikies to go the bash was one thing, ordering the murder of a shareholder troublemaker another. Both came down to business. But the murder of innocents?

Swann wanted to call Marion and the children, but he didn't want to alarm them, implicate them in what happened next. Better to do the necessary, whatever it took, even though it was Hogan pulling the puppet-strings, expecting Swann to proceed directly to the address. Instead Swann dialled Gould, who everyone thought was dead – a ghost who wouldn't be traced. Gould deserved to know, had been spared by good fortune, but that luck was about to end. 'Start packing, old mate. This time for a long haul. I'm on the way to see Trevor Dragic. If you don't hear from me in an hour, then scarper, don't look back ...'

'No need for that. I still haven't unpacked from last time, or washed for that matter. But Frank – the Exetar train's taking off. Trucks hijacked, a murder this morning – environmental consultant found floating in the river, just off Burswood. Clear signs of a hostile takeover, from the bottom up. What do you think about –'

'Don't worry about Exetar. Just get ready to leave. One hour. I'm nearly at the address.'

It was like talking to a child. 'I agree. Exetar's a scratch – clear evidence of organised crime influence. I'll start looking at the next tender. Hercules Construction. But also – I got a line on Calhoun, the owner of the security company Quinlivan's occupying. Details forthcoming ...'

Swann let him go. The sun was falling to his left, the warm burn on his face and forearm, wind gusting over the limestone hills and the smell of swamp creeping through the remnant bush. The city left behind – now came large allotments with handpainted signs and dirt driveways, giant tuart and marri by the roadside; ploughed earth and market gardens, greenhouses and Vietnamese women in conical hats and bright scarves. Swann saw the sign ahead – Wattle Grove Smallholdings, letters scrawled in red paint over a grey jarrah plank, the dusty road winding through wattle and banksia scrub.

He drove past the turnoff and looked for somewhere to park, away from the road and invisible from the farm. Two hundred metres ahead, a little cutaway edged into a stand of sheoak and wattle. On the rise above were six giant granite blocks piled into a pyramid and painted like dice; white surfaces with black markings – a warning to those on the Bindoon Road. The road was empty of traffic. Swann pulled across and eased the Holden over the dry crust of dirt and gravel, parked inside a natural cover of wattle. The Statesman would still be visible from the road, but only if you were searching. He cut the engine and patted the dash, crossed himself for good luck, tested his hand for the shakes, swallowed nothing from a dry mouth. He'd never killed a man in cold blood. He'd never had to torture a name out of a man and, if that name emerged, kill the man. Wrap the man in a blanket and drive the man far away. Bury the man where he would never be found. A sequence of events that was not the ending, but just the beginning.

One thing Swann held to – if the contract was legit, and if the name emerged, and if Dragic was killed, the second man would fall away. He'd proved that by letting Gould go. If Dragic was dead, then there was no contract, no point in the shooter moving forward. That thought got Swann out of the car, the two pistols and the box of shells in his jacket pockets, peaked cap pulled low.

Over the sagging strings of wire, into a nursery field with red-turned earth skirted by grey sand, pudding rocks and limestone rubble. The homestead lay across the fields, sprinkler turning over an acre of tomato plants. Even from a distance Swann could see the unnatural green of the marijuana buds, tall over the green fruit. There was no cover towards the front of the property, so he continued along the brushline, expecting dogs at any moment, his .22 throwaway loaded in his gun hand – the sound of a .22 not unusual in an area plagued by rabbits. From the back of the homestead an array of sheds and shipping containers fronted the bush, gave him cover to approach the house. Silence and a sense of dread; ears tuned to the slightest anomaly; cicadas like jet planes, instincts humming with the strain, eyes charged with an electric focus. What he hoped: Dragic to see him coming and they go at it – self-defence. What he hoped: no others in the house. No witnesses, or potential victims. Still no dogs. Swann edged towards the back of the house and tested the screen door, unlocked. He eased it with his foot. No dogs, or sounds within. The screen door hinges, he could see the shine of grease. Nudged the door open and slipped inside, let his eyes adjust, the smells of paprika, boiled cabbage, bacon fat, dog. Gun hand leading, room to room. Heart flipping like a fish. Tinnitus buzz of blood in his head, the roaring silence. Finally, the lounge room. Could see the back of Dragic's dyed black head, tilted, reclined in an easychair, looking out over the fields, his investment. Still no dogs. The sound of flies. Swann smelt it. Old blood. Like pig iron; sweet rust. He followed the wall around the chair, saw the bullet hole in Dragic's eye; seeping jelly and blood, the other eye staring at him. Dragic's bare feet, impossibly white against his black jeans, black carpet, pool of velvet-black blood. Three toes severed on his left foot; secateurs nearby, bubbles of blood where his toes used to be.

A controlled crime scene. A disciplined killer. No sign of unnecessary beating; the minimum amount of torture to extract information. Nothing personal. No exit wound in the skull – clearly a .22, probable multiple shots in the same eye socket.

Almost as though Swann had done it himself.

But the job only half-done. Hogan's work. Hedging his bets. It was Swann he wanted, not Dragic. Drug-dealing thugs turned businessmen were a dime a dozen since the mining boom. Dragic was someone who didn't play the game; impatient, incompetent – lacked the temperament – Swann had proved that in court.

This was Dragic's punishment, and Swann's reward – also a punishment, but also an opportunity.

Hogan's law.

If Swann walked away, Hogan's men would come for him. The false money Dragic put on the street, motivation enough for Swann to murder him. And Hogan would have a trump. Swann didn't know what – except that he would have it.

The only course of action, to follow through, as though the murder was his. Another step towards the body, and he may as well have killed Dragic. Expecting sirens. Were they watching from the road? Back outside, the smell of the ocean riding the sea breeze, the banksia woodland whispering; the gloaming light feeding on the shadows, illuminating every object, sharp and distinct, watchful even. The sound of his boots on the gravel, inside the sheds. An old blue tarp. A shovel. Keys in a Datsun ute.

Swann realised that he'd been holding his breath, sipping little hits of air, holding at bay the image of Hogan's men, arriving in numbers. He exhaled, put his hands on his knees, felt the earth turn, watched the light fade around his feet.

33.

For the first time in weeks, Swann was grateful for the early hour. He hadn't slept, and the day's work ahead was a blessing. There are things you can hide from in the daylight hours, people you can only reach when the sun is shining. After leaving Dragic's farm, he'd called Dennis Gould from the car, told him the situation, that he might need to run. Hogan might be waiting for him to bury the body, then make the arrest. But there were no lights in the rear-vision, all the way to the pine plantation north of Wanneroo – the closest patch of navigable bushland. Like all pine plantations, a graveyard air at night, but Swann was grateful for the lack of underbrush, walking trails and neighbours. He chose a hollow between rows, soft beach sand, inaccessible to the machinery that broke, skinned and loaded the pine, ploughed the earth. Enough moonlight to dig by. It was humid in the hollow; sweat dripped off his nose, the dust of each spadeful coated his wet skin. Two feet down the sand compacted. Swann prayed he didn't hit tamala limestone, the shovel-head scalloping the grave until he was four feet down, then in the hole itself, sinking into the cold damp sand, the surface at eye-level, then above, and still digging. Fireman's carry then dropped Dragic into the grave.

He drove back to the farmhouse and parked the ute, hosed down the shovel, locked the house. Looked for his footprints all the way back to his car, and where in doubt, roughed the surface with a leafy wattle switch. Pulled the car out onto the empty road, walking the switch along the tyre tracks, his footprints, tossing it into a ditch.

On the drive home he was alone on the outer roads, but in the city the Statesman passed taxis, civilians, coppers, each of them looking at him, he noticed, behind his tinted windows. Swann had hunted men now like himself, another mask to wear. Details like clues – the red dirt in his tyres needing to be hosed off, the same with his boots. Afterwards, lying beside Marion in bed, a great distance between them, Swann was unable to sleep. Going back over everything. Everything back to normal. Like it never happened. Then going back over everything, again.

Swann lay awake in his bed and looked at his watch, the minutes painfully slow. The street believed that Dragic had done a runner to Macedonia. Swann needed to build upon the rumour, reinforce it and make it real. But some knew otherwise. Hogan, and the man Dragic had hired to potentially harm his family. According to Hogan, a member of the Junkyard Dogs. A down payment made. The bikie would need to be told. The sun coming up behind the scarp, wattlebirds and magpies beginning the dawn chorus. Swann got up to boil the kettle, make tea for himself and Marion, another shower – follow the routines. There was a note from Marion on the chalkboard by the fridge. Gerry Tracker was in Fremantle Prison, on remand. A concerned friend from inside Corrective Services had called it in, obviously on Tracker's instructions.

Swann left Marion asleep, turned the ceiling fan up a notch, shut the door quietly behind him. First port of call – a payphone in Fremantle, on the corner of Market and High, nobody about except two drunks who'd wandered over from the dunes, draped in their blankets, leaning on a bench seat soaking up the morning sun. Swann dropped the twenty-cent piece, looked down at his feet, the ancient stains of blood and oil soaked into the porous concrete, layered with a fine windblown sand, dozens of cigarette butts. The call was a risk, because Riley was Hogan's fizz. Swann let the phone ring on. In Riley's Federation semi-detached, with its bare floorboards and cool stone walls, the chime would echo loud. Despite the early hour, Riley picked up. He was the club president, always on duty. 'Riley. The Junkyard Dogs' sergeant-at-arms. Personal number. Now.'

There was the sound of a lighter's hiss, a little suck as Riley's mouth made a seal around the first of the day. Flicking through a rolodex. 'Clem Gunston. Two six six, three five three one. Didn't hear it from me.'

Swann hung up, dropped another coin and waited. There was a chance that one of the Junkyard Dogs was freelancing for Dragic, that Clem Gunston mightn't know, but three men had taken Dennis Gould for the drive.

'Gunston. This better be fucken good.'

Swann covered his mouth with his sleeve, spoke through it. 'Only gonna say this once. Dragic is in the ground.'

A pause, no hurry. 'Got any proof?'

'Try to get hold of him. You won't. Better still, those plants in Wanneroo, they're yours.'

'Don't know what you're talkin' about, mate.'

'Whatever you been paid, doesn't matter. But there's no more comin'.'

'How'd you get my number?'

Swann hung up, replaced the receiver and leaned on the booth. Felt the shiver of released anxiety rise up his spine, exit the back of his head.

*

The freeway was empty on the drive in, too early for commuters. Dozens of joggers, keeping to the riverside tracks, their bright fluoro tracksuits snagging in the pure morning light, each of them wired for sound, walkman headphones bobbing up and down, the river unruffled to the horizon west. As he neared the city, the first convoy of trucks rose over the Narrows Bridge, their battered flanks and dusty tyres and drivers in identical grey collared shirts, caps pulled low. The car phone rang, and he lifted the console. It was Marion, her voice sleepy and warm, like any other morning. 'Just making sure you got the message about Gerry Tracker. His friend, didn't leave a name, said Gerry's asking for you. Won't talk to anyone else.'

Swann started to reply, got it caught in his throat, the guilt in his voice. He coughed. 'I'll tee up a visit. Thanks. I love you.'

'I know. You sound exhausted. Come home early, we'll go to the beach. I love you too.'

Swann swerved as a truck drifted into his lane, the driver's face a mask of alarm. He pulled over towards the West Perth exit, scrolled down the windows and welcomed the sun on his face, inhaled the smell of diesel fumes and baking concrete, felt the Statesman pull along the curving road, his eyes ghosted by the image of Dragic's grave and the smell of pine, the moonlight glistening on his arms.

34.

The situation wasn't fucking ideal. Des Foley shifted his arse on the mat, let a buttock find its shape in the sand, take the pressure off his hip. Old injury, after a spill on a stolen Yamaha, just another thing to put up with. Even noticing it told him how his mood was darkening. The boy across from him, giving off that vibe he hated about young men – twitchy, sullen, never know what the idiots are going to do next. In prison, always trying to prove themselves; make a name, deflect the attention of the perverts.

This boy should know better – had already done some time. They'd run out of Longmore Boys Home reminiscences. The yard, footy comps, stuck in the classroom zoning out. All the other stuff – the circle-jerking, the smell of spoof everywhere, gash on everybody's minds – awkward to joke about wanking and blow jobs when you're in a hole with another male – didn't want the kid to get the wrong idea. But Christ, he was hard work. Made Foley feel like his jailer, which in a sense he was.

The kid wanted to move, to get things moving, to get out somewhere and do something – a stupid play. Gerry Tracker would make the first move, Des had told him, let them know what he needed, what to do. All they had to do was wait. Think of it as doing time. Either converse with your cellie – speak seven different kinds of shit, didn't matter – or even better, go inside yourself, make yourself stronger, have a good hard look and make the resolutions, adjustments – or daydream instead, nature's fucken television set, drift along on the good times and the fantasies of good times to come.

But no – the kid was caught between – neither in himself nor outside. Eyes shifty and bugged out one minute, wounded and glistening the next. Fucking jiggling his leg even. Breathing through his mouth. Eyes returning to the pistols in the bag beside Foley's pillow. Any minute now, the kid was going to make a move, and Foley would have to restrain him, or worse. His allegiance was to Gerry Tracker, his old mate, and himself. The kid running would put Foley in danger too.

At least it was quiet in the house above. The old man asleep in gin-soaked dreams, until the dark. And Foley's hip, really aching now, needed to stretch but there wasn't room.

Most kids in this situation would humbug Des until he relented, told the stories of the banks and his life on the run, the prisons, the prossies, the guns and the cars; milk him for information and useful knowledge. But Gerry's boy didn't seem interested, and Foley sure as hell wasn't going to play to an empty house.

Des started laying the cards down, on the blanket, again. Glad that the boy didn't ask, knowing his response would be edged. 'The name of the game is fucken *patience*.'

Most blackfellas Foley knew loved a laugh, Gerry Tracker especially. He was a hard man in prison, did some hard things to survive, but it was his humour that made people admire him, even the screws and the skinheads. But the boy wouldn't even ask about his father. Des didn't understand that. His own father a prick of the lowest order, stole from them on his visits, temper like a grenade. If Des had a father like Gerry Tracker, bit of a legend in the system, Des would want to know. But the kid didn't want to know.

The words in Des' mouth sounded false. Trying not to sound like his own mother, who'd tell the boy to toughen up, don't let the bastards get you down, keep that ember of fighting spirit deep inside. But he had to try. 'I've never really been out the goldfields. Tell me about your mother's country. What's it like this time of year?'

The boy glanced, looked back at his feet. Little shrug, but he did start talking. 'Now's the best time … still cold at night, not too many flies. There's this namma hole still got water – like a big swimming pool, fulla taddies …'

Just as Foley suspected. The kid didn't want to talk guts and glory. Not a crim at heart. A good kid, thrown in the deep end. The kind of kid belonged somewhere else. Talking easily now, every now and then a little prompt from Foley. 'They got those little people out there?'

The boy nodded. 'Yair, they's all over. Little fellas, bad smell, same mob as here. Mummery men. Into everything. Either like you or they don't …'

The Tracker boy started talking about experiences with the little people, eyes alive with living the stories, still avoiding the main source of hurt – his mother's early death. But he got there in the end, and Des Foley listened, right up to the point when Gerry Tracker had gone bush to collect his son, the haunting visible in the boy's eyes now, tremble in his voice. 'There was something off. My dad was still asleep, just as the sun was comin' up. I walked out the backyard, circled with this cyclone fence. Every foot around the fence was a big black crow, maybe fifty of 'em, and they was all lookin' at me. It was the old ones. I woke my dad up, he took one look and we was outta there. He's never been game to take me back, even for a visit ...'

Des Foley looked around the perimeter of the stumps, the weatherboard cladding radiant with the light outside, the eternal dark beneath the house. He wasn't easily spooked, didn't fear man or beast, but the story of the crows, and the image of Gerry Tracker on the run from a law Foley didn't understand, made his skin tingle.

35.

Swann flagged the premier's offices with the debugging wand, with Lurch the security guard watching his every move. Because he wanted to check, Swann searched the premier's drawers until he found the receiver linked to the landline, pulled it out. Lurch thought to say something, shifted his weight, but a look from Swann decided him against it. Swann turned over the silver-cased receiver, sleek and modern, expensive. There were only a couple of local PIs with the motivation or the knowledge to run a surveillance operation using equipment of this price and sophistication. He would need to know who – most PIs were ex-cops and Swann didn't like the idea of working around a potential enemy. He also noticed that the bag of cash had grown in size, loose notes and banded notes and rolls of notes were visible at the bag's mouth. Which was what Lurch was really watching him for.

Swann sat in the parliamentary carpark and smoked a cigarette, his view of the city that was growing ever-louder with rush hour, pedestrians stalking the pavements down Hay Street, buses throwing out orderly lines of suits and frocks and kids from the suburbs. He dialled Dennis Gould, got him on the fourth ring, voice bleary with exhaustion, launching straight into a summary of the second tender belonging to Hercules Construction, all good news on the surface of it – local companies long associated with public works, gathered under an umbrella held by construction heavyweight Robert John; an old-money family going back to the first gold boom in the 1890s, got the contracts for most of the country rail network, most of the ports and the Narrows and Fremantle Traffic Bridges. A natural rival to Exetar, Hercules' tender was more expensive because, as far as Gould could tell, their timeline for completing the project was two months north of Exetar's. As to which was more realistic, that wasn't

Swann's concern, a matter for the Ministry's resident engineers and town-planners, although there were no anomalies so far – all their accounts in order, no red flags on the names.

Exetar – just a couple of loose ends before they put a line through the tender. Gould had tracked down Tommy Calhoun, the director of the security company currently occupied by Gary Quinlivan. Swann took down the street address and the number, although he didn't call ahead.

The double-brick and tile house was in Thornlie, front porch shaded by a stand of giant casuarina, their dark nuts and resiny-brown needles strewn across the hard-packed drive and yard. Swann parked behind a newish Holden panel van, gold duco buffed to a high sheen, and the burnt-out chassis of the same make and model, puddles of rubber, glass and plastic on the macadam. The house was dark and silent, built like a bunker into the hill that sloped up from the river. Behind an asbestos fence, an ancient swing set creaked in the breeze. Prominent, handpainted *Mind the Dog* sign. Swann rapped the front door, stood back and waited for a minute. Tried again, louder this time, and longer. The sounds of a shuffle, a dog's chain, and the door cracked, blown by the wind.

'Tommy Calhoun?'

The man peered past Swann, both directions, his muscled arm gripping the choker on some kind of black mastiff, panting, eyes bugging, front legs off the ground.

'Whatchya want?'

'A chat.'

Swann identified himself, and his purpose. The dog ceased its whimpering, began to growl, a long low growl at war with its friendly eyes, suggesting the growl would win out. Calhoun clucked, and the dog quieted. Like dog, like owner. Calhoun's eyes were at war with his body language. Proud eyes, and aggrieved, but shoulders slumped in resignation.

'Come in, ya dickhead. Get us both killed.'

Inside the house, the shades drawn, smell of stewing garbage from the kitchen, chop fat, ashtrays and stale beer. The signs of a man alone, but also the remnants of a woman's touch, not yet undone: the art and photographs on the walls, the neat arrangement of the leather couches, brightly coloured cushions, white shagpile carpet. Kids' toys pushed into corners, folded kids' clothes on the dining room table.

But no sense that Calhoun's family were around. Swann could guess. They'd be staying at a mother's, a sister's, a caravan park somewhere, until all this died down.

Calhoun was hiding in his own home. Swann glanced into the windowless bedroom off the kitchen, saw a semi-automatic rifle, a brace of American grenades, tear-gas canisters and ammo in clips and boxes – the perfect room to make a last stand.

Calhoun saw the glance, gave a shrug of the shoulders. 'Wanna beer?'

Swann could see it in his eyes – not used to being cooped up, cut off from the world. Hadn't been answering his phone. Sitting in darkness at night. Loneliness on top of worry. Worry on top of shame. Shame on top of anger.

Waiting.

Too proud to take the holiday with his family. Sticking around, a petty act of defiance. The world of security goons a small one, and everything to do with reputation. Private armies made up of ex-cops, soldiers, crims and thugs. Calhoun owned one of the biggest, now taken off him.

'All I want is the names,' said Swann. 'I've seen Gary Quinlivan. He's not going to standover anyone. Who were the others? And why?'

Calhoun grunted, padded past Swann into the tiled cave of the kitchen, took a beer out of the fridge, cracked and slurped, wiped froth off his moustache, beady, angry eyes. 'You payin'?'

Swann snorted. 'I'm investigating what looks like a hostile takeover of your security agency. You don't want to talk –'

Calhoun put up a stop sign. 'Hostile takeover. I fucken like that. If it was sold to me that way, might've been easier.'

'How was it sold to you?'

Calhoun put a finger-gun to his temple, pulled the trigger. 'May as well have been a public arse-reamin' – that's what it looks like to my rivals, my staff, my missus.'

'The names.'

'Yair, and what about my name? Two months, the bastards told me, but I ain't coppin' that. I used to be a sniper. Death from a mile away. That's how I'm gonna do it ...'

Calhoun showed Swann his eyes, but he wasn't convincing anyone.

'Maybe that won't be necessary. Start at the beginning,' Swann said. 'Start now.'

The way Calhoun described it, shoulders hunched and mitts around his tinny, voice straying into wheedling, catching himself when he heard the self-pity, the first move had been onsite vandalism, disabling earth-movers and cranes, theft of explosives and site vehicles, all of which made him look incompetent. When Exetar demanded explanations, he started looking closer. Right under his nose: the trucks and truckies. Total replacement of the drivers, with no warning. When the vandalism and stealing didn't stop, the site manager complained to Calhoun, who told him about the trucks. The site manager made some inquiries, made some threats. That night he had a Molotov put through his front window, kids and wife watching *Countdown*, only escaped out of good luck. When the next day Calhoun dragged a driver out of his truck and beat him with a pipe, the other drivers had gang-bashed him, driven him off-site with boots to the arse, in front of everyone. That night, blew up his panel van. Three men marched inside wearing balaclavas, slapped around his missus, put a gun to his head. Two-month vacation, for him and all his staff. Starting now. Hostile takeover? More like a fucken invasion. And names? Take your pick of the city's lowlife. Calhoun was no angel, but he followed the law when he could. None of his staff with a history of larceny. Violence, yes, perhaps, but his company gave violent men a second chance, some structure, a pay cheque. These new blokes, they're career crims: bikies, bash-artists, hoons. Italians from Leo Ajello's crew. Not even union men. No union'd fucken have 'em.

'The upper management. Exetar. Do they know what's going on?'

'Not much they can do. Strike. *Nothing* they can do.'

'Let me guess. Since Quinlivan took over, no more thefts, vandalism, threats.'

'Yep. Nope.'

'What I don't get is,' Swann continued, 'why muscle into a construction project right near its completion? So they pad out the salary bill with a few sleepers. Small potatoes for the bikies, for crims like Leo Ajello.'

Calhoun didn't know, looked to the empty in his hands, stubby fingers tapping. But Calhoun didn't know about Exetar's Burswood tender. The premier's commitment of taxpayer money. The opportunity to get in on the ground floor, from day one, and milk the public tit. The Burswood project would take years to complete. Now Swann understood. Gus Riley had mentioned his men working on the site as drivers. They were training for the next job. Swann could see the headlines already, years down the track. Burswood cost over-runs. Project delays. Massive spending blowouts. A secret margin on every purchase and expense – thousands of purchases and thousands of expenses. Local organised crime getting their noses into the corporate trough. Using their street skills for intimidation and extortion and violence to control the site. Exetar eaten out from the inside. But who was controlling it? Conlan brothers' money was behind the East Perth development, and also Exetar's bid for Burswood. But Conlan's Harrowgate money was behind each of the tenders. Swann wondered. In a world flooded by cheap finance, it must be a stipulation, a requirement, but ordered by who? Had to be the premier, and Heenan, brokering the tenders even before the election, a focus on local employment and local money. Good for jobs, good for everyone.

Swann left Calhoun in his darkened kitchen. The mastiff followed him to the door, looked out at the empty street, wouldn't cross the threshold.

36.

Terry Accardi was parked before the stand of paperbarks, in the corner of the crumpled and potholed lot where the junkies usually congregated. His idea of a joke, perhaps – the unmarked Belmont shouting obvious cop. Across the foreshore men and women wearing wristbands and headbands and sunglasses jogged before the glare of the river, the sun sheeting down from the west, the sound of the traffic on the Narrows like a hive of angry bees. Swann parked alongside and lit a cigarette and had a look around. Before leaving Calhoun's house he'd done a check of his car for bugs, or tracking devices – after last night and the lack of sleep, the suspicion of Hogan tailing him was reasonable. The strategy behind Hogan setting up Swann for Dragic's murder, then banking it, was still not clear. Which is why Swann needed to get with Accardi, and put it on the record.

A battered, brown Datsun 120Y entered the carpark then U-turned when it saw the Holdens. Swann got out and looked around, then joined Accardi in the Belmont, lifted a paper bag off the passenger seat and put it behind, the rear seats laden with ziplocked glassine evidence bags.

'That all from the bloke in the river?'

Swann could see jeans and sandshoes, socks and an office shirt, all wet. A wallet, cigarettes, gold wedding ring.

'Just come from the autopsy. Looks like a cut-and-dried, should I say, clear case of drowning. Wasn't dead before he went in the water. I have to drop this off at Central, go back to the deceased's wife, follow-up interview, then his colleagues. What do you have for me?'

'Tell me about the dead guy.'

Accardi gave him a look, didn't really have the time. Swann looked back, let his silence do the talking.

Accardi nodded. 'Michael Cassidy. DOB April forty-six. Lived a block from here, back nearer the zoo. Wife, no kids. Degree in botany. Environmental scientist for the Ministry of Development. Like I say, went into the water alive. Strong swimmer, according to his wife. Waiting for the tox reports. Car found parked near the mouth of Claisebrook Creek, presumed where he entered the water, body drifted on the tide down to the flats near Burswood. That's it, so far.'

'He have any juice at the Ministry?'

'That's an interesting line of inquiry. This involve your background checks of the Burswood tenders?'

'Might do. If I was going to drown myself in the river, I wouldn't choose there. No bridges, little current, pretty shallow.'

'Fair call. His colleagues'll have a better idea. Tell me what's going on.'

Swann laid it out – the whole Exetar shebang. Put in the new context, the enviro's drowning not a few hundred metres from the East Perth development started to click, Accardi's hands tensing on the steering wheel. But problematic, too. The parasites bleeding Exetar, at this stage Leo Ajello, Riley's Nongs and Gary Quinlivan, was a perfect match for Accardi's remit from the Federal Police – organised-crime money moving into legitimate business fronts. As a Homicide cop, the enviro's death was a legitimate way into his parallel federal investigation, his role open-ended and unofficial, using Swann as his eyes and ears. Swann watched Accardi play out the angles. If the drowned man was murdered, Accardi could investigate more widely, but not without potentially putting his local peers offside, bringing suspicions of secret agendas. If Ben Hogan got a sniff that Accardi was playing both sides of the street, his career was over. The Feds wouldn't want to know him either.

'There's more. What is it?'

An uneasy moment, knowing that it had come. Swann's decades in the force, his early years on the street, all his training and experience – the wisdom of telling a Homicide cop about his involvement in a murder, despite his relationship with Accardi – didn't sit right. But his younger friend needed to know. Swann was working for Accardi, who was working for the Feds. Ben Hogan could snatch Swann any time he liked, pin him for murder. In that event, the case might even fall to Accardi. Swann laid it out, exactly as it happened, could feel Accardi shrinking from him, soiled goods. Swann's voice a monotone. Got to the part about the burial,

Accardi put up a hand. 'Don't want to know, Frank, except whether you were followed. No body, as you understand ...'

'Hogan has the murder weapon. No doubt he can supply a witness.'

'Not like him to play games. What the fuck does he want?'

'Hasn't said. But it's coming.'

They looked across at the city, floating there on the heat haze, the shimmering river, dome of clear blue sky. 'I haven't asked until now. Do the Feds know about me?'

'No, they don't.'

Swann patted Accardi's shoulder, little paternal squeeze, longer than he needed. A goodbye like any other, or a final parting, only the day would tell.

*

Official visiting time at Fremantle Prison was over, but Swann knew the watch commander of the afternoon shift – Tony McIlroy – a six-foot-four Scotsman who lived on the same street as Swann in a stone cottage that looked like it had been built for gnomes. Swann called ahead and asked to see Gerry Tracker. No, he didn't want to see Tracker in his remand cell – the visiting room would be fine. It would be an ordeal for Tracker that'd involve waiting, being searched and still more waiting and being searched, but Swann didn't want to stretch the relationship with McIlroy too far – he had a feeling he'd be visiting frequently.

The great limestone walls of the prison loomed over the carpark, catching the late afternoon sun. The steel front doors were open to allow a delivery, overseen by a rifleman on the rat-run above. The day had been hot, and Swann could see in the eyes of the guards on duty that something was up. A tension in the air that might relate to a particular incident, or might not – the general build-up of resentment and anger when the temperature soared. The prison was built like a medieval fortress and the only change since the 1850s was that the cells were more crowded. Many of Swann's childhood friends had ended up in the jail as either crim or screw and he knew the stories well. The guards ran their own race, organised by a gang called the Purple Circle, rorting the overtime system and some of the commerce inside, but that was to be expected. The thought that Ben Hogan had a murder charge over him weighed heavy as Swann sat in the stinking waiting room, imagining Marion and his daughters and grandkids visiting him. He could understand why some men chose to do their time easier, cutting off all contact with loved ones.

Gerry Tracker had been beaten: his right eye was closed and his lip split, his nose bridged with a deep cut. One of his wrists was bandaged, and he favoured his right leg as he hobbled into the room, no light in his eye as he approached. Swann offered a cigarette as Gerry eased himself, wincing, into the hard chair. 'You feel it? This place is set to fucken blow.'

Swann nodded, glanced at the two guards leaning by the door, keen young men. 'Any particular reason?'

'Not that I can tell. I'm in isolation, but I can feel it through the walls. Thanks for comin', Frank.'

'They got sick of you holding out on Blake, eh?'

'Pretty much. I know you can't do anythin' but it's somethin' one of them said.'

'The gun?'

'Yes, but more than that. Somethin' about the car Blakey stole. None of that came up in court, but these guys ... they were too old to be uniformed constables. And they knew how to bash. They're either ex-detectives, sent back to uniform, or they were Ds in borrowed clobber. I've been worked over in interrogation rooms before, and these guys were fucken elite bash-artists. Reckon they're gonna be visiting me again in a couple days.'

'What are they holding you on?'

'Resisting arrest. Petty shit, but with my record ...'

Swann offered Gerry another cigarette, which he lit off the end of his first, pinched it off, secreted the butt down his sleeve.

'Have you heard from Blake? We've got to get that gun back.'

Gerry exhaled a stream of smoke. 'That's the thing, Frank. What I need from you ...' Gerry leaned forward, and began to whisper, breaking up his message with louder comments about the food, the heat, the conditions.

When he'd finished, Swann sat back, lit himself another cigarette. 'Jesus Christ. Gerry. C'mon, mate.'

'I know.'

Harbouring Australia's most wanted, plus a wanted son. Swann's first duty – split the two up. Get young Blake well away from Des Foley. Get the gun back to the sergeant.

Gerry Tracker leaned forward and began to whisper again, describing the set-up beneath the neighbouring house, the best way to make his approach without getting shot. What to say to Blake, about the gun. To trust Swann, to return it anonymously. To pass on Gerry's message. Des Foley could look after himself. But Blake needed to tell Swann what he knew about the car. There was something off about it. Swann would know what to do, based on Blake's answer. If it was nothing, Blake should hand himself in, serve out his time. If it was something, he needed to get back to country, hide among his mother's kin, out in the goldfields. Gerry would come once he'd done his time.

There was shame in Gerry's eyes, aware how much he was asking, but he had no choice. Life and death for his son. Blake's future in Swann's hands. Gerry's eyes moist, blinking it away.

Swann stood, shook Gerry's hand. Gerry Tracker couldn't know how much trouble Swann was in, needed this like a hole in the head. So tired he was floating, feet like balloons. He left Gerry with his cigarettes. The guards would try to confiscate them, but Gerry had a way with words.

37.

Swann stood at the back fence in the laneway and waited for the old man cradling his rifle to move from the sleep-out windows. Gerry had warned Swann about the old boy, indicating that his eyes weren't good but his hearing was acute. Several times over the past years a gunshot had rung out. None of the neighbours called it in – they didn't want Tom Pickett institutionalised. Swann saw Pickett's shadow retreat into the house and vaulted the fence. Took out his pistol and turned the safety off. Des Foley was a hothead, and Swann wasn't going to be slow on the draw if the escapee started firing. Cop thinking – in the back of his mind the understanding that if he took down Foley and gave him to Accardi, the young detective would be set for life – above recrimination. Likewise, if he gave Foley to Hogan – the slate might be cleared.

The moonlight cold on his forearms, as he crouched in the dirt and wild oats at the rear of the house, hidden from the old man above. He sniffed the air but there were no cooking smells coming from under the house, or conversation. Too early for them to be asleep. Here goes nothing. Swann waited until the shuffling above him died away, then rapped on the weatherboards twice – hard and loud. Then waited. Rapped twice again. Waited. Repeated.

He heard the boards lift away and Blake Tracker's hopeful face appeared, dissolving instantly into hatred. He saw Blake signal behind, began to whisper to him, the message from his father, keeping his voice calm and clear. Did he remember Swann?

Blake's eyes focused hard on Swann's moonlit face. 'The guy who drove the EK Holden? Diff troubles?'

Swann nodded. Blake withdrew into the darkness and motioned for Swann to follow. He crawled on his hands and knees along a trench dug into the chalky limestone and sand, came to a dugout, still in darkness. Torchlight in his face, Des Foley behind it, horror-show shadows, Browning pistol. Swann saw the look of recognition come into Foley's slit eyes, his mouth tightening, laying down the pistol and reaching for a filleting knife at his side, shifting his weight.

Swann began to speak, quietly without pause, never taking his eyes off Foley's knife hand. Foley was shirtless, blood dripping in a lace across his chest. Blake had been giving Foley a tattoo, cutting incisions with the knife, pressing ink from a Bic pen into the stripes now welts – the fist-sized outline of a kelpie's head carved across Foley's breast. Foley's other prison tattoos were confined to his torso and upper arms, knowing at an early age what his fate was going to be, not wanting anything visible and identifiable.

Foley listened while Swann passed on Gerry's message. What Gerry wanted, for Blake. Careful not to pressure Foley. The tattooing a sign of intimacy that Swann was wary of – Foley the mentor, might want to demonstrate to Blake how to handle an ex-cop when your back's against the wall. Swann's gun was returned to its holster. He finished the message, and waited, looked around the dugout. Neat and ordered, like a prison cell; everything packed away, but to hand.

Foley shifted his weight, a small gesture that relieved a lot of tension. His eyes still burned in the torchlight, his face a mask of shadow. Made a little mouth towards the kerosene lantern, Blake Tracker nodding, then kneeling and lighting a match and turning the wick until a glow filled the dugout. Sat back against the wall and waited – his fate still in other hands.

Foley turned off the torch, sat forward on his bucket, ready to parlay. Agreed that Blake should go with Swann. Told him of their plans to return the gun. Showed Swann the cash to accompany the weapon, and sweeten its return. Asked Blake to tell Swann about the guards, flapped his wrist to hand over the conversation.

Blake Tracker spoke quietly. Swann watched the kid's glances towards Des Foley, who nodded for him to continue. Swann didn't know how far back Gerry Tracker's relationship went with Foley, but it had to be significant. Blake shared his revelations about guards standing over him, demanding that he coerce Gerry into smuggling. Foley was right – they'd want significant money before they'd forgive Blake's escape.

The kid too proud to ask his father for help, or more likely didn't want him to get in trouble again. Time would tell. Swann interrupted – 'Gerry ... your dad, he mentioned that the policemen who arrested him were going on about a car. Not the gun, but a car. What do you know about that?'

Blake's face folded. Hands searched for each other. Sucked in a breath.

'Blake? Tell the man. He's gonna help.'

Blake Tracker hung his head, closed his eyes. He'd seen a lot, but whatever it was, he'd locked it away deep. Looked into the shadows, where they couldn't see his face, little shake of the head.

Swann tied a different tack. 'The detective who chased you. Who you took the gun from. Can you remember his name?'

Little nod of the head. A gruff whisper. 'Never forget 'im. Detective Sergeant Carter.'

'Faark.'

Swann looked to Foley. 'You know him too, eh?'

Foley sniffed, spat. 'I know the prick. Served on your watch, dinnie? Back when you were at Central.'

'I was uniform, he was CIB. One of Don Casey's bagmen. Armed Rob squad. No wonder you know him.'

'The very man. When he was in Armed Rob he invited *me* to work for *him*. Fuck that, I told him. Then it was game on.'

Swann and Foley understood at the same moment, looked to Blake, still looking away, shoulders small. Swann spoke first. 'Blake. Whose car did you steal?'

The kid shrugged. Swann continued. 'Where did you steal it? You remember?'

Foley grunted. 'And what was fucken *in* it?'

The kid roused himself, eyebrows raised, fists clenched. 'They was in the boot. An old couple, naked, tied back to back. Their faces was all purple and blue. They both dead.'

'You know who they were?' Foley asked.

'Knew later. Was in the paper. Missing couple. Could never say the name. Gr-somethin'.'

Swann filled in the rest. 'The Grednics. Marko and Agata. Marko Grednic was Conlan's accountant. Director on one of his property development ventures. Wanted last year for questioning by the Costigan Royal Commission, some line of inquiry about corporate tax evasion. Never made it to the stand.'

'Fucken hell, Blakey. Wrong car to nick. Where'd you get it?'

'Was a Merc. Never driven a Merc. Saw it parked over there in East Perth, near the cricket ground. Parked on a hill. I was walkin' up from behind it, saw the keys sittin' there on the back tyre. So I got in. Didn't even start the thing. Just sittin' there when I hear the siren – right bloody behind me. So I cranked her up and went for a tear. Over the Causeway, down Canning Highway, onto the freeway, this fucken Belmont on my arse, couldn't shake it. I just wanted to get near home, peg it on foot. But the thing had no grunt, slippin' clutch or somethin'. So I get near home and tried to lose the copper with a bush bash, cut into the swamp near home, lost it on a turn and pranged into a tree. That's when the fucken boot popped open. And the copper was right there, drawn 'is gun and everythin'.'

'The copper. Carter – he wasn't gonna take Blakey in. He was gonna shoot him down,' Foley added.

'I can see why. Case of bad timing, Blake. Carter knocks off shift, goes to where he or someone's parked the car for him. His usual job – tie up a loose end. He would've killed the Grednics, or been there when it was done. His next job to get rid of them. So he draws on you, you get the gun off him. Why'd you take off again in the Merc?'

'The Belmont was parked some ways off, still runnin'. Didn't know if that D was alone. So I got the Merc going again, backed her up, the boot still flappin' open and closed. I know all those tracks, by heart. Normally I'd burn the car, but I couldn't – just couldn't – not with them in it.'

'What did you do with the Mercedes, Blake?'

Blake looked at Swann. His forehead beaded with sweat. The thing that he'd never told anyone else. Not his father, not his legal-aid lawyer, not his cellmates. 'I didn't go far. Didn't know how many coppers would be out there, lookin' for me. I closed the boot, drove it to Bibra Lake – there's a jetty there. Deep water. Just buckled up and drove it off the end. Got the belt off as it sank, and swam away.'

'That's a loose end, right there,' Foley murmured. 'That Carter's just a bonehead, but Ben Hogan. He wouldn't like that. Loose end could unstitch the whole plan.'

Swann didn't reply. Foley was right. The question was why the car theft hadn't come up before. The Tracker kid had been accessible, in custody. Why were they looking for the car now?

'Blake, this is important. Was there anything else in the boot, apart from the bodies?'

Blake nodded. 'Loads of stuff. That was a big boot. Bags. A suitcase. Some cardboard boxes.'

Foley patted Blake Tracker on the shoulder; the kid looked spent. It was time to get him home. Swann turned his attention to Foley, not knowing his plans, not knowing if he'd ever see him again. 'Tell me about Mostel. Why you've been following him. It doesn't make sense.'

Foley shrugged. 'Sure, while we're getting on. Sure. But first, why you wanna know? And Blakey – do us a favour mate and go and wait outside. This is yours.' Foley passed Blake Tracker a sleeping bag. No goodbyes. To Swann he passed the sergeant's revolver, showed him the chamber, loaded with two.

When Blake Tracker climbed through the weatherboards, Swann lit a cigarette and offered one to Foley, who shook his head. Old man Pickett shuffled along the corridor above them, the boards creaking. 'He guarding you?'

Foley shook his head. 'Think he's still guarding his mates, some Kokoda ratholes. You get used to it. Not so different being inside, listening to blokes shoutin' and wailin' all night long.'

Foley's face was lit with a reddish glow. If he was nervous that Swann might draw on him, or disclose his hide-out, it didn't show. Eyes patient, observant and faintly amused – two grown men in a hole underneath the house of a war-haunted veteran.

As though reading his mind, Foley said, 'Funny, isn't it? Few years ago, we would've shot each other dead, soon as blink. How'd a bloke like you end up being a copper anyway? I didn't know Gerry had copper mates, though it doesn't surprise me. Sociable fella. He'd never give me up though, for any money. A proper mate.'

Foley didn't need to ask him – the question was implicit in his last statement. What kind of man was Swann? The kind to shop Australia's most wanted, or be worthy of the trust of a mutual friend?'

To put him at ease, Swann told Foley the condensed story of how he met Marion, a detective's daughter, how at the time he could've gone either way. Swann guessed that Blake Tracker wasn't one for conversation, because Foley was eager, kept prodding the story along. Swann reached the point, exhaustion weighing him down. Returned to

Mostel, and Foley's motives. By way of an answer, Foley took out a small leather satchel, showed Swann the false passports, the US currency, the US treasury bonds.

'Bloke reckons he's a bit of a player, doesn't he?'

Foley's interest in Mostel was purely personal. Mostel's response, putting money on the street – an idiot move. Big tickets on himself, trying to build a reputation. Most of Perth's gangsters were trying to move out of drugs and gambling into corporate crime, where the real money was. Mostel moving the other way. Swann described his own interest in the man, how he fit in with the premier's new direction. Foley nodded, took it in, prodded the dried blood on his chest, admired his new tattoo, cracked his neck. There was no need to spell it out. Common enemies make for strange alliances. They could help one another. Foley grinned. 'Well, you know where to find me. I haven't worked out how, but I'm gonna take that fucker down.'

A handshake, and Swann stood, crouched over, moved towards the darkness at the edge of the house.

38.

The kid. Swann woke with a start, heart racing. The dream of diving to muddy depths, popping the boot of the Mercedes, skeletons launching out and grappling at his arms, his feet, holding him under.

Swann looked at the clock – just gone nine. Four hours sleep. He heard Marion in the kitchen, beating eggs, the sizzle of butter, kettle coming to the boil. He rolled his legs over, put his head in his hands, felt the weariness as a terrible gravity. He forced himself to stand, walked down the hall, to check: Blake Tracker was still asleep in Sarah's room, his legs too long for the bed, tangled in the doona, little snores. The puppy asleep on the floor beside.

Swann drank two glasses of water from the tap – Marion's eyes on his back. He kissed her, his arm draped around her hip, took the wooden spoon and scrambled the eggs. When she put her head on his shoulder, he murmured, 'Some things I've got to tell you.'

'I know. We'll eat first.'

They sat at the old wooden table, scored and stained with the marks of their children, ate everything on their plates, took their coffees out to the back porch, sat looking at the garden, the sunlight.

Swann described it all – Dragic's body, and what he'd done with it. Accardi's investigation and what they'd learned about Exetar. Last night's meeting with Des Foley and Blake Tracker, Blake's story about the two bodies. What he planned on doing today, to end it, so that he could walk away. The wildcard what Hogan would do with Dragic's murder – most likely make Swann back off from Quinlivan and Exetar, which he would gladly do.

'It's my rostered day off, then I'm on nights,' Marion said. 'I can look after the boy. If you're not back tonight, I'll ask Blonny to drop around, keep him company. He has to go back inside, doesn't he?'

'When it's safe. I'll call.'

'Drop in on Janey, will you? She didn't phone last night. Sure it's nothing, but ...'

'Will do.'

They kissed, Marion tousling his hair, gripping his arms. A neighbour's cat walked the fence line at the back of the yard, another's dog began to bark. The day was getting hot. Inside, the phone began to ring. Heenan, probably, wondering where he was. Swann let it ring as he dressed, cigarette burning at his lips.

*

Heenan was waiting at Parliament House, sitting in the big chair. No sign of Lurch the security guard. Heenan blanched when he saw the look on Swann's face, put down the phone.

'There's disquiet,' he said, by way of explanation. 'Party whip's an underperformer –'

'Not by accident, I'm guessing.'

Heenan quit his stalling. 'I don't owe you anything in the way of an apology. I've been distracted. Actually, I've been working my arse off. Damage control. There are some powerful lobbyists circling. Some of the ministers, well, they're impressionable ...'

'You mean they've been bought, on the way to being bent. Move over a bit.'

Swann extracted the wireless wand and waved it over the desk, the ping. 'Look, it's a bug. Who put it there? Not for me to know. Move away from that bag of cash for a minute. Let me check that too.'

'C'mon, Swann. Easy up. It's not like –'

'Heenan, I've always liked you. But you can see where this is headed, right? I'm giving you my notice, now, today.'

'But Frank, the tenders.'

Swann started packing up. 'Yeah, the Burswood tenders. I'd be advising you to put a line through Exetar, for a start. A company whose security's done by bikies. Whose site manager gets blown up. You're too young to remember what the Conlans were like. People like that don't change, Heenan. I would advise you to steer clear of Exetar and the Conlans, but the premier, he doesn't know you put me on that, does he? All that bullshit about not trusting his public servants.'

'Ok, you're right. That was me. *I* don't trust the public servants. But more than that …'

'You don't trust *him*. Your own boss. Dear leader. You want to protect him from himself. You want me to catch him out, before it's too late. Before he or the Conlans get caught with their fingers in the till.'

'Well, have you? Caught him out?'

'Heenan, you don't want to be around when it blows. And you don't want me around it. What's happening to your ministers just happened to me. My fate's now in the hands of a man who's previously tried to kill me. Don't ask for details. I walk away now, I might get out alive.'

Heenan slumped, wrung his hands. 'I'm sorry for that. I understand. I'm overwhelmed. I mean, listen to this …' Heenan reached into the bureau drawer and took out the receiver, pressed rewind. When the spool finished he hit play.

Swann recognised the voice. An ex-premier. Asking, then demanding twenty thousand dollars for services rendered. Namely the service of keeping his mouth shut, doing nothing. The premier telling him to shove it, cool and ruthless. The next call, not so cool or ruthless. Another voice Swann recognised. A minister. Demanding a meeting. More canny than the ex-premier. Speaking in general terms, no names or figures. Promises made to people, needing to be kept. A nice donation to the party at stake. Reputations on the line.

Swann clicked the latch shut on his Gladstone bag.

'Be seeing you, Heenan. Send someone to collect the Statesman. A pity, but there you go.'

39.

In the Statesman, Swann cranked up the air-conditioning, enjoying his last drive. He tuned the radio, just in time for the news. Following this morning's acquisition of the Fremantle Fuel Company from businessman Sam Mostel, for a reputed twenty million dollars, the premier was now up in the Kimberley, spruiking a diamond mine. Clifford and Welsh reportedly calm about their fate. Their execution set for two days. No sign of clemency from the Malaysian president. A car thief, dubbed the Porsche Boy, led the police on a chase overnight through the southern suburbs in another stolen Porsche, the tenth this month, police admitting they had to give up the chase – their Holdens unable to keep up. Reported sighting of Des Foley in Toodyay, camped near one of the haunts made famous by Perth's favourite bushranger, Moondyne Joe. British pop singer Boy George and his band Culture Club to tour early next year; dates to be announced. Boy's single, 'Do You Really Want to Hurt Me', here it is ...

Swann killed the radio, lit a cigarette, scrolled down the electric windows, cold air on his face, warm air on his arm, the traffic purling around Mounts Bay Road where protesters were blocking traffic again. Swann pulled over at the foot of Jacob's Ladder, intending to U-turn, when the car phone started to ring. He lifted the receiver and parked across from an artificial lake, little family of ducks huddled in the middle.

'Frank?'

'Terry, how can I help?'

Terry Accardi. Swann could hear muzac in the background, and guessed the detective was calling from a payphone in a shopping mall. 'Frank. No time to meet, this line is secure, correct?'

'Can't be sure, Terry. I'd prefer to meet.'

Suck of breath. Long pause. 'No time today. That deceased person we discussed. Bruise marks on his shoulders. Some lacerations on his wrists. Not the work of our blue manna crabs, apparently.'

Just as Swann suspected, the scientist entered the river in the shallows near Claisebrook Creek, because of the adjacent carpark. Not far to drag an unwilling man with bound wrists out into waist-deep water, hold him under until he's dead. Unlike the scientist, his killers not privy to an understanding of the river and its currents, its placid waters away from the main channel meaning his body hadn't drifted as they'd expected.

'I'm on the way to his laboratory. Very interested to hear about his recent testing –'

Swann cut him off. 'We need to talk, Terry, but in person. I'm afraid I'm going to be a disappointment to your colleagues in Canberra. Competing interests have arisen. Call me when you have time.'

'Understood.' No trace of emotion, or disappointment, although Accardi would be feeling it.

Swann drove into the city, guilt breaking the flow of his thoughts. The old mystery: how he could live with fear but not shame. His tactical withdrawal felt like a defeat, although it was the right thing.

But first, a couple of loose ends. He pulled into the cutaway behind Fast Eddys, waited for a young man in baggy shorts and oversized gym shoes, basketball singlet and cap, feeding coins into the payphone while shouting – something about his BMX bike being stolen; knows who it was; gonna go and sort the prick out; will be late for dinner.

Swann intervened when the kid began smashing the receiver against the red-brick wall, cursing and kicking. Swann flipped him around, looked into the hateful eyes, nasty little moustache, didn't have to say a word. The kid dropped the receiver and shaped up, some kind of kung-fu stance. Swann ignored him, took out his change and dropped a coin, grateful to hear a dial tone. The kid backed away, pulled a little knife out of his back pocket with shaking hands. Swann stared at him but lost interest, focused instead on the ringing phone, the kid wavering now on the periphery of his vision, building his dignity back up by shouting as he withdrew, kicking bins and parked cars, going elsewhere to share his misery.

'East Perth Lockup,' came the hard voice. Swann asked for Sergeant Carter, was told he was on night shift. Try at ten tonight.

Carter on the ten-to-six turnkey shift, meaning he'd be home and asleep. Swann returned to the Statesman, sat with his feet on the pavement, rising heat radiating under his chin, flicking though the White Pages. Carter was a common name, but Xavier wasn't. One X. Carter of Inglewood, just up the road.

The house was a Californian bungalow with chunky stuccoed foundations blood-red with bore water. The stained-glass front door was recessed behind a deeply shaded porch. Xavier Carter had done well for himself. The house was built onto a long rambling block, well-maintained garden and newly cleaned terracotta tiles with little Viking curlicues on the roof-peaks.

Swann parked under a flowering bottlebrush across the street, among the many cars whose customers were in the pub around the corner. He left the Statesman and carried the heavy paper bag containing the revolver and two thousand dollars cash across the road, down the garden path and onto the porch. He laid the parcel on the sisal mat and returned to the car.

Carter surprised Swann by answering on the first ring, and even more by not interrupting.

'There's a paper bag on your doormat. Inside is something you lost two years ago, plus a generous incentive to forgive. I hope you can forgive, Xavier.'

Carter didn't answer, but he didn't hang up either. Swann saw the front door crack, a chubby hand reach around and drag the paper bag.

Rustle of paper, Carter's smoker's voice, just like Swann remembered it.

'Tell the little coon that this is a good start. Even better, I bring him in. He takes his medicine, he does his time. I get to wear my detective clobber again.'

'Not going to happen. Those prison guards he got one over, he made them look bad by escaping – they'll neck him, as you know. So two things. First, you need to get the father out. No more bashing. He doesn't know where the Mercedes is. *I do.* Second thing, you overturn the conviction against the son. For doing that – I tell you the location of the car. Intact. Contents in the boot. Intact.'

Carter thought about it. 'Takes a judge to overturn a conviction. For an Abo, I don't think so.'

Swann set his voice. 'You tell your pocket-judge the charge of resisting arrest is fabricated. Come up with a story about losing the gun, about finding the gun. You get the court transcripts put away under FOI for twenty-five years. Nobody'll ever know.'

Carter would need to run it up the chain. At the top of the chain would be Hogan. But Carter had been well schooled. Said it like he couldn't help himself. 'And you're what, some coon-lovin' lawyer type? Got money, obviously.'

Swann withheld his answer, just a beat. Like Carter had strayed close. Then confirmed it. 'That's of no concern. We do this properly, we both get what we want.'

'Yeah, a fucken lawyer. How do I get in contact?'

'Do your part. I'll be in touch.'

Swann hung up, reversed the Statesman round the corner into the pub carpark, heard the laughter, a nice clean break on a pool table, jukebox blaring Michael Jackson's 'Beat It'.

40.

Swann dialled as he drove. He joined the freeway at Charles Street, gliding the Statesman into the right lane, Parliament House unseen on his shoulder. The northerly lanes of the Narrows Bridge were crowded with traffic, the result of a tail-ender, men and women gesticulating in the smog-haze. Beneath the bridge, the wide river shimmered in the windless heat, but Swann felt a chill when he thought of the environmental scientist, face thrust into the mud, dark water and the boots of his murderers the last thing he saw.

Dennis Gould answered, flashing Swann out of the image. 'Sorry, Swann, just got back. Heard the phone on the stairs.'

'Dennis, I'll be around later to explain. Drop everything. That thing I mentioned earlier. I meant to call you, but –'

'I've got news. Spent the day at the stock exchange, with an old colleague. Foreign markets his cuppa. Some odd behaviour that I couldn't explain, at home. Not *his* odd behaviour, although he has taken to wearing braces, shoes so polished they're a danger to aeroplane –'

'Dennis, I'll be around shortly. We'll have a drink.'

'You *are* serious then.'

'Yeah, I am.'

Swann exited at Manning Road and checked the time. It was just gone three. The car phone rang, Swann expecting Heenan's liquorish voice, but instead got Ben Hogan – voice of a commanding officer, blunt and contemptuous, expecting to be obeyed. 'Turn right off Manning Road, park up by the golf club, fairway seven.'

Swann took a long look in his rear-vision, the white Belmont crowded with suits, Hogan invisible in the back, being chauffeured.

'How'd you get this number?'

Hogan sniffed, his version of a laugh. 'Fairway seven.'

Rubbing it in. Fairway seven where Ruby Devine was murdered, where the consorters met their snitches.

Swann parked up, freeway on one side, separated by a cyclone fence, vast fairways and greens before him, stands of tea-tree and marri marking the course. The Belmont pulled over seconds later, with a dramatic little skid, controlled intimidation. Swann climbed out of the Statesman, lit a cigarette and watched the four detectives exit the Holden and gather round. Hogan had ambushed him like this before, the beating he copped on that occasion a preface to being hauled to the cells.

But there was no beating this time. The three other detectives lingered at a discreet distance. Hogan took a lean on the Statesman, ran a hand through his wind-ruffled hair, pushed up the sleeves on his jacket. 'What the fuck do you think you're doing?'

'*Here*? I wonder myself.'

'You don't do *anything* unless I tell you. You're not walking away from the premier's office. I want you *there.*'

Swann pulled on his cigarette, eyed Hogan with distaste, the expression returned. 'You're not looking too flash, Hogan, despite your threads. Feel free to unburden yourself.'

'You assumed wrong, you mutt. I want you back in there. Ear to the ground. You know the rest: if you –'

Swann flicked his cigarette at Hogan's feet, little shower of sparks. 'Jesus, you must be desperate.' Hogan stepped closer; Swann could smell his cologne, the spearmint on his breath. Eyes over Swann's shoulder, voice low. 'Better the devil you know, Swann. You were part of it once. We've kept these cunts down since Adam. What do you reckon's gonna happen if coppers like me disappear? Blokes like Leo Ajello, the Corvos and Adamos – the bikies? Right now, those pricks work for *me*. They know the rules; they know their place. Those bastards'll take over – you know it. And not just them. Crims'll flood in from everywhere.'

'Tell me about Ruby Devine. You were here when it went down.'

'That was a business decision. A political decision. Nothing personal.'

'Personal to her three kids.'

'Shut the fuck up and listen. This is my way of reaching out. With a warning. Something very bad is about to happen to you. I find myself in the unusual position of trying to intervene, because right now you're useful. Soon as you're not ...' Hogan clicked his fingers.

Swann leaned closer. 'You feeling left out? Whatever it is, buy your way in.'

'I'm not worried about our premier Farrell. Normal transmission will resume.'

Swann had to try. 'That friend of mine. Last seen snatched by bikies. Who pulled the trigger?'

'You looking for a reach-around too? I know Gould wasn't killed. I know he's back in his hole. For *now* ...'

'You seem to know plenty. You need to be specific about what you don't.'

'Time will come. Believe me.'

Hogan stepped away and snapped his fingers again. The three detectives arrived so sharply Swann had a thought – not just working for Hogan. *Protecting him.*

Another snap, and the nearest detective pulled a Ziploc bag from his jacket. Inside was a dull grey shape. Exhibit A. The pistol used to shoot Trevor Dragic, and the shell casings.

*

Swann drove to Stormie Farrell's on autopilot, barely noticed the passing streetscapes, the air becoming cooler as the Statesman glided into the bank of shade by the river. Hogan had thrown him, and visiting Stormie and Janey on Marion's request would give him time to decide.

The Thunderbird was still there on the limestone ridgeline, as were the charred remains of Stormie's earlier tantrum beside the driveway. Swann saw a curtain shiver, but otherwise no sign of life. No rockabilly or laughter, no fantasy road trips. Even seasoned drinkers like Stormie had to come down sometime.

Swann reached the top of the driveway and was about to take a step around a strange barricade of assorted furniture – upturned chairs, desks, a couch – when he looked down and saw the ankle-high fishing line catching the light. The fishing line was taut and led in both directions to an empty banana box weighted by bricks. Swann walked closer to the box nearest the front door. The line passed through the handles of the box and went vertically up to the roofline. Placed there was a precariously balanced sherry bottle – Stormie's idea of an early-warning system.

Swann stepped over the trip-wire and raised a fist to knock. Stormie yanked the door back, took Swann's arm and pulled him inside. His eyes were fierce, and a bit watery with the effort.

'That coward is back in the picture, Swann. And I blame you.'

Swann followed Stormie down the corridor and into the kitchen, newly gutted to make the perimeter of tables and cupboards that stretched across the back porch, looking out over the backyard.

'Too old to fill sandbags. Lack a bloody Bren gun too. Owen gun'd do me in a pinch. Cover that whole fence line if the meathead comes over it.'

Swann didn't know what to say. Stormie stood before him, expression of a rabid Jack Russell, smears of Kiwi boot polish on the backs of his hands, his cheeks and forehead.

Janey entered the kitchen from the bathroom, looked drawn and spooked, exhausted.

'Janey, what's going on?'

'I told you what's going on, Frank,' Stormie cut in.

Jane moved to Stormie's side, put a hand on his shoulder. 'I can speak for myself, thanks Stormie. Reckon I know what this looks like to Mr Swann. Bit weird.'

'You got me,' Swann agreed.

But Stormie wasn't having any of it – raised a hand like a commando on patrol. 'I'll tell you what's going on. Janey here called a friend, lady of the night, works the park down there on Beaufort Street. Apparently that dog-faced runt ex of hers is back, asking after Janey. He's heard that you took her out of the battered women's place. Reckons you might be her new man. Jealous as hell. Been going round to all the girls with your description. Offerin' 'em a twenty for a name. Only a matter of time before one of them girls twigs, puts you in for a quick fix of the old morphia.'

Swann looked to Janey for confirmation, who gave a little nod, sniffled. 'So you've decked this place out like the bloody Alamo, just in case he gets my name? This isn't what Janey needs, mate.'

'There's the thanks I get. What'd I say, Janey, eh?'

Swann looked to Janey again. 'What's he on about?'

Janey went to speak, but Stormie got in first with a rhetorical clenching of his fists. 'Are there any fucken *men* left? Are there? Any? If you'd finished that prick off, Frank, we wouldn't be here. I did you a large, mate, and this is the thanks I get.'

'Janey?'

'I didn't give Stormie the number. He's got this call-back thing on his phone. He called Mel, my mate, back, and told her to spread Stormie's name around, and to give this address.'

Stormie grew an inch, and his face went hard. 'You don't run from scum like that, Frank. You invite 'em in for a friendly cuppa, say "sugar", and blow their fucken lights out.'

Swann shook his head. 'This friend of your's, Mel, she reliable enough to remember the message, pass it on?'

Janey gave a quick shake of her head, so quick that Stormie didn't see it. Swann tried to hide his relief. Janey, going along with Stormie's theatrics, although Swann didn't doubt his intent. He took out a pen and wrote the number of the car phone, and passed it to Janey. 'Call me on this, anytime. And Janey, please call in to Marion, let her know how you're doing. She worries.'

Janey threw her arms around Swann, just as quickly detached herself, well used to the presence of a possessive boyfriend. Swann said again, 'You need anything, call me.'

Stormie rocked on his heels. 'Fucken Bren'd be alright. Owen'd be handy too. Yeah, nah, too much to ask, isn't it? Bit of logistical support from the great man.'

Swann left them to it. If what Janey's friend Mel said was correct, Janey wouldn't be safe at Swann's home. He'd have to talk to Marion about it, find somewhere new for Janey to hide out.

41.

Swann knocked on the door of Gould's apartment, inserted the key and opened the door. Gould looked at him, noticed the lack of a bottle, made a face. Swann followed him into the lounge room, made a face of his own. He pulled back one of the heavy curtains; the block of smoky light illuminating the carpet laid with piles of paper, overturned ashtrays and coffee mugs. But Dennis Gould was immaculately dressed in a blue pinstripe with polished shoes and crisp white shirt, freshly shaved and barbered.

'Must've made an impression, Dennis. Taken years off.'

'They wouldn't let me in the front door if I didn't look the part. Stockbroking's all about image, Frank. Half the blokes on broking desks round the world don't have a clue, but they make sure to look good, sound good, smell good. Speaking of which – you wanted me to stop working, but you didn't bring any booze.'

Swann opened his jacket, took out a half-bottle of Jameson. Gould saw Swann's holstered pistol and, as he did whenever he saw a gun, shivered. Swann cracked the cap and passed the bottle. Gould drank the shoulders off, wiped his mouth with the back of his hand, huffed out some fumes, crossed himself.

'What's the problem?' he asked.

'Word's out that you're back. Hogan knows.'

'I only popped out for an hour.'

'It's not that. Hogan always knew. Somehow.'

Gould's searching look broken by another swig. 'This is one of those gigs, isn't it? A step behind, always.'

Swann nodded. 'Doesn't feel like I'm working the inside, that's for sure.'

'That's kind of what I wanted to show you. The second tender, Hercules

Construction. Like I told you earlier, Hercules is the umbrella company for more local firms – pretty experienced, although not to the scale that Exetar has accomplished. Ticks all the boxes re directors, subcontractors, et cetera, nothing untoward. Seems to be plenty of liquidity and potential for taking the next step. Conlan is listed as their premier financier, but when I made a few calls, turns out that Conlan's pulled the plug on their money, yesterday. You want some?'

Swann shook his head at the bottle. He was having trouble maintaining interest in Gould's research, thinking instead of Hogan's motives for wanting him near the premier. But the whisky had set a fire in Gould's eyes that Swann didn't enjoy seeing. Dennis Gould was either working, or drinking, and once he stopped working and started drinking there'd be no sense out of him, so he let him ramble.

'That was unusual enough for me to investigate. Conlan's bank, you'll remember, was financing each of the tenders. Whoever wins, the Burswood development will be built using Conlan money. So why pull the plug on Hercules? I visited my friend at the stock exchange. He hadn't heard, so we looked at recent transactions on the market. Turns out someone's buying shares in Hercules, significant transactions. Sure you won't join me?'

Swann watched Gould drain the bottle, toss the empty onto the couch, at a loss now with his hands, looking around for more. 'Go on, Dennis. I'm following, just.'

'Small chunks of Hercules stock but overall in big volumes.'

'We know who's buying?'

'That's the thing. More trades the past two days than in the past year. Got my mate excited. Like he's missing out on something. Forgot I was there. Started following the company names, making calls. All roads leading back to London. Took a long time and a lot of calls to trace the shell companies, registered all over the place, but enough to get a clear picture. One way or another, all of the companies are part of the Handos PLC empire, owned by one Graham Greylands.'

'Grim Greylands, even I've heard of him.'

'Because he's a notorious bastard. Gold mines. Pharmaceuticals. Brewing. Rumours of funding mercenary-driven coups in Africa. You name it. And the obvious question –'

'Why's a big wheel like Greylands buying into a local construction entity?'

'Precisely. We don't know. We may never know. But what we *were* able to ascertain, with a few well-placed calls to London brokers, is that Maitland Conlan's Exetar, as part of its worldwide shopping spree, has been buying up big in Handos. Very big. And of course leveraged by his brother.'

'So it's payback. Greylands is buying into an Exetar competitor? And Conlan hears, pulls the finance on it.'

'Exactly. To what end Greylands is stalking Exetar, I don't know –'

'Maybe that *is* the end. Swinging dicks. But why doesn't he buy Exetar directly? Surely he's got enough backing.'

'Frank, that is the bloody question. *The* question. Perhaps he knows about the organised crime influence we uncovered, or something else about Exetar that we don't? Either way, the amount he's bought into Hercules, it's what's called a poised position. Not a majority ownership, but not much more needed.'

Swann understood. 'If Hercules gets the tender, he buys himself across the line, takes a majority interest. If not, he flogs what he's bought, no harm done.'

'Exactly,' Gould said. 'So, what do you want me to do about it? I mean, focus on?'

Gould's wringing hands, desperate for a drink. It couldn't hurt. It wouldn't make any difference to Swann. 'Look at Exetar again. Try to find out what Greylands knows. But be careful. Hogan and Quinlivan are together in Exetar, at ground level. So look higher up. If Hogan knows you're here, others might.'

'But Trevor Dragic. He's out of the picture, right? For good, yeah?'

Swann nodded. 'Yeah, for good.'

42.

It was near midnight when Swann headed out of the city, radio tuned to the classic station pre-set when he'd taken the Statesman. He knew the call from Hogan was coming. He had something that Hogan wanted in the sunken Mercedes as possible leverage, but Swann needed that material to get the Trackers clear. He didn't want to go near the two bodies, not at night, not with Hogan watching him. He dialled the East Perth Lockup as he drove, kept the classical music in the background, good cover for a lawyer type. Got Carter on the line, in the middle of his shift. Carter confirmed that the deal was on, wanted to see some of the contents of the Mercedes. Swann declined, strained his voice; the conviction needed to be quashed, the father released from Fremantle Prison, otherwise no deal. Would call again tomorrow. If no progress, Swann was going to the media with the whereabouts of the bodies, the Mercedes, the documents.

Windows down, Swann could smell the lingering heat in the eucalypts of the Kings Park bushland; no sound but the purring V8 engine and the sharp notes of a violin, working around a cello. Swann let himself relax into the seat, could smell the river now, briny and warm. The car phone began to ring, and Swann pushed aside his jacket, heavy with two firearms, lifted the receiver. It was Terry Accardi.

'That meeting tomorrow. I've got some interesting news that might, well ... persuade you to rethink your earlier decision. Tomorrow morning, at the usual?'

Swann agreed, planted the phone into its cradle, continued west away from the black acres of river and the darkened ridge of Mt Eliza. It would be good to pass everything onto Accardi, let him take it from there. There was self-interest involved, too. If Hogan framed Swann for Dragic's murder, even if the case didn't fall to Accardi, he would be in the right position to make crucial evidence go missing, namely the gun and shell casings. By insisting Swann stay in the picture, Hogan had also put Swann in the frame to help Accardi. It would be the young detective who Swann tipped off about the Grednics' skeletons, if necessary.

The car phone trilled as Swann stopped at some traffic lights in Claremont, watching drunken girls with tanned skin in short skirts and tank tops and boys in jeans and collared shirts spill down Bayview Terrace. He lifted the receiver; heard the screams. A man screaming – Heenan, hysterical, not physical pain. There was no traffic behind him and when the lights turned green Swann stayed at the lights, listened to Heenan sobbing now, waited for it to subside.

*

The door to Heenan's twentieth-floor apartment was open. Heenan was slumped on the edge of his bed, dazed and mute but the tears still pumping, his pink Lacoste shirt soaked, nipples and fat rolls visible across his chest. On the bed, facedown and head turned awkwardly, silver wig askew, was a naked woman. Swann pushed Heenan aside with his knee, put a finger to the woman's neck, took it away, put it back to check.

'You fool. She's still alive.'

Heenan, tangled in Swann's feet, and near catatonic with shock and exhaustion, sucked in a deep wheezy breath, kept sucking it in, a balloon expanding, scrambling to his knees. Swann kept his finger at the woman's neck, pulse weak but regular, deep in the overdose. Swann could see why Heenan thought she was dead; she was barely breathing, taking a breath every ten seconds or so, barely a breath at all.

'Call the ambos, now.'

'No, Frank. C'mon ...'

Swann grabbed Heenan by the hair and threw his head back, caught the bedside table, sent a lamp spilling. The woman began gurgling, her lungs imploding, heart ready to burst, drown her in blood. He hefted her over, began CPR, filling her lungs. Heard Heenan stagger away, make the call, run the tap, throw water on his face while Swann kept putting air in her lungs, dizzy with air himself, could feel himself start to hyperventilate, too much oxygen. Kept going, lights in his eyes, felt himself spinning. A hand on his shoulder. An ambo, and he fell aside, slumped on the floor beside the bed. Took a shallow breath and held it, felt his lungs tremble, exhaled and repeated the process. Could stand now. Went to Heenan in the kitchen, hands on the benchtop, staring down into the marble.

When Heenan spoke, his voice was a whisper. 'She wasn't like that, Frank. Not when we got here. I was drunk, couldn't even do it, passed out. When I awoke, she was there, so *still*. I thought ...'

'She one of Dot Coulter's girls?'

Heenan looked up. 'How'd you know that?'

'I recognised one of Dot's girls on the riverboat.'

Heenan nodded. 'Conlan only uses Dot. We were at a party near here. Started as an office party, in Maitland Conlan's boardroom. Ended up more a ... Jesus Christ.'

'Was the premier there? You see something you weren't supposed to?'

Heenan thought about it, wobbled at his knees, still drunk. 'No. I've seen the others like that before. *Flagrante delicto*, so to speak. It's why I ... partake too. So they know I'm no different, not likely to –'

'Then what? What do you remember? That girl, I checked her purse. No fits, no gear. Someone came up here, gave her a hotshot.'

Heenan shook his head, furrowed his brow. The tears started; the panting breath. Then stillness, eyes widening. 'Not something I saw, Frank. Something I said.'

'Go on.'

'I said to Larry Conlan. I told him ... what you told me. About the Exetar tender looking shaky. He doesn't know, of course, that I asked you to –'

'You mentioned my name?'

'Yes, Frank, I'm sorry. I was angry. Sick of him treating me like ... so I ragged him back. Just a little.'

'That doesn't make sense. The power he has over the premier. He could just get you fired.'

Heenan slumped. 'That's what *he* said. That's when I said ...'

'Spit it out.'

'What you told me. About organised crime. The bikies, and the Exetar tender. I wasn't specific.'

'Specific enough. The Burswood project's worth near a hundred million. You don't think that's worth Conlan killing for?'

'I was drunk, Frank.'

The ambos entered the kitchen, a young man and an older woman, faces that had seen it all. The woman looked at Heenan, her voice cold.

'She's stable. Refusing to come with us, to Royal Perth, against my advice. Must've had a big tolerance already.'

Swann thanked her, Heenan looked away.

'I hope you paid her well,' she said to Heenan, who still wouldn't meet her eyes.

'Where did she inject herself?' Swann asked.

A strange question, but the ambo didn't blink. 'Looks like straight in the neck. Veins are collapsed on her arms, probably everywhere else too.'

Swann followed them to the door, locked it. Took Heenan aside. 'How much cash do you have? She's not going back to work. Not after what she's seen.'

'Not much. Not ... that much.'

Swann nodded, as Heenan thought it. The cash in the premier's office.

'And I'd get your locks changed.'

Swann entered the bedroom, the woman trying to buckle her high-heels, unsteady. The ambos would have given her an upper, to get her heart going, but her eyes were unfocused, her satin dress unzipped and her wig still askew. Swann knelt beside her, buckled her shoes, zipped her dress, straightened her wig, stood her up and passed her bag. Looked into her eyes.

'Don't worry,' she slurred. 'Dot recruited me from St Kilda. I'm not hangin' round here. And since you're not askin', I'll tell you. There were two of 'em. Didn't see their faces, but I saw their boots. Bike boots. Leather.'

Swann took her arm. Heenan was waiting in the kitchen, shirt tucked, wearing a peaked cap pulled low, car keys in hand.

*

The lights in the kitchen were on. Swann walked down the side of the house, peered through the window, and there were Marion and Blake Tracker, seated at the formica table drinking tea and playing cards. He could hear the turntable spinning Charlie Pride, one of his father-in-law's records, at a guess chosen by Blake. The back door was unlocked. He shed the revolver and pistol, took off his shoulder-holster and rolled the lot in his jacket, placed it on an upper shelf in the laundry. Blake was already at the kettle, but Swann shook his head, reached for the good stuff – Matusalem dark rum – on top of the fridge. He took it down and rolled a glass off another shelf and kissed Marion on the ear, looked at her hand. They were playing twenty-one. Blake took up his hand again and waggled his eyebrows, made Marion laugh. Each of them exhausted, unable to sleep, no words necessary. Swann poured himself three fingers and corked the bottle, drank off half the glass and slumped in his seat, nearly slid away. He offered his cigarettes around the table, lit up and exhaled and closed his eyes.

He felt Marion's fingers reach for his own and took her hand, kept his eyes closed, sipped the rum. He had sat at this table decades ago and held hands with Marion while her father, George Monroe, told stories about the job, for Swann's benefit.

A strange relationship at first – the hardened detective and Swann, the tough kid and occasional criminal, in love with a policeman's daughter. Marion told him that her father had seen something in Swann, but it wasn't until later, just Swann and her father at the table, drinking longnecks and smoking, that he learned the truth. His future father-in-law telling him straight that Marion was stronger than Swann, and so he saw a match. But what Marion's father saw in Swann wasn't good; the worst aspects of his own personality, barely checked. Swann trying to be respectful, knew he had a lot to learn, didn't understand what the middle-aged man meant, sitting there in a white singlet, scars and tattoos on his arms, handsome face all hard angles – eyes that saw through the darkness.

Unspoken between them, the morning paper's front-page photograph of Detective Sergeant George Monroe with a cracked shotgun over his suited shoulder, the gun he'd used to kill a cop-killer. The corpse out of picture – a young man Swann's age who'd boasted that he was going to kill a cop, had done it there in Bentley on the driveway of his mother's yard, had run to the hills and holed himself up in a logger's shack, calling down hell. Marion's father like most of his detective peers, a WWII veteran, took no pleasure in killing but his eyes were cauterised by the lives he had taken of men who wanted to kill him.

Marion's father was drinking for his own reasons, but filling up Swann's glass and leading him into falling-down drunkenness, an old Scottish tradition to test his psychological and emotional core. They drank for twelve hours straight, Swann afloat on a sliding floor, but moored to the dark eyes and the other man's fierce sobriety that would never leave him no matter how much he drank. In between stories the older man counselled Swann that a family would steady him, put the fighting and stealing and fucking into a different reference point, acting as a rein on his worst impulses. Told Swann that either way he wasn't destined to live a normal life, and that taking on the discipline of responsibility was a survival technique that would guarantee him a longer life, and spare the community the collateral damage. He counselled Swann to never mention this to Marion, who would be making her own sacrifices in turn. Her wildness was a reflection of Swann's own, and their bond of love was exactly that, a binding that contained a spiritedness that would sustain them together but destroy them apart. Swann took the older man's words on a promise, but later knew them to be true; Swann never happier or safer than in her arms at night, in the cool darkness on the edge of sleep.

Swann felt the squeeze of Marion's fingers, sensing his drift towards sleep, pulling him back. He opened his eyes, saw that Blake was smiling mischievously as he fanned another hand, pushing a matchstick into the centre of the table. The sun was coming up; a magpie warbled in the driveway, a train trundled towards the port. Swann stood and felt his legs buckle, replaced the bottle and wandered towards his bed.

43.

The river was calm as a lake in its blue depths and amber shallows, pelicans seated on the stanchions of Canning Bridge as Swann passed the Raffles, the Abe Saffron–owned pub where coppers were always welcome. He'd just hung up the phone, Carter assuring him that today Gerry Tracker would be presented before a judge and released, all charges dropped, as a sign of good faith. The overturning of the conviction against his son would require some good faith on Swann's part. Some physical evidence – say a photograph of the Mercedes. Swann had laughed at Carter. Overturn the conviction, or the location of the Mercedes and its contents would be given to the media; the Grednics' disappearance still played well with the better investigative journalists. Carter laughed back at Swann. Did the Abo boy really want murder added to the charge of stealing and assault? Swann raising the stakes – the papers in the trunk made for interesting reading. Carter swore and told Swann to call back in an hour.

On the radio: no sightings of Des Foley, the Good Morning Bandit, meaning that Foley was good to run. A snippet on the state's acquisition of power infrastructure in the South-West, questions raised by the shadow finance minister about the fact that it was only recently sold to a private bidder, Sam Mostel, and that the buying price appeared double the original selling price. The premier unavailable for comment, touring the government's latest private-sector investment; a swathe of land in the Ord, a joint development project with Barry Conlan's Exetar, the land supposedly diamond-rich. Another car stolen by the Porsche Boy, another aborted car chase. Clifford and Welsh, hours from death. The prime minister's request for clemency denied. And next, the latest number one single from Australian Crawl, 'Reckless'.

Swann left the radio on, the measured drumbeats of the song

accompanying the bass thuds of the laden trucks rolling over the Narrows Bridge; the South Perth foreshore occupied by kids kicking footballs, joggers and rollerbladers on the path closest to the shore.

The carpark was empty of junkies, which was unusual. Terry Accardi was due in fifteen minutes, and Swann parked in the corner near the paperbarks, where two crows and a seagull tussled over a bloody sheet of butcher's paper. The car phone rang, and Swann lifted the receiver and crooked it into his neck, expecting Accardi. But it was Hogan, terse, agitated.

'Swann, whatever you're doing, stop doing. I warned you yesterday –'

Across the river, a small puff of dust from one of the middle floors of the Central Police Station, followed by the sound – a blunt, ugly thump, followed by more dust-cloud – a horizontal black and brown spear over the Causeway, then an eerie silence, the crows and the children and the joggers and rollerbladers pausing to look, shielding their eyes from the sun.

Hogan had cut the line. On the foreshore, normal life resumed; the sounds of children squealing with delight, bickering and slamming cricket bats on trees, crows cawing, parents scolding, the trucks drumming over the Narrows.

The cloud of dust to the east was gone. Only seconds had passed. Long, hollow seconds, but time enough for Swann to understand.

Terry Accardi's office. Blown out onto the Causeway traffic.

*

News vans and reporters on foot. Car alarms railing at the wide blue sky. An ambulance edging through the crowd of rubbernecks on the footpaths of Adelaide Terrace; Swann parked between the looming police building and the snarled traffic at the Causeway roundabout.

Heenan had called and wanted to know. The premier was flying back from the Kimberley in a Conlan private jet. Swann was asked to stick around and pump the journos; even better, get the good oil from an ex-colleague. But there were no ex-colleagues on the street who would speak to Swann. The building had been evacuated. A hundred detectives and a couple of hundred uniformed clerical staff and senior brass huddled in the carpark under the blazing sun, a barrier of black-clad TRG troops with pump-action shotguns at present-arms.

Swann scanned the milling crowd, looking for a familiar face, waves of heat prickling over his skin, heart thudding, light-headed with adrenalin. He lit a cigarette and left the car, caught snatches of conversation, dream language, floating in the air. It was the Aborigines, their militant Brewery protest gone mental; it was the mafia, drugs, always about drugs. Or Des Foley, taking a crack at the old enemy, bank robber turned cop-killer. Then a crackle of loudspeaker, the warping of feedback, a gruff voice warning spectators to stand away, let the ambulance through. A press conference in the carpark about to commence, the station superintendent in full uniform, flanked by TRG; their black helmets a backdrop of uniform menace.

Swann pushed his way through the crowd, journos three deep as the super began to speak, squinting into the sun. Tragic news. One of our own. A young and promising Homicide detective. Would appear to be a letter bomb. No motives as yet. No leads. The entire force at the disposal of the Homicide squad. No holds barred. Full weight of the law. The Super's words drowned by the journalists' questions, a jostling choir chanting *what can you tell us about ...*

There was nothing for Swann at the scene. He returned to the Statesman, sat behind the wheel, put his head in his hands. Accardi was working the case of the murdered enviro, who'd been looking at Exetar. A Conlan company, and Conlan-funded, but it was Hogan who'd warned Swann off Exetar, Hogan who'd called him the moment the letter bomb blew, must have known about their meeting. Wouldn't hesitate to kill another copper if he stood in the way. Swann next, of that he could be certain. And despite this, despite the blood in his face, his fists clenched, the dark congestion in his chest – with his eyes closed, Swann saw the perfect logic of all his years leading to this moment: driven out of the blackness of his feelings towards an image of crystalline definition; the moment when he would look into Hogan's eyes and release his fury.

44.

Swann saw the HG Kingswood three cars back, confirmation that Hogan's men were tailing him again as he climbed out of St Georges Terrace, past Parliament House, up towards the treeline banking Kings Park. The car phone was off the hook – he was sick of Heenan's importuning. Swann turned the Statesman into the park, speeding along the row of lemon gums, tourists taking happy-snaps of the city at their feet, joggers in fluoro headbands and kids on BMXs riding the trail beside the road. Past the cenotaph obelisk, through the roundabout and the giant fallen karri, a hard right away from the botanical gardens, running into the forest. A glance in the rear-view: the HG keeping pace, crowded with suited bodies, passenger hands on the dash as Swann gunned it, the Statesman lifting in eagerness, the HG stuggling to keep up, giving Swann time to slow as he approached the artillery memorial. He reached into his rolled jacket and drew out the two loaded guns, laying them on the seat until he glided the Statesman off the tarmac and onto the woodchip track that led into the bush. The car chewed up the track but made it to the first rise, Swann jacking the handbrake so that the car lunged forward, skidding over the top. Swann hit the ground running, could hear the HG whining up the track behind, building speed towards the ridge, saw the looks on the faces as the Statesman blocked their way, driver slamming the brakes and shanking the wheel; the Kingswood fishtailing into a jarrah, smashing into the driver's door. Swann aimed the .22 pistol throw-down in his left hand, kept the .38 revolver for whatever happened next, watched the rear passenger door crack open and saw the pistol in the hand of a young detective and fired his own: two shots from point blank into both legs, followed by a kick, the .38 covering the front of the car, the .22 now aiming straight at Hogan's face.

Hogan's eyes – genuine fear there, hand on the man beside, pushing the service revolver away. Hands raised in surrender, pushing at the boys in front to do the same. Swann waved Hogan out of the car, saw that he was wearing a bulletproof vest beneath his suit jacket. Not standard issue – bought it with his own coin. Why?

Hogan stood beside his shot colleague, who was now on his hands and knees retching into the grey dirt. 'There was no need for that, Frank.'

Swann took a short step with the leading leg, a feint with the right – Hogan walking into Swann's sweeping left fist, pistol butt catching his temple. Dropped to his knees, hands reaching out for Swann in punch-drunk vertigo, grabbing his colleague instead, sliding round onto his back. Swann stood over him, .38 still covering the men in the car, pointed the pistol at Hogan's head. A terrible gravity drawing on Swann's wrist, a burning line between bullet and forehead. The gunshot surprised Swann as much as Hogan, a little jerk of the wrist the only thing that saved him, cordite spray on Hogan's cheeks, deafened. He felt it in his ankles, knees, hips – the buckle and sway of violence at close range, only his gun-hand steady, and that just training. Now Hogan came alive, eyes flinching, seared by muzzle-flame and powder-blast. Hands reaching up for the barrel, trying to speak but only puffs of sound, Swann kneeling closer; bringing the pistol to Hogan's neck, beneath the chin.

'Conlan. It was Conlan.'

Hogan's voice eerie with displacement, as disembodied as Swann felt. Swann understood that he'd stopped breathing, barked, gulped at the air around him, pressed the barrel deeper. Finger rigid on the trigger. Understood now that the voice wasn't Hogan's, had come instead from the car. He looked across to the front passenger, his hands out the window in surrender, another young detective, eyes like Christmas baubles.

'Mr Swann, it wasn't us. It was Conlan. Inspector Hogan, he tried to warn you. We didn't know.'

Swann staggered up, covered them all, the words out of the young detective's mouth coming automatic.

'What the press don't know yet – there was another letter bomb in Canberra, at the Feds. It was found in time. Postmarked Perth. A bulletin went out. Wasn't passed on in time. Nobody knew that ... Terry was working for the Feds. Not until a man named Sam Mostel called us, said he was passing on a message from Conlan. "Sniffer dogs like Terry Accardi get put down. You're next." Inspector Hogan had it on speaker. We all heard it. It's recorded.'

Beneath Swann, Hogan groaned. There was no fear in his eyes now, just hatred rising on the humiliation, weak man's juice. He spat out the side of his mouth, tried to sit up, jacket askew. He managed to grunt. 'Jones, get out of the car. Introduce yourself to Swann.'

Swann looked to the detective but it was the other passenger in the back seat who climbed out, had the bulk and poise of a heavyweight, nose broken a few times but his eyes not punchy. He came around the car, no expression on his face. Swann saw Jones notice his shaking hands, his own juice departing. Jones kept his hands showing, stopped beside Hogan, but didn't help him up.

'I won't shake your hand, Mr Swann. They appear to be full.'

British accent, touch of Geordie. Calm under a gun. Military background.

Hogan roused himself, got to his feet. Swann saw the iron in Jones' jacket pocket, wondered when Hogan was going to reach for it. Hogan spat again, wiped blood from his face. 'Jones here is a Falklands veteran. Royal Marines Commando.'

'And now?'

No answer from Jones. Hogan looked at his profile. 'He works for Grim Greylands. In your line of work. I'm assuming you've –'

'I've heard of Greylands. In fact, his name came up in conversation just yesterday.'

Little smile from Jones, flicker of his hands, indicating for Swann to continue.

'He's buying up Hercules Construction stock, taken a poised position. You've been sabotaging Exetar, from within. What's a Pommy tycoon's interest in the Burswood tender?'

Hogan coughed. 'You wouldn't believe me if I told you.'

'Try me.'

Jones cleared his throat. 'Two birds with one stone. Maitland Conlan is a bug under Mr Greylands' shoe. And there is money to be made in the long-term development of this state's mineral assets.'

Hogan saw that Jones wasn't going to elaborate, stepped in. 'It appears as though Maitland Conlan got impatient on the St Andrews long eighteen sometime last year. Wouldn't wait for Greylands to clear the green on a par three. Launched a rocket-shot from a heavy driver straight at Greylands when he was putting, hit his favourite caddy behind the ear, nearly killed him. Waltzed up the green like nothing happened, sank his putt. They came to blows – Greylands decked Conlan. Soon after, Conlan started buying up Handos stock, financed by his brother's bank. Greylands outsmarted him, basically forced him to sell it all back, got shorted badly. To the tune of near half a billion. Didn't seem to touch the sides. Which made Greylands curious. Jones here is a vehicle of Greylands' curiosity.'

Jones shifted his weight, nodded. 'Which is where you come in.'

Swann shook his head. 'You're telling me this is all about a game of golf?'

Slight nod from Jones, bemused. 'Correct, in the first instance. Now it's about ego. And principle. The teaching of a lesson. And money.'

Swann shot a look at Hogan. 'You're Larry Conlan's man, always been in his pocket. What's in it for you?'

Hogan sneered. 'Those Conlan bastards are planning to build a casino at Burswood. Cut me and the wogs right out. The Italians will be out of business, and their business is my business. I offered to parlay, to provide security, most of the subcontracting on the Burswood building site, for a small percentage. But he refused.'

'Then Gary Quinlivan contacted you from London. Let you know about Greylands' interest in Conlan.'

Hogan shrugged.

'What's that got to do with Terry Accardi? I know he was working on the Exetar environmental scientist's murder.'

'Nothing to do with that. With Jones' help, we've been bugging Maitland Conlan's phone. He got a tip-off from a Federal. About Accardi working out of school, looking at Conlan's links with organised crime. Being run by a Fed handler, the one that got a little message in the mail this morning.'

So Hogan hadn't known about Swann and Accardi. Instead, Accardi had been betrayed by the organisation he was hoping to graduate to.

'Murdering fizzes is your line of work. Who sent the bomb to Accardi? I want a name.'

Hogan nodded. 'Part of Conlan's rise to prominence, his being taken under the premier's wing, is that I've lost control of certain members of the outlaw motorcycle community. Rather than them paying me, Conlan is paying them.'

'The Junkyard Dogs.'

'Correct, and facilitated by Sam Mostel, Conlan's accountant, now right-hand.'

'You invited the Outlaw Mob over, to try and patch the Junkyard Dogs. Get back some kind of control.'

Hogan looked surprised. 'A desperate act. One that Heenan tells me you stymied with your interference. Jones. Over to you.'

Jones nodded. 'It's Mr Greylands' belief that the Conlan brothers' business empire, both the bank and the companies, is a house of cards. The merest tap, and it will collapse. Taking your government with it, it looks like. What I need from you is the documentary evidence. I've tried to obtain it myself, by payment and blackmail, but no luck so far.'

'When did this process begin?'

'Late last year. Around the time Conlan started buying Handos stock.'

The time the Grednics disappeared. Grednic was Conlan's chief accountant, knew everything about the business. Swann looked to Hogan, who had a hand in the Grednics' murder, at that point still working for Conlan. When Blake Tracker stole the Grednics' Mercedes, Hogan lost the incriminating paperwork.

'Carrot or the stick?' Swann asked.

Jones smiled. 'That's up to you. A sizeable retainer for your services, a significant bonus should you succeed. But if you don't ... the Conlans find out you were working for Accardi, your atomised friend. You have of course demonstrated today your willingness to avenge Accardi. What I'm offering you is a chance to do that, while getting paid. As if that weren't incentive enough, I understand there exists evidence that you played a part in murdering an old rival, Trevor Dragic. And that this evidence is in our possession. And that ex-cops prefer not to serve life sentences, for the simple reason that they don't get to serve them out.'

The cold clarity in Jones' eyes. The professional crime scene at Dragic's farmhouse. It was Jones who'd killed Dragic. Because Dragic had killed the Grednics, together with Carter, or left the Mercedes there for Carter to collect.

Dragic had been tortured, but had he broken? Swann knew Dragic better than Jones, better than Hogan. If Dragic had been tasked to kill the Grednics, collect the incriminating paperwork and hand it over to Hogan, there was little chance that he'd hand everything over. He'd keep something as insurance, and as a potential doublecross earner.

There was the Grednics' Mercedes and the materials in the boot, submerged for a year and likely ruined. There was Dragic's farmhouse. There was Conlan's bank vault.

'How long have I got?'

Hogan scuffed dust off his jacket. 'Not long. The premier's under the Conlans' thumb. We know for a fact that they're pressuring him to announce the Burswood tender in Exetar's favour. We need something in case he goes early. If he doesn't, we need something to demonstrate why he shouldn't. Something that'll destroy him if he does.'

'You need to take down the Junkyard Dogs' hierarchy. The men who sent the bomb.'

Jones cracked his neck, glanced at Hogan, who hissed. 'I'm not going to mourn a rat. But as chief of the CIB, one of my own getting murdered – that's a case that's going to be solved. Don't you worry about the Junkyard Dogs, or Sam fucking Mostel. Those bastards broke ranks. They're going to pay for that. An example will be made.'

Swann turned, walked the track to the Statesman, felt their eyes on his neck, the target on his back. They were going to kill him the moment he was no use.

45.

Swann fishtailed off the dirt track onto the bitumen trail that ran through the park towards the city. Turned on the local radio, the talkback all about Terry Accardi's murder; the speculation, the fallout, the loss of a promising detective. Rumours abounded, some of them unlikely and some of them moronic: 'With a name like Accardi, he was probably working for the mafia, had a falling out.'

Swann turned off the radio, hit the freeway north, turned onto Scarborough Beach Road and headed towards Wanneroo. The road out to the pine plantation was quiet and still as the heat built in the breezeless morning. He didn't bother hiding the Statesman at the entrance to the market garden, but instead cut down the dirt trail raising a parachute of dust. The marijuana plants were vivid green and rising higher over the tomatoes, the row sprinklers still ticked over the heated earth. There was no car at the farmhouse, but two Doberman puppies roused themselves off the porch and looked at each other and looked at Swann and ran towards him on unsteady legs. They bumped his knees and licked his hand. Swann looked up for their owner, saw his silver hair and flannelette shirt behind the screen door, cradling a shotgun.

Swann raised his hands, let the puppies lick his boots. Old man Dragic cracked the screen, slipped onto the porch, aimed the shotgun at Swann's belly. The puppies looked at Dragic and whimpered, cowered towards him. Recognition in the old man's eyes. Knew that Swann was the man who destroyed his son's reputation, bankrupted him, made him desperate. He would know that Trevor wanted Swann dead, would assume that Swann had killed him.

'The men who killed your son. They wanted something.'

Dragic spat into the dirt. 'You know who killed Trevor?'

Swann shrugged, *yes*. 'You know who I am. I'm not a murderer.'

The old man grunted. 'Every man is a judge, jury, executioner. Only fate decides when it's time. Perhaps your time came. Perhaps now it's my time.'

Leaned forward to distribute his weight, prepare for the recoil.

'The men who killed Trevor, they were looking for documents. He wouldn't talk. They're still here.'

Speculation, speeded words, Dragic's eyes watering like he was ready to burst. Then a switch as Swann's words hit, the old man allowing himself to feel the pride, a remnant product of his fathering – the fact that Trevor hadn't spilled. He nodded, relaxed his shoulders, brought in his front foot.

Swann needed to keep Dragic talking. A sullen violence, product of grief and old-world pride, there on the surface. 'You didn't report his murder.'

'I don't report nothing to nobody. It happened here, it stays here. My revenge, when it comes, will be dealt here.'

Swann had buried Dragic in the dirt not a few kilometres north, but he asked the old man, 'Where is he?'

'That, I don't know. Where he is buried. But I found his dogs up there, in the bush, poisoned. So I buried instead his guns, his dogs, clothes and what you're looking for. My boy, I teach him: take your secrets to your grave.'

He turned, and Swann followed him through the house, which smelt of meat sauce and drying herbs, the puppies greeting them at the back door. Old man Dragic handed Swann a shovel, and he followed through the sheds past a vegetable plot to a stand of wattle; a Christmas tree beginning to flower; a child's swing hanging from the bent back of an old paperbark. Beside the swing was a mound of turned earth. Knee prints in the soft earth, deep and numerous. Raindrop spatters on the grave, when it hadn't rained for months. The old man, alone here at night, returning time and again, weeping over the empty grave of his only son. On top of the mound was a plastic cowboy rifle and black hat, pinned with a silver star. The puppies threaded Swann's legs, began to nuzzle and dig.

*

Dennis Gould's apartment was hot enough that the papers spread around the floor had begun to curl. He sat before Swann in his silk boxers and smoked a cigarette and scanned the ledger. The rolls of fat on his belly were beaded and silver lines of sweat trickled out of his hairline down his neck. Swann's mind was elsewhere. On the radio had come the news of a riot inside Fremantle Prison, in B wing where Gerry Tracker was being held. The afternoon heat had broken forty-three degrees, and you could add ten degrees inside the old cells. Prisoners had bashed a guard and taken hostages. A fire had spread to the adjoining wings. Most of the prisoners were in the yard, in the baking sun, avoiding the flames. Squads of TRG troopers were getting ready to mount an assault. The premier was unavailable for comment.

Gould grimaced and smoked and scratched himself, going down the lines of the balance sheets and bank statements and wire transfers without a hint of excitement. Swann hoped that there was something – the price for the ledger had been to give old man Dragic the names of Hogan and Jones. When Swann mentioned Trevor Dragic's likely involvement in the Grednics' murder he had shrugged, grunted, kept drinking his homemade wine.

Gould closed the ledger, looked disappointed. 'No smoking gun, I'm afraid. There are clear indications the Conlans have been using bottom-of-the-harbour tax schemes, but so has everybody else. And it's difficult to prosecute. There's evidence of asset-stripping between the listed companies, and of transferring large amounts to unnamed financial institutions, most likely offshore tax shelters, but that too is common and equally difficult to prosecute. All we've got here is clear evidence of juggling accounts, borrowing from Peter to pay Paul within the Conlan Empire. It's enough to arouse suspicion that Exetar and Maitland Conlan's other companies are struggling financially, but not enough to prove insolvency, failure to disclose and stock manipulation. Sorry, Frank.'

'It's alright. Dragic wouldn't have known what to look for. A stab in the dark.'

'I'll keep them safe. If we get a broader picture, based on more detailed information, we can run with it.'

The sun was setting, but no breeze blew from the coast. The darkness in the room seemed to magnify the heat. Swann passed Gould the bottle of Jameson and wiped the sweat off his forehead, his hands shaking with nerves, out of sync with the slow turning of the day, the quiet suburban lives around him. For Swann the world was turning faster.

*

He sat in the parliamentary carpark, the Statesman alongside the peach Commodore. The receiver in his hand scanned for wireless signals, of which there were many. The strongest signal was the most likely. He adjusted the dial on the receiver until the red hand on the meter touched the red shade that indicated a solid fix. A quick call to Norman Gorman after leaving Gould's house had decided him. When Swann asked the blind telephonist whether he'd been listening to the premier's phone calls Norman had sighed, yes, on occasions, but wished he hadn't. He was only able to eavesdrop between taking and transferring other calls, and so only heard snippets. Asked to describe the premier's state of mind, Norman had answered: agitated, furious, defensive. Norman didn't know that the premier's line was being bugged on his own instructions, so that Farrell would be careful about what he said, but Norman's answer was helpful. The young policeman's death, according to Norman, had invoked a slanging match with an older man whose voice he didn't recognise, all veiled threats and coded phrases that hinted at common interests and a close personal relationship turning sour.

Swann locked the receiver onto the wireless signal, exited the Statesman and popped the boot of the Commodore. Whenever the premier's line initiated the recording to the receiver inside Parliament House, that receiver would in turn trigger Swann's receiver. Its batteries were fully charged, with six hours of tape ready on the spool. He locked the Commodore's boot and returned to his car, cranked the ignition and cruised out of the darkened carpark towards the curling sulphur lights of the freeway.

46.

Des Foley parked the dirt bike in Shafto Lane, away from the eyes of the few drunks and street-people on Hay and Milligan. He was dressed like a dero, cap pulled low over his bearded face. There were a few people on Murray Street down towards the mall and a prowl car parked near Wolf Lane. He shuffled up the road in his heavy coat like any of the other derelicts headed towards Kings Park for the night. At the entrance to Conlan's bank, Foley glanced inside to make sure no lights were on, walked to the end of the block past Fast Eddys and came back the other side of Wellington Street. He jumped a fence and climbed a wall, made his way through the shadows towards the bunker-like shape of Harrowgate Investment Bank, keeping out of range of the single security camera covering the rear doorway. The building behind Foley was a record store, only a blank wall with no windows. He tested the downpipe nearest the back; solid steel. It was thirty feet to the asbestos roof behind the salmon-brick fronting, no eaves. Pressure perpendicular to the drainpipe would rip it off, so he braced his feet and hands and made the first jump and shimmy, making sure his weight ran vertically down the pipe. The week hiding beneath old man Pickett's house had drained his muscles and weakened his tendons, and so he climbed quicker than usual. It wasn't far to fall, he told himself as he gripped the pipe with feet and hands, moving from fixing brace to fixing brace. He made the roofline and rolled over, sat with his back to the wall and took out his tools. He'd done a preliminary reconnaissance of the bank a couple of years previously, but had decided against hitting it, had gone for a savings branch instead. But it wasn't cash on Foley's mind tonight. The safety deposit box key in Mostel's leather satchel was stamped Harrowgate, and whatever the box contained, it wouldn't be Mostel's wife's jewellery. The frustration of waiting for the police and media attention to ebb away had only made him more determined. If he could get something incriminating on Mostel, shed some light on whatever scam he was running, then he could use that to destroy the man.

Foley glanced at his watch. Just gone twelve. It was safer to make noise while there were people and traffic around. He could spend half an hour prising off the hooded roofing nails from the asbestos sheets, or he could take advantage of the material's brittle nature and kick himself a hole. He chose the latter, stepped back and slammed his boot down, once, twice, heard the sheet crack on the third attempt. Knelt and pulled the sheet back, heard the nails groan out of the jarrah beams, put the sheet aside. The hole was just enough to drop into, making sure that he maintained the weight on his hands, placing his feet carefully on the ceiling joists. Now he turned on his torch, saw that the ceiling hadn't been reinforced. He crawled over to the weight-bearing walls that framed a series of offices, separated from the floor of the bank. There was less likelihood of a motion sensor or a security camera inside an office, and it was the best place to hole up and wait for the manager to arrive. He chose the largest corner office and crouched, began to cut at the plasterboard with a gyprock saw, made a hole large enough to shine the torch into, looked down and saw the manager's desk, perfectly positioned for him to drop to. Foley sawed a bigger hole and placed the slab of sisal-reinforced plaster in the roof cavity beside him. Lowered his toolbag down onto the desk. Braced his hands on the nearest joist and swung down into the hole, dropped the five feet onto the leather blotter; a minimum of noise. The manager's office had a single window that overlooked the floor. Foley stood back and tried to picture the office from the floor, the manager arriving in the morning, killing the alarm, the chime of his keys, moving towards the office. The hole in the ceiling would be visible from the window, but assuming the manager didn't check the window first, he would unlock his door and then meet Foley. He would be polite. 'Good morning' was the first thing the manager would hear.

47.

Swann could smell the burning prison from South Fremantle; it had the nasty taste of plastic and rubber, burning garbage and mattresses. He'd driven past the massive stone walls on his way home, orange and magenta light flaring inside roiling smoke columns that rose a couple of hundred metres before dispersing and drifting across the town. TRG vans stationed at intervals, in case the men got through the walls, the snipers on the rat-runs over the yard not patrolling, but leaning on the rails and aiming into the yards. Ambulances and fire trucks, unable to get through the gates. Media vans and news helicopters. Locals gathered in the street to watch. Cheers and shouts from behind the walls. A couple of hundred family members crowded into the carpark, worried and agitated, beginning to abuse the TRG and screws changing shifts.

Blake Tracker wanted to join them. There was talk on the radio of transferring prisoners by bus to Canning Vale. Even a glimpse of his father was worth the chance of getting caught. He was dressed in clothes borrowed from Des Foley. It was a good disguise, except for his plaster-cast wrist, that Marion had dressed and set at home. But Swann talked him around. Prison guards from all over the city would be called off shifts to help at Fremantle, including from the juvie facilities. There was every chance that Blake would be recognised. The attitude of the police and guards at the prison was obvious – skittish, aggressive, their orders to shoot on sight, to not let the situation get further out of control.

Marion had packed a bag and gone to Sarah's house for the night, perhaps longer. Blake would stay there too, but first there was something that might help his father.

'Your father's Datsun truck, does it have a winch?' Swann asked.

The kid understood, nodded. 'Yes. But I'm coming. You don't know which jetty, or where. I can go in, attach the winch-hook.'

It would save time that Swann didn't have. 'Alright, but only that. Then you sit in the truck.'

*

Away from the suburban streetlights, the tannic water of Bibra Lake was impossibly dark in the moonless night; the day's heat dissipating over the ring of swamp trees, the haunting call of a boobook owl in a rivergum.

Swann backed the truck down the sandy track towards the old bones of the jarrah jetty, the swimming hole for generations of local kids. The jetty was barely wide enough to take the truck, but it didn't flinch as it took the weight. Without being asked, Blake stripped down to his jocks. Swann passed him the Dolphin torch. 'Sure you're ok to do this?'

Blake walked out past the leaf litter, arms wrapped around his body despite the heat. Kept the torch off until he'd swum to the last jetty pilings. Long legs following the glazed yellow light down into the brown depths, the soles of his feet glowing among the leaves roused off the lake bottom, a kid with a good set of lungs; down for nearly a minute. Big rush of bubbles and a bobbing head, treading water with big eyes, fear there despite the brave face.

'Found it.' He was treading water twenty metres away. So the car had pitched off the jetty and rolled further out. 'How deep?'

'Not deep. 'Bout twelve feet.'

Swann began to roll the winch chain off the spool, hoping there was twenty metres. Blake swam over and waited. The torchlight, Swann noticed, was directed into the water beneath Blake's treading legs, back into the dark towards the car and the murdered couple.

Swann drew the chain out in arm-lengths, links clanking shoulder to hand, counted twenty-five before the spool ended. Had a last look around the shoreline, then lowered the cast-iron hook. The boy turned and swam, eager to get the job done and get out of the water. When most of the chain was in the water it became too heavy, and he dropped it, took to duck-diving and dragging the chain along the bottom, the torchlight panicky, returning to the surface to draw breath. On one of these resurfacings he started swimming rapidly towards the jetty until he reached the shoreline and staggered and slipped over the muddy bottom, fell onto the sand, gripping the car keys taken from the ignition. There were goosebumps on Blake's arms as he stepped into his clothes, not looking at Swann and not looking at the lake either.

Swann moved to the side of the truck and engaged the winch, holding down the rusted iron lever, felt the truck body stiffen and jerk as it took the weight, and began to crunch the links one by one over the spool. When ten metres of chain was on, he felt the strain lessen, instead of increase, which was unusual. Five metres to go and Swann thought the hook might have separated from the Mercedes, so easily was the chain coming in. Swann looked to Blake just as the chain spurred on a metre, then a great splash as something broke the surface; the boy jumping with his fists raised.

Swann cut the power to the winch. 'Shit, Blake, we're in luck.'

There it was, the boot of the black Mercedes, like the mouth of a deep-sea monster, the silver decal glinting in the torchlight. The nose of the Merc was down with the weight of the engine, but the boot was floating on the winch hoist, meaning that it still contained a pocket of air. A year underwater and there was a chance something might be retrieved.

'Toss me the keys, and wait in the truck.'

Blake didn't need to be asked twice. He climbed onto the jetty and into the cab. Swann clambered down onto a beam at surface level. With one hand supporting himself on the chain, the light from the torch playing over the water further out, he slid in the keys, barely rusted, and turned the lock. It took a few attempts, but the lock caught, popped.

Swann steeled himself for the stench. He reached above for the torch and shined it inside the boot. Two skeletons, laid upon an oily slurry of dissolved paper and flesh, twin bullet holes in both skulls. He could only see three exit holes. Water had entered the boot, but only until it reached an equilibrium with the trapped air. The Grednics' bodies had been at the rear of the boot, first to take on water. Cardboard boxes of files had been turned to slush, except for two, wedged into the wheel-arches above the waterline, and a suitcase that had presumably floated. Swann hefted the boxes of files and the suitcase onto the jetty, climbed onto the boards and loosed the winch a couple of turns, enough so that the boot took on water. Swann wanted the Mercedes to sink, and he climbed back down and slammed the boot, a slash of water over his legs, left the keys in the lock, unhooked the chain from the towbar and watched the Mercedes settle, then roll forward and slip beneath the surface. Swann stood and watched the churned water become clear. No sign now that they'd disturbed the dead.

It was on the drive back to Coolbellup, Blake staring into the cone of light rising up Winterfold Road, when the thought occurred to Swann. 'Blake, when you took the revolver off Carter, the detective, can you remember how many bullets were in the chamber?'

'Two bullets. That's for sure. I thought about them a lot, when I thought about the copper coming for me. One for him, but if he got too close, one for me. Just like in the movies.'

Two bullets, just as Swann remembered. He'd assumed that the fifteen-year-old, on the run, had loosed off a few shots in the bush. Two bullets left in the revolver from the six-shot chamber. Two shots each into the Grednics' skulls. The more he thought about it, the more it made sense. Carter's service revolver, used in a double murder, an execution made on the behest of the Conlan brothers; Grednic privy to all of the Conlans' financial secrets, and Grim Greylands looking to buy them.

Carter had his revolver back. Swann didn't think that he'd be in a hurry to destroy it. He needed it to demonstrate to the bosses that he was capable of retrieving his service weapon. Three exit wounds in the Grednic skulls. The Grednics had been murdered elsewhere, put into the boot after they'd bled out. There was a small chance that in one skull there might remain a slug matching Carter's revolver.

Swann returned Gerry Tracker's truck to its park by his front door, let himself in with the keys and left them on the fridge. It was late, and by the time Swann returned to the Statesman, Blake Tracker was asleep on the front seat. He drove the boy west into White Gum Valley to Sarah's house. The house was rented under her boyfriend's name, as were the phone line and all the utilities, a precaution suggested by Marion at the time. Swann's home wasn't safe, but they would be safe there.

Swann guided the boy up the front steps, let himself in, showed him to his bed on the sleep-out couch. He was asleep again before his head hit the pillow.

Outside, Swann lit a cigarette and leaned on the Holden, looked up at the stars cartwheeling across the night sky, thinking of Terry Accardi, remembering him as a kid from the neighbouring streets, always in the black stubbies and brown singlet, bare feet, a wharf rat like Swann had been, his ageing parents unable to keep him in line. The look on his face the first day in uniform, proud and nervous, mischief in his smile. Swann grateful that Accardi's parents weren't alive to see their only son buried. That role would fall to Swann.

He thought of the Conlan brothers then, their smug faces on the river last week – the world before them, theirs to take and shape and destroy. Looking up at the stars Swann made a promise, whispered it back to himself, knew that Accardi would approve.

48.

The sun began to rise over the Darling Scarp, with a blush of colour on the ridgeline and the remnant chill darkness over the sand plain. Swann drove to Gould's apartment but parked the Statesman a block away in the hospital zone. He carried the suitcase and the boxes, their weight adding to his exhaustion, up the four flights of stairs and, instead of using his key, knocked on Gould's door. Gould answered immediately, the wild, haunted look of sleeplessness and anxiety. Inside, he flicked through the first file in the first box, cracked a big smile. 'More like it. I can use this.'

Swann looked around the apartment, had a bad feeling, sharpened by the smell of death on the boxes. Better to be safe. 'We need to move. Hogan knows you're back. Up until now it hasn't mattered.'

Gould's rictus grin, the fear of a home invasion like the last, Leo Ajello's thugs shattering his kneecap with a ballpein. 'One of the apartments I inherited, it's empty at the moment. Haven't found a new tenant. It's right across the hall.'

'Perfect. Leave most of the other stuff. Boil the electric kettle. Like you've just popped out.'

They carried the Grednics' material across the hall, entered the east-facing apartment, streaks of orange light breaking over the lowlands. This apartment smelt no better than Gould's. Swann opened a window, the easterly still cold off the desert, but that would soon change. Gould began unpacking the files from the boxes, laying them out in a grid. Swann looked in the cutlery drawer for something to crack the suitcase lock.

Murmurs in the corridor; Gould's ears pricking, relaxing when the voices became familiar. Swann located a steel knife that broke at the first attempt. 'Fucking Samsonite.' Under the sink he found a screwdriver, began to prise around the lock, broke the rubber seal, no water coming out. It took three minutes of patient work, levering and cracking until he'd broken the metal frame of the lock. He then placed the suitcase on the ground and began to stamp, once, twice, felt the lock weaken. A final stamp and it broke. Gould left the boxes, holding the suitcase firm while Swann worked the screwdriver back and forth, the male and female parts separating. He lifted the lid. Cash, and plenty of it. Two passports in plastic covers. A cashier's box with a key. Some jewellery in a plastic bag. A Rolodex. More files: manila bound in cotton ties. Printouts and envelopes. Stamps and letterhead pages. Organisational charts. Bank statements, receipts, money transfers.

'This looks the goods, Frank. Even if it's a year old. Grednic wouldn't have taken it otherwise, wherever he was planning to run.'

Swann nodded, climbed on one knee. The faux-leather couch wasn't far to crawl, anticipating the relief of closing his eyes, dousing the burn with darkness. He was halfway there when the banging started in the hall. Gould froze. Swann made for the door, looked out through the peephole, saw four of Hogan's men gathered outside Gould's door, including the mercenary Jones, a side-arm loose at his groin. The door kicked in, one man outside to control the hall, the others rushing in. Swann conscious of his breathing, his feet at the line of the door, the breeze behind his back. The detective in the hall eyed the door across, glancing left and right, murmuring into a walkie-talkie. A minute and the men emerged. Jones holstered his pistol, for a terrible moment looked at the door across, but was interrupted by the man with the walkie-talkie, passing it over. Jones walked and talked out of Swann's line of sight, towards the staircase; the others followed.

Hogan had demanded that Swann call. There was every chance he'd put out a warrant for him on the police radio-bands, thousands of eyes and ears better than a few detectives'. A warrant for Dragic's murder.

Swann needed to stall Hogan. A few more hours and Gould would have the files sorted, a narrative translated from the ledgers and statements that Swann could use.

Gould was waiting on his word, poised over the files. Swann nodded that it was safe. 'Sort that into what's useful, and what's not. I need to give Hogan something, and copy the rest.'

He waited a beat, opened the door. Gould sucked in an audible breath. Swann stepped into the hall, crossed into Gould's apartment. Listened for the sound of the mens' return. They hadn't tossed the place, which meant that they'd likely be back. He sat before the phone and dialled the number from memory – Central. Asked for Detective Inspector Ben Hogan, was put through immediately.

'Swann, when I get a team to you, you're gonna wish –'

'I've got something for you.'

Time to take what he could, before the end.

'Go on.'

'You've been speaking to Carter, about the Grednics' Mercedes. Carter has been speaking to me.'

Hogan was silent, a whole new vulnerable flank exposed. Swann not mentioning Carter's gun, used to kill the Grednics, didn't want it thrown in the river.

'Alright Swann. What you wanted. Gerry Tracker's release. It's signed. And soon, the Tracker boy's conviction annulled.'

'I'll believe it when he walks free, and I see the paperwork.'

'You may have noticed there's a riot going on at Freo, and Tracker's in the thick of it.'

'You let the Freo screws know, I'll handle the rest.'

'What's your interest in two Abos, anyway?'

'You wanted material on Conlan, I've got it. At least I had it. I saw it when I buried Dragic. It was under the dash in the ute; fell out when I went over a pothole. Didn't know what it was at the time, so I left it in the car. Dragic's father's in the picture now. He won't give it up. Reckons it's worth something. I reckon it is too. Told him you'd be dropping by to pick it up. When you've got that, and Gerry Tracker's out, and I receive the pistol used to shoot Dragic, and the casings, and a lab report that proves the casings belong to the gun – I'll tell you where the Mercedes is. Whatever Grednic had on Conlan – it's all in there.'

'You might not live that long.'

'That's not real smart, Hogan.'

'Don't blame me. Blame your mate Heenan. Seems Larry Conlan is having a bit of an … episode. Likes the powder, does Larry. Explains his blowing up young Accardi. Usually it's Dot's hookers he takes it out on. Heard he gave Heenan a hard word. More than a hard word. More akin to a medieval torture session, is what I hear. Heenan told him that you're looking into Larry and Maitland's business affairs. Now, normally, that mightn't –'

Swann glanced at the smashed front door to Gould's apartment. He wouldn't hear them coming. 'Get on with it.'

'Well, in his current state of mind, given to … extreme gestures, apparently the Conlans have set the entire Junkyard Dog pack onto you. Ordered them to bring your head.'

Swann hung up, rang directory, got the number for Dragic's market garden. Dialled and waited. The phone picked up, but no words, the old man listening. Swann filled the space. 'The man who killed your boy. He's coming to visit you. An Englishman. He thinks you've got something of his. I told him you'd be expecting him.'

A cough, clearing of throat, in the background, puppies whining. 'That is good.'

The line gone dead. Another call, this time to Norman Gorman at the switchboard. 'Norman. I've been hearing things. Bad things. You?'

Swann could imagine Norman's face, the waxy skin and Somme-era moustache. Eyes that were blind, but had seen it all. 'You wouldn't believe me if I told you, Frank. Out of control barely describes it. Well, you'll see for yourself. I'm presuming you want a connection?'

'I'm after Heenan.'

'I haven't heard the dulcet tones for nearly two days. But you can ask.'

The connection was made, the line began to dial, the pick-up. 'What?'

Not Heenan, or the premier's voice. Maitland Conlan. In the premier's seat.

'Conlan, this is Frank Swann. I want to speak to Heenan.'

Conlan's response a belly laugh, a slap on the leather blotter. 'Heenan is helping us with our inquiries. As you will be soon. Some friends of mine are looking for you, *mate*.'

So it was true.

'Heenan had nothing to do with anything –'

'Maybe not, but he's got a big mouth, and big mouths need to be sewed shut.'

'Too late for that, Conlan. I've got the Grednics' car. All the papers Grednic was going to hand over to Grim Greylands, I've got them. I'm giving them to Ben Hogan.'

'Name your price. I'm a businessman. You have goods to exchange; I'll buy them.'

Swann chose his words carefully, calmed his breathing, spoke quietly.

'You tell the premier, if he calls the Burswood tender in your favour, he's going to be in a world of political pain.'

Conlan unaware his words were being taped.

'What makes you think he has a choice?'

Swann hung up, replaced the receiver with sweating hands, that floating sensation again. A final call to make. Asked directory for the Canberra number, Federal Police switchboard. Told the operator he wanted to speak to the policeman who'd received a letter bomb yesterday, heard the tension in her voice when she told him to wait. A long minute passed. Couple of clicks as the recorders activated. A deliberately modulated voice. 'Johnson. How can I help.'

'My name is Frank Swann. Terry Accardi was my friend. I was working for him in my capacity as a private investigator and ex-policeman –'

'I know who you are. We did our background checks.'

Swann wary. The leak to Conlan about Accardi's investigation had come from the Feds, not the CIB.

'That's interesting; Terry told me he hadn't mentioned my name. Was it you who leaked his name over here?'

The response Swann wanted. Rush of blood. 'You fucken ... my life was threatened too.'

'But your package was mysteriously intercepted, just in time.'

'All incoming mail to this facility is scanned. The scan picked up the bomb. An emergency protocol was initiated. The bomb was defused.'

The game gone long enough. Swann cut to it. 'This is what's going to happen. First, you stop recording this call, or I don't proceed. Then I'll tell you what I want from you ...'

Swann waited for the clicks. When they came he spoke, and Johnson listened.

*

The emperors with no clothes. Gould's words, after a skim through the contents of the files. Maitland Conlan's business empire was, as Grim Greylands suspected, essentially bankrupt. Most of his companies, including Exetar, were operating while insolvent. Whenever there was a sniff of rumour, or revelation from a disgruntled employee, Maitland's brother Larry flooded the company with capital from Harrowgate Investment Bank. But Harrowgate too was bankrupt, according to Gould.

Apart from Larry Conlan's lavish lifestyle, he was borrowing heavily from some dubious sources, the regular overseas financial institutions having cut him off, demanding repayment at penalty interest rates, and all of the transactions and all of the threats were contained in Grednic's files. Depositors to Conlan's bank, which included the Catholic Church and several of the local councils and universities, the various local unions and superannuation trusts, were going to lose everything. Money entering the Harrowgate front door was going out the back door faster than ever. The Burswood development was an opportunity for the Conlans to plunder the public purse, refresh the coffers, keep the show rolling along. Until then, one push and their empire was going to fall over.

Swann called ahead and parked in the street. Through the Statesman's driver window he handed the first thousand dollars of Grednic's cash to McIlroy, the Fremantle Prison guard, with instructions to get Gerry Tracker ready for extraction. The second bundle contained five thousand dollars for the screws at Longmore, to settle the Blake Tracker matter. McIlroy didn't ask, patted Swann on the arm and let him go with a warning.

'We had a dozen or so bikies in the street last night. No patches or rego plates. They charged your place. After they left I walked down there. Old Salvatore was cleaning up the damage. You'd best keep away, Frank.'

Swann thanked him and reversed out of Nelson Street, took the shortest route to Coolbellup, air-conditioner blasting to keep him awake. During daylight hours, old man Pickett was likely asleep. Swann vaulted the front fence and walked down the back. Heat radiated from the cottage roof and walls, the asbestos box baking in the sun. Swann shuddered at the image of the old man inside, sweating through his dreams.

He gave the knock on the weatherboard portal, waited for Foley, heard the scrabble of the limestone, a chink of dark. Foley ushered him inside, glanced around the yard, looked just as wired as Swann felt.

Soon as Swann slid into the dugout, Foley presented him with a sheath of papers, fixed with a bulldog clip.

'What's this?'

'I robbed Harrowgate this morning. Got the bank manager to open Mostel's safety deposit box. This was all there was.'

'Nothing on the news about it.'

Foley shrugged, pointed with his chin at the papers in Swann's hand.

Swann looked over the first sheet. The final piece of the jigsaw. Mostel's insurance. Not only accounts and ledgers. The man had also written a story. Outlining in detail, in case of his death, exactly what he had done for the Conlans over the past year to keep them afloat. Obviously aware of the significance of his predecessor's disappearance. The rewards he'd demanded – some of the small projects such as the Brewery development, some of the state energy infrastructure, a place at the trough. Swann flicked to the last page. The manuscript was even signed and dated, to two weeks ago. Ink fingerprinted. The final words of caution: *dynamite in the wrong hands.*

Or the right hands.

'I came here to destroy Mostel. Is that going to do it?'

Swann nodded. 'Well and truly.'

'I can leave it up to you?'

'One last thing.'

Swann talked Foley through his plan. Told him about Conlan, about Mostel and Accardi. The final nail.

Foley agreed, began to pack.

*

The Conlans lived on the fiftieth floor of the tower they'd built – Conlan Tower, the city's tallest building. Swann parked in the underground carpark, walked towards the nearest lift, Foley a step behind with his motorcycle helmet on, holding a bag full of newspapers gathered off Coolbellup lawns; a fake courier.

The mirrored lift rose, stopped to take on office types, drop them off. Swann not looking, eyes closed, just the smells of perfume and cologne, Foley's unwashed body, the awkward atmosphere of lifts. Swann opened his eyes as they passed the thirtieth floor, counted the numbers until they reached 47, 48, 49, where the numbers stopped. Floor forty-nine was the offices of Maitland Conlan and Exetar. Maitland might even be there, along with Mostel. There was a private lift that went to the final floor. An electronic code needed. The lift doors opened and Swann stepped into the lobby beside Foley, still wearing the helmet. Behind cool glass walls were carpeted dividers separating workers in an open plan. Nobody noticed them. Swann watched the workers busy in their cubicles while Foley cased the ceiling, the painted cement sheets laid on steel frames, air-conditioning vents every twenty metres. Beyond, the view of the river snaking upstream towards the hills, haze of a bushfire burning to the south. No sign of panic or anything untoward. Jamming the lift and going up through the lift roof into the shaft was one option, but Foley's least preferred. Swann followed him around the curved, painted wall towards the toilets. Inside, they took adjoining stalls. Swann left his door unlocked, sat on the toilet cover with his throwaway pistol on safety. Listened while Foley climbed over the cistern and onto the stall walls and pushed up a concrete sheet at the edges. It looked heavy. He propped the sheet with the motorcycle helmet, hoisted himself up and into the roof-space. Swann left his stall and sat in Foley's place, climbed the cistern and slipped the sheet back into its snug.

Foley returned after five minutes, knocked on the ceiling. Swann lifted the ceiling-tile up with the helmet.

'There's a guard stationed outside the lift. Looks like a Junkyard heavy. Fucking hand-cannon on him. Lift opens onto a room, goes two ways, one to each brother's apartment. Nothing going on one side, hardly looks used. The other side ... fucking Mostel's there, tied to a chair. Next to him's the fat man I saw him with last week. Both look pretty bashed up. Mostel saw me, I think. The other bloke was out cold, or sleeping.'

Swann heard the door, let the tile down, crouched while a man pissed in little constricted tinkles, whistled 'Islands in the Stream'. He took his time washing his hands: water, soap, rinse, towel, deep sigh upon departure – the whole ritual, which gave Swann time to think. He lifted the tile. 'Mostel will know the code to the lift. Get it out of him.'

Swann waited, the chill air in the toilet freezing the acid sweat down his back, little trills of anxiety rising up his neck, pricking his scalp. Foley back in twenty minutes, the knock. 'Fucking comedians. The code is one billion, in numbers.'

'You wait by one of the doors. You hear the lift open, you come from behind. You armed?'

Foley nodded over his back; the black nylon shoulder bag. 'Gotta sawn-off rifle, offa the Junkyard bastard tried to kill me. Give me two to get in place. Something goes wrong; you hear a gunshot, you get your arse up fast.'

Swann left the stall, then the bathroom, carried Foley's helmet under one arm, walked to the private lift, glanced down the corridor either side. Pressed the button, the door gliding back. Ordinary vestibule with dark mirrors wrapped around. He closed the door, waited two minutes and punched the numbers, took a deep breath, clicked the safety catch on the Beretta .22 and put the helmet at his feet, stood side-on, gun-hand extended. One floor, seemed an eternity. An eternity for the door to tremble, begin its soundless slide. Nothing in front of him. Then the shadow of a giant magnum revolver turning on a slow arc, Swann turning at the same time, raising his arm while the giant bear of a man lowered his own, eyes meeting, snap of recognition, the man beginning to smile. The .22 aimed at the bikie's face, the magnum aimed at his own. Swann's might kill, more likely wound. The magnum would take Swann's head off. He backed into the lift, forced the man to follow round, left his back exposed. Foley moving on silent feet, a silent charge, the rifle butt raised above kamikaze eyes and mouth open in a silent shriek, caught the bear-man behind the ear, the force of the blow carrying him into the lift, taking out Swann's legs, slamming him into a wall of shattering glass.

No gunshot.

Foley smashed the bikie's head a second, third time. Took the magnum revolver and uncocked the hammer. 'That was lucky. You wouldn't believe it, these things have a fucken hair trigger.'

'You did good. He was out before he hit me.'

They dragged him into the anteroom, into Larry Conlan's apartment, spots and smears of blood over the camel-coloured carpet. One big room: messed up circular bed against one wall, large dining table. Cocaine on the dining table, on a mirror spotted with blood drops containing powder. Someone going hard, most likely Larry Conlan, given his alleged mental state. In the wall-to-wall mirrored bathroom, beside the jacuzzi and bound to two dining chairs, were Mostel and Heenan, the latter still unconscious, gurgling, head sagging at a bad angle. Mostel's face all pulp, the weapon on the vanity beside: a gold-plated hairbrush.

Foley didn't waste any time. He grabbed Mostel by the hair. 'The safe. Where is it and what's the combination?'

There was still fight left in Mostel. Tried to laugh, coughed and spat blood instead, panic in his eyes. Foley wiped blood from Mostel's chin on his hand, held it up. 'They sure did a number on you. See that frothy blood. That's an embolism. You've got a collapsed lung. Now, where's the safe and what's the combination?'

Mostel began to cough, fear in his eyes, could feel himself rupturing inside. Bent forward and let the stream of blood and saliva run from his mouth. Shook his head.

'What's that mean? You won't tell?' Foley raised the rifle. Swann put a hand on his arm. 'I think it means there's no safe. Have a look.'

Foley went out while Swann untied Mostel's hands, moved to Heenan, coming round. Swann finished the job with a glassful of water on the face. Heenan came to the surface from a great depth. Instant recognition, straining at his bonds. His wounds superficial, but it was his first beating. Ears would be ringing, concussion vertigo making him dizzy, the terrible nausea. Swann helped him to his feet, guided him out of the room, sat him on Conlan's bed. Moment of panic. The bikie was gone. Swann ran to the hall to see the lift-light blink off. Turned to see Mostel stagger towards him, pink blood gushing out his mouth, bank left towards the balcony, disoriented and oxygen-starved.

'No you fucken don't!' shouted Foley, turning from the cupboards pulled open; Swann recognising the garbage bag he'd filled with Conlan's cash, stowed beside the tycoon's shoes. He followed Foley to the balcony, watched Mostel swing a leg over, no idea what he was doing, then gone into the whistling wind. Nothing but the view to the hills. Mostel on his way, fifty storeys down.

'Good fucken riddance,' said Foley, who wanted to watch the fall.

Swann grabbed his arm, pulled him back. Moved to Heenan, helped him towards the lift. Foley stuffing the half a million cash into a canvas laundry bag, arrived just as the lift door slid open. They got inside, Swann punched the numbers. The floor below, people milling around, the bloodied bikie gone. The next lift, the forty-nine-storey descent, Foley with his helmet back on, only Heenan drawing attention, face swelling badly. In the underground carpark, Swann shook Foley's hand. Foley reached into the canvas bag and pressed a fat wedge of money into Swann's jacket. No words needed. Never met, never to meet again.

Heenan staggered towards the car but Swann blocked him. 'You're safer on your own, Heenan. Get yourself to the RPH, then lie low. I'll be in touch.'

Swann reversed the Statesman, put his foot down and punched the Holden towards the block of white light.

*

The traffic on St Georges Terrace had the Statesman locked in, creeping forward, little jerks and starts, the lights changing slowly. Swann felt vulnerable; not tying the bikie down had been his sole mistake. Now he was propped like a target in the best environment possible for a bikie with a gun. Just in case he didn't make it, he called Gould in Subiaco, where he was headed.

'Everything useful, make multiple copies. In the event of ...'

Light-headed, surreal, *in the event of* sounding like the certain pronouncement of his own death. For once, Gould kept his mouth shut, did as he was told, could feel Swann's fear down the line. Next, a final good deed before he called Marion, he dialled Stormie Farrell, to get the word out to all the unions, to get their money out of Harrowgate. Stormie Farrell's word was gold, Swann's conduit to a panic that would spread from the unions to the councils to the general public. There was no answer, the phone ringing out. In his rear-vision Swann saw the first bike, a black bobbing helmet, visor down, weaving into a position three cars back, and Swann understood. There was no way to communicate to the Junkyard Dogs that Conlan was broke, no cash left to pay them for their paramilitary duties. He shanked the steering wheel when he saw the bikie reach into his side-saddle, still stationary, so he cut down a lane through a red light and took the freeway south, the Statesman eating up the road and hitting 100, 120, 140, weaving between the commuters and taxis and buses, heard the throaty roar; jet engine clearing its throat, watched the bike come up the emergency lane, Swann cutting in front, two parallel lines intersecting at speed, except that the bike swerved, came around Swann from the outside, no gun in the driver's hand or look as he passed but accelerated ahead; one hundred metres, two hundred, sat there and waited. Swann heard another bike come from behind, another Harley at its maximum speed, single rider coming on his right side, Swann looking for the weapon but the bike pulling into the farthest right lane, pulled further ahead and sat there, waiting.

He was being positioned. A gunman riding pillion due anytime soon. He kept his speed up, wanting to draw the attention of a traffic cop, but there was no sign, he was on his own. He dialled Hogan, steered with one hand, dirt and gravel on his left side, still doing 140; one slip and he was in the trees. Hogan answered, terse, ready to launch a tirade, Swann telling him where he was headed, what Hogan needed to do if he wanted the Grednic papers. Another bike, single rider, black helmet and settling between lanes a hundred metres back, then another, moving at speed up the far right lane, boxing him in; further back, a black wedge of riders breaking left and right past the startled faces of drivers around him, rolling thunder, and there it was, not a Harley but a BMW, faster and more responsive, pillion passenger drawing out a sawn-off shotgun, taking aim, Swann ducking as the rear window blew, the back of his head ripped by glass and buckshot, only distance saving him, could feel the wind on the pulp and scalp and exposed skull; slammed on the brakes and swerved right, caught the bike's front wheel and sent it toppling forward, airborne and the riders flying, arms wide like skydivers but landing on the tarmac, gone beneath the wheels of a truck and taxi. Swarming bikes, falling around him, Swann waiting until the last second before cutting a hard angle down the Manning Road exit, the centrifugal force crushing the breath out of him, the bike pack split, but there were four on his tail. He led them down the straight road, could see uncertainty in their actions, once or twice speeding to catch him then settling back, waiting for the others to regroup. He took the advantage, his plan to swing around onto Leach Highway, get some distance and lose them in the southern suburbs, put his foot down and hit 160, the Statesman lifting into the headwind. Swann glanced over his shoulder, was hit with a flash of blinding light and then he was gone, floating; a figure aflame in a black landscape, just wind and pain and flame and darkness; came to on the wrong side of the road, had crossed a median strip, felt behind his head and down his neck, exposed spine, pellets lodged there. A panic that started in his feet, a fear like no other. Fingers on bone and cartilage and lead, warm and slippery with blood. The Holden's steering was awry, damaged by the smack of cement on sump at speed. Swann heard the bikes beside him, slammed on the handbrake and slid into a right-angle turn, trying to keep his head straight, the light-headedness and the panic lost in flashes of light, coming in and out, light and dark, life and death. Found himself on Stormie Farrell's street, the swarm behind him, sirens too; drove up the dirt incline of Farrell's drive and skidded, heard the smash of metal on metal, the shattering glass falling from a great distance.

The sensation of ghost footsteps, of stepping through black water onto silver sand, quicksilver bubbles, the darkness clearing, a perimeter of flames, beyond that Stormie Farrell's open front door. Swann looked down, saw the pistol in his hand, heard the bikes in the street. He staggered inside. Slammed the door shut. Entered the room off the hall, took a position by the window, shot it out, one bullet gone. A black leather shape framed by fire. Swann shot him, saw him fall. Black blurs down the side of the house; heard gunshots in the street, sirens. Dozens of shots; different calibres, the old .38, a semi-automatic rifle, shotgun blasts. He knelt, crawled, dragged himself down the hall to the kitchen. Pulled himself up on the sink, aimed a wavering hand up at the sky, felt himself falling. Slid to the ground. Gunshots. The ceiling a flashing canvas, everything haloed by flickering orange light. Silence. The back door edged open. Swann felt the dark presence but couldn't raise his head. Tried to raise his hand but couldn't. Paralysed. No pain. The earth beneath him, steady and heavy and him on its surface, looking out. A shadow. Hogan, leaning into his view, head haloed by angelic light. Dark angel. Look of great satisfaction.

'Jones is dead, Swann. Your doing. And Carter arrested by the Feds, taken to a Fed facility I can't get to. Your doing.' Hogan cracked the chamber of his revolver. 'I've just killed four men, to get to you first. That leaves two bullets. That's a nice pool of blood around your head. Like one of those Russian ... ikons. I'll finish with your head. How about that? But first –'

Swann felt his body jump, float, thought he'd keep floating, but no. Nothing. No pain. Just the weight. Hogan laughed. 'I see your spine is fucked Swann. I just shot you in the stomach.'

Hogan smiled, leaned closer. Last rites. Death whisper. 'I could ask you where Grednic's files are. But I know. I'll find Gould. Which leaves the coup de grâce. Pity you won't feel it. I'm not going to waste an opportunity like this. Blame it on the road warriors outside. It's been a long time coming.'

Swann didn't close his eyes. He looked down the barrel, the dark borehole, past it to Hogan's haloed face. Hogan was waiting for something. Swann gave it to him, channelled the flame and the darkness into his eyes, flung it upwards. Hogan burst in a wave of blood, his face and torso erased in a moment of terrible sound, meat-spatter against the wall beside, and then the falling red mist, the legs falling across Swann's legs, the ringing in Swann's ears and then the sound of dripping blood.

Stormie Farrell leaned over him, shotgun smoking.

49.

Swann asked to be sat, so he could see. The brace on his neck meant he couldn't turn his head. Feeling had returned to his hands and feet. He clenched his hands and wiggled his toes, just to make sure. It was the gunshot to his stomach that had nearly proved fatal. The bullet had penetrated his bowel and shattered his hip. Galloping sepsis had set in, his vital organs shutting down even as the surgeons operated. His heart had stopped at one point. They had nearly given up.

All of this told to him by Marion and his daughters. When he came round his hands and his feet were held, but he couldn't feel them. Teardrops on his lips when they had kissed him. He too had cried, for them. For what he had done.

Now he sat and looked out of the Mount Hospital window down the Esplanade to Burswood, listened to the Federal copper describe Terry Accardi's last piece of evidence, the finding that got the environmental scientist killed. Examining his random samples of the Burswood site under a microscope, the scientist had noticed that the soil was similar to the soil taken from the Exetar building site in East Perth. Then he had looked closer. The samples were not just similar, but identical. In expectation of securing the Burswood tender for Exetar, Maitland Conlan had been trucking the contaminated soil from East Perth out to a disused quarry on the edge of the city, then turning the trucks around and sending them back to the inner-city Burswood site, the toxic soil used as infill. The low floodplain soil was now too contaminated to use as the premier intended, as a mixed-use low cost residential housing development. Too contaminated now even for a golf course or park. According to the Federal copper, Burswood was now intended to be the site of a giant casino, precisely as the Conlans had always planned.

Not that they would get to enjoy the fruits of their scam. When Dennis Gould passed on the Grednic papers, soon followed by Mostel's signed confession, to investigative journalists at the *Daily News*, the *West Australian* and the *Sunday Times*, the breaking news had sparked a stockmarket panic, and a run on Harrowgate. The premier had moved to pump one hundred million dollars of taxpayer money into the bank, allowing the Catholic Church and other friends to get their money out, but that only delayed the inevitable. Harrowgate went under within days, soon followed by Exetar and all of the Conlan subsidiaries across three different continents. Grim Greylands had his victory, and was there to pick over the remains, buying them up at bargain prices from the receiver who delivered money back to the banks the Conlans owed. Greylands withdrew from the Burswood tender after Jones' death at the hands of old man Dragic, although his body was never found. The threat of the federal police investigation into Accardi's murder spread into Ben Hogan's role as Greylands' flunky, which saw the British tycoon withdraw at speed. The premier had survived so far, but there were calls for his resignation, to stave off the royal commission that the media and others were demanding. As Stormie Farrell predicted, his son had swum with the sharks and been eaten alive. Government patronage of men like the Conlans was as old as the state itself, but the mask had slipped, and the face behind wasn't pretty.

Swann ceased his dictation. It was all there. Amended only in the writing to give Accardi the credit. His investigation on the Feds' behalf, his death a result of a Fed leak, his forthcoming medal in recognition of his service. No comfort to anyone except Swann, and the man who stood next to him, straightening his uniform jacket, adjusting his officer's cap. Accardi's funeral was due to start in half an hour. It wouldn't be well attended. Marion and his daughters would be there, some of the neighbourhood people, a few Fed representatives. A couple of reluctant CIB superiors, no replacement for Hogan having been found. Hogan's own funeral, a hero murdered by bikie thugs, sponsored by the state, held in St George's Cathedral, a cortege across the city to Karrakatta. The federal investigation into Hogan's role in the Grednics' murder continuing. Hogan had been working for the Conlans at that point. Both brothers were still free, for the time being. The bikies who'd planted the Accardi bomb presumed killed in the shootout at Stormie Farrell's house. Omitted from his account the role that Des Foley, old man Dragic and Blake Tracker had played in securing the vital evidence. Foley was still Australia's most wanted, but Gerry's charge had been dropped, and Blake's conviction annulled.

Swann shook the policeman's hand, and the press of his fingers felt good. The shotgun pellet that lodged in his spine had nicked the spinal column. There would be ongoing consequences, although it was presumed nothing serious. A secondary injury to the area could be catastrophic, however. He had been lucky, and soon he would be able to walk again. Walk on the beach beside Marion, the sun on his face, the wet sand beneath his feet. The good life, the life he had always wanted, the life he had always known.

ACKNOWLEDGEMENTS

All characters in this novel are fictitious. Any resemblance to real people, living or dead, is coincidental.

I owe a debt to my first readers – Mark Constable, Sean Gorman, Andrew Nette, Dave Honeybone and Kerri Guardia. Thanks to Lyn Tranter, my agent, and Michael Robotham for his recent advice. To Peter Whish-Wilson for the financial background, and to fellow crime writer Alan Carter for our regular chats in the pub. To Fremantle Press for taking this on, and in particular my editor Georgia Richter, and publicist Claire Miller. It's been a pleasure.

And for Bella, love and gratitude always.

MORE GREAT CRIME FROM FREMANTLE PRESS

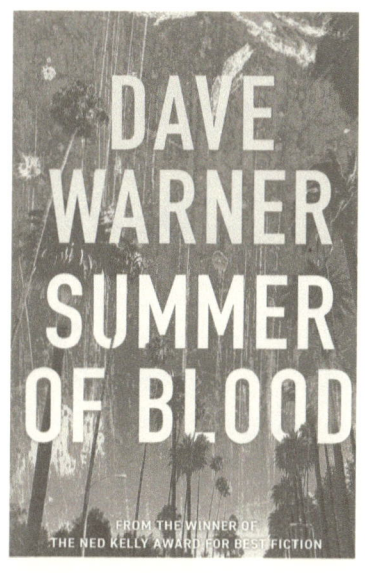

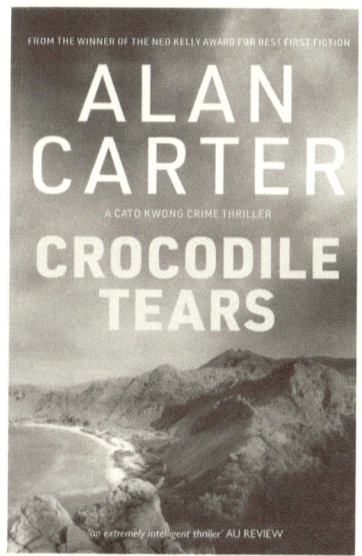

www.ingramcontent.com/pod-product-compliance
Lightning Source LLC
Chambersburg PA
CBHW020600030726
47497CB00007B/2029